On the Origin of
Findo Gask

by

David McCreight

D1440194

ISBN-10: 1484916573
ISBN-13: 978-1484916575

www.davidmccreight.co.uk
cover design by David McCreight

For Paul Mutch

(even though he's a big hairy eyebrowed twat)

Chapter 1

Friday April 12th, 10am

I used to be a child prodigy but now I'm just a lazy teenage shit. Mum and Gran tell me I'm lucky to live in such a beautiful village in such a beautiful part of a beautiful country but fucksticks to them, these are the same people who tell me girls will be interested in me for my personality and that my great great grandmother was a mermaid. Kilmuir, their beautiful picturesque village, is a tiny isolated pit of a dump on the stupidly named Black Isle – not black, not an island – set in the middle of the nothing-to-do capital of the world, the Highlands of Scotland: a place which you'll find isn't nearly as friendly as it pretends to be in the brochures. I'm Findo Gask, I'm 16 and I'm very probably Scotland's ugliest inhabitant. Actually that's unfair; I'm very probably Europe's ugliest inhabitant. I live with my Mum and my Gran in my Gran's shitty, tiny house, because Mum pissed our old place up the wall playing online bingo or poker or something. Dad's been dead for years. Thanks Dad.

I solved the universe today. Seriously, the whole universe, completely solved once and for all, and I wasn't even trying, it just sort of occurred to me as I was eating a chocolate mini-roll. Mind you, even though I am now the discoverer of the most fundamental advancement in human thought ever, it turns out that the answer to the universe is so simple that it doesn't even involve any maths, so I'm not sure anyone will bother to believe me when I tell them. So even though I have now totally solved the universe, it's not as if I'm going to get a Nobel prize out of it, let alone a shag. Anyway, I'm supposed to be sitting here revising for a pointless History exam and I don't think the essay question, 'In the context of the industrial revolution, solve the universe', is all that likely to come up. However, the industrial revolution without any reference to why the big bang happened is very likely to feature, but as I can't be arsed with any of it I'm going to eat some more mini-rolls and watch more TV.

Chapter 2

Nursery School to Primary 4

My earliest memory is of being sat on a table so I could have my photograph taken and of the table edge digging into my chubby legs, but my first memory that matters to me is the moment when I decided to learn to read. I was three and I was sitting on the floor in the canyon between two chairs in nursery school watching some other children running about the vast room with crayons, or sitting on the floor picking at themselves, when I had the revelation that turned an unthinking infant into the well rounded member of the human race that I am today. In my three year old brain, and pay attention as this is about to get tricky, it went something like this: 'I'm me, and the me that I am lives behind my eyes, so maybe the other children have a me that's behind their eyes too, but then their me can't be the same as my me, because my me is mine. So maybe they all have a me which is like mine but not like mine because it's in them: and that's what makes them, them, like my me makes me, me.' It was a hell of a lot for my young brain to spring on itself and I sat there for a very long while adapting to the new reality of the world. The other children ran and crayoned and picked just as they had been doing a minute before, but now I saw that they did it as fully conscious individual human beings; and as a newly fully conscious human being myself, I put my finger up my nose and went among them.

Later that afternoon I tried to explain to my Mum that I now knew she was a person in her own right, and so were all the other people and so was the dog, but I found I didn't have the language to do it and it was obvious from her patronising tone that she wasn't going to take my important thing seriously, and my important thing needed to be said. So I decided at once to learn all the words and what they meant so I could tell her exactly what I was trying to tell her, without her looking down on me as if I was some child and not just as human as she was. So as soon as she went back to making my dinner I set off to learn all the words. Well; all the letters, and then all the words.

Of course I had no idea that there were so many letters, and to even begin to understand how many I had to learn all the numbers too, though at least there seemed to be a bit of a system in place for those; whereas with the letters you seemed to be able to chuck them about and mix them up any old how. After dinner Mum expressed some interest in helping me and then got bored and told me I'd learn it all when I went to school. So bollocks to her, I applied myself to the task all the same and with her occasional half-arsed help and Dad's sporadic but enthusiastic input, green crayon in hand, I forged ahead. By the time I did go to school and finished off Primary one, I was told I'd be skipping P2 and be put up straight into P3 because I was doing so well with my letters and numbers. That was disconcerting at first, because those children in the other class were so much bigger and older than me, but it did mean I wouldn't have to listen to the noise of all the children my own age learning the alphabet out loud while I was trying to get on with reading my novel. By this time I'd noticed a change in Mum and Dad's attitude towards me too. Now when I wanted to know stuff, Mum would pretend to be patient with me for a few minutes longer than she was really being patient, and Dad would listen intently and give me deeply unsatisfactory answers, but then a day or so later he'd drop a scruffy book in my lap on whatever subject I'd been bending his ear. Then later he'd pretend to listen intently as I pointed out to him exactly where he'd originally been going wrong.

The reason for all this unexpected attention seemed to be because my teacher had whispered the word 'prodigy' to my parents, as it seemed that a five year-old reading at a level beyond most of the teaching assistants was considered unusual, even after a close look by the inspectors at the teaching assistants. But as far as I was concerned I still hadn't learned all the words and what they meant, and was in fact having a lot of difficulty even finding a grown-up who would tell me definitively how many words there were. So while I was being told I was a prodigy, it didn't mean anything to me beyond it getting me books and attention, and if I didn't want attention, it got me left alone with a book. And I would have been happy if the world had gone on like that forever, but the boys in my new class had decided that a prodigy, rather than something to be marvelled at, was better suited as a receptacle for flicked dog shit. Someone who should be a receiver of dead legs and be at the bottom of every 'pile on'. A prodigy should have spit dribbled down the back of his neck, he should be the star of the game 'execute Findo' and his shoes should be on the roof. Even when the prodigy was growing big for his age and would be shaving by the time he was ten, a six-year-old prodigy should be herded with pointy sticks into the iced-up burn in January and bricked up into a cupboard when the workmen went on their lunch in May. In the intervening months he should be treated very badly but with far less invention, and then in June his dad should be killed. Just to be clear, it wasn't the boys in my class that killed my dad, it was a man with a beard called God.

At first I'd thought he'd died because of his little problem, because the passenger in his taxi who survived said Dad had gone straight through a red light without even slowing down, and Mum and me both knew from the way she used to scream at him in the car, that every now and then Dad would forget that red meant stop. But Gran said it had been down to God's will, and that God had taken Dad to be with him, and Uncle Robert and Auntie Roberta said God only knew what happened, and the Reverend at the funeral, where I had to wear a borrowed black jacket, said it wasn't for us to understand God's plan. I'd heard of God before of course, but I hadn't paid much attention to him as no one had ever mentioned he took such an active interest, but now everyone agreed that God had slaughtered Dad for some reason of his own, but none of them were willing to explain to me why he might have done it. So I determined to find out, got hold of a bible from my Gran's and started to chase God down.

I was kept off school for a couple of weeks until Mum stopped drinking and started to get bored of using me for a hankie, and when I did go back no-one picked on me for a while. They just had me confirm that my Dad was dead and then they stared at me like I was a poisonous vegetable. A couple of days later a couple of boys asked me in the playground if I wanted to play, I said I did, one of them tripped me up, the other shouted 'Pile on!' and everybody piled on. As far as they were concerned everything was back to normal, but at the bottom of the growing pile of limbs, all the breath squeezed out of me and a huge screaming hole inside where I never knew my Dad had been until he wasn't there, and now with nothing to put in it in his place, nothing was feeling normal for me. When the pile of boys eventually disassembled itself and got off laughing, instead of sloping away somewhere as I usually did, to put my rib cage and my pride back together; I filled the void for a moment by going super mental ballistic. I thrashed, pummelled and scattered every gap-tooth smirk that came into reach, until the hands of a teacher lifted me off Ross McKenzie's jellying face and whisked me inside and down the corridor and into the headmaster's office.

Mr McRae was authority personified. He was old and had a voice like thunder and he didn't take no shit. I'd never been in his office before. I stood dwarfed by the height of it, dwarfed by the size of his desk and dwarfed by his aura. Forty years of dealing with little highland boys in all their depravity had given him a roar which could reverse a stampede and a towering presence which would instantly overawe any mere six-year-old child who'd been brought in to be faced with their crimes.

'What happened Findo?' he asked me, not unkindly, but with absolute don't piss me aboutness. I could have explained that I'd had enough of being piled on or that I missed my Dad or how in the moment when I'd elbowed Mikey Marshall in the stomach when he was trying to pull me off Ross McKenzie, and Mikey Marshall had gone down; how I realised that I was actually a lot bigger than most of them and maybe I was entitled to be angry with them all for always ganging up on me. It wasn't my fault I was smarter or uglier or couldn't run as fast as them, but then why should I have to explain that to anyone anyway. Mr McRae raised an eyebrow and waited for my answer. I could have said 'don't know' which was the standard excuse, but I did know and just didn't want to say. I felt a endless hole inside me and had filled it for a moment with smashing Ross McKenzie's face in. How could a headmaster, an old man, be expected to understand that? So I remembered the best answer to everything that my Cousin Dan had taught me to say when I was younger, and I looked Mr McRae in the eye and told him to:

'Go and do a fuck'.

I was no longer a prodigy, I was now a disgraceful foul-mouthed little boy who'd be taking the rest of the week off. They called it a cŏmpassionate suspension, and as far as I was concerned, it was better than being jumped on for sport by every other boy in the school every lunchtime and break and before the bus came in the afternoon. They didn't exactly leave me alone in the playground when I came back again, except for Ross McKenzie who didn't even join in at the edges of the bullying now that one of his eyeballs had a tendency to roll towards his ear. And although all the rest of them never tried to pile on me again, they settled for calling me endlessly inventive names while staying out of range, confident I could be very easily outrun. And then, when baited to distraction, my angry lumbering after them caused endless delight as the stupid way I ran meant I never caught up with anything but previously occupied air.

The way I ran wasn't the only physical attribute my tormentors could choose from to pick on me for. Not to put too fine a point on it, even for rural Scotland, The Gasks are sitting-on-a-wall-at-the-end-of-the-village ugly. I'm tall but my legs and arms are too short for the rest of me, my nose is big and my chin recedes directly into a roll of neck fat; and the rest of me is pretty fat too. My under-bite is far beyond the hope of orthodontics and my ears are at substantially different heights up my head. My only redeeming feature, if you can call it that, is people say I have nice eyes. Whenever women used to visit my Mum for whatever reason women find to visit each other, I'd be called into the kitchen to be shown off, and the visitors would always say: 'Oh, he's got such beautiful eyes, your boy, doesn't he, oh yes, beautiful big eyes he's got, yes.' And then the visitors would glance round the claustrophobic kitchen table at each other and I could see in their faces them warning each other: 'but for Christ's sake don't mention any of the rest of him.' Instead they'd say again: 'Such beautiful eyes, lovely eyes, yes, lovely, yes. Gorgeous big brown eyes he's got, he gets them from you,' they'd say to my Mum, and Mum would pretend to be flattered and then everyone would pretend not to notice I'd got pretty much everything else from her too, because as terrible to look at as I am, my Mum looks like someone hit a pig with a troll. And so being polite adults, there'd be a slightly too long uneasy pause and then someone would change the subject to the weather.

Six year old boys are not quite as polite as ladies collecting for charity bakes, so as a result I've had more nicknames growing up than I ever knew what to do with. Off the top of my head there's been: Experiment, Frankenface, Dog, Dogboy, Sausagedogboy, Uglycunt, Frogeyes, Tosser, Caber the Tosser, Neandertall, Lurch, Igor, Mutant, Moooootant, Big Shit, Fish Shit, Bigfishpoo, Monobrow, Eyebeard, Shouldn't-have-a-Beard, Finboy, Fatboy, Fatboy Gasket, Ugly in a Basket, Banjo-Bridge-Boy, Banjo, Banjodog and Ding-ding-ding-ding-ding-ding-ding-ding-ding; and those were just the ones that stuck. Some I had for weeks, others for years, some were specific to groups and some to individuals. One arsehole decided my name should be Sea slug and he persisted with it, convinced of its hilarious genius, and yet to the total indifference of everyone else, until his Dad pushed someone off an oil rig and he moved away.

So at six, by day I was taunted and by night I chased down God. Why did he do what he did, how come he was such a shit and did he ever say he was sorry?

'What'll we do today Jesus me boy?' says God.

'Let's create Findo Gask, Dad,' says Jesus.

'Brilliant idea my lad. Kazzamm! ... oops.'

'Don't fink you were concentrating there Dad.'

'Don't fink I was son, oh dear would you look at that. Never mind, fuck 'im, and remind me as soon as I remember to do in 'is old man too.'

'Nice eyes on 'im though Dad.'

'Oh yeah, I got the eyes good. Careful there Jesus, your 'ands are bleeding on the good carpet again.'

'Sorry Dad, just can't seem to get sticking plasters big enough to cover the 'oles.'

It took me until I was eight, mostly working alone but sometimes talking to Gran when she came round, to finally pin God down and fully understand his mind. Apparently, lots of people studying their whole lives had got no nearer the mind of God than they had been when they started, but as soon as I realised God probably had a cockney accent, I had it sorted out beyond question in no time at all.

God was nuts. God was a vindictive, crazy random murderer who would happily kill people just to make a point to some other people, but then leave them all alone to figure out what that point may be for themselves, and then if they got it wrong he'd probably kill them too. Yet all he really had to do was show up for five minutes and explain what he wanted from everybody: and when you're omnipotent, omniscient and omnipresent it's not as if it's really such a difficult thing to do, but oh no, not God. That Cockney shit didn't care, didn't answer, didn't listen and would sweep aside civilisations on a whim, the touchy bastard. He might tell one or two people with a history of mental difficulties, how good and lovely and caring he was, but everyone else, he'd give the plague and starve them and burn them and drown them, and if you didn't believe in him he'd kill you. And if you said the wrong thing he'd kill you, if you thought the wrong thing he'd kill you, and he might, for a laugh, give you a dose of boils and destroy every aspect of your life for a bet.

He sent his son to die, but then brought him back to life, so no grief for God there. He sent his son to suffer, but didn't do any suffering himself, as he already knew exactly what was going to happen as him and Jesus had agreed how they were going to stage the whole thing in advance. By the end of the New Testament, the God family is all happily alive and hanging out in heaven together, demanding that everyone should be grateful for their non-existent sacrifice. And oh yes, after you're dead, at the end of time they're going to judge you. They've not been very clear on the criteria, but basically you have to be good. But good by whose standards? God's? A murdering, vague, hypocritical, love me or I'll kill you all, cockney gangland wide-boy? The people who actually get into heaven will be expecting Jesus to be sitting on his father's right hand, but they shouldn't be too surprised if they happen to find Stalin sitting on his left, while the holy family and friends are waiting for Hitler to come back with the chips.

Of course that was just what I believed when I was eight, and because I'd started seriously frightening some of the younger children, and a sensitive teacher called Miss McPhail, with stories of hell-fire and the world of shit that their souls were all in, I found myself in Mr McRae's office again. This time, rather than suspend me for violent behaviour and appalling language, he asked me if I'd considered the possible non-existence of God, and whether I'd be interested in looking into evolution as a far more plausible alternative to an angry invisible man in the sky. Well I hadn't, because that was the kind of thing God killed you for and sent you to the eternal furnace for mentioning. But Mr McRae didn't seem bothered by that at all and pulled out from a pile, and handed me a thin book called 'Understanding Evolution for Intelligent 11–13 year-olds', and he told me to tell him what I thought of it when I'd finished. Enormously pleased with the title of the book alone, I ploughed through it in a day, and again the next day and twice the day after that, just to be sure. I emerged from the back cover in a waking dream with the realisation that while everything I'd believed was true, simultaneously, everything else I'd believed wasn't. A man with a beard had killed my Dad, just like Gran and everyone had said: but his name wasn't God, his name was Mr Charles Darwin. God hadn't done anything to my Dad because God was a bullshit invention hungover from the stone age, but a tricky concept to stamp out in the minds of the simple who kept telling their kids it was true. But God didn't point his finger and kill people, because God had no fingers or any existence to attach them to. God, for all his threats and bluster and all his human back-up insisting on his manifest reality and power, simply didn't exist. The universe and everything in it was clearly divinity free, and I felt a weight in my brain that I'd forgotten was even there, fizzle away. There was no one else inside my thoughts but me, there was no grand plan but choice and luck and chance, and there was no crazy judge sitting at the end of time to remind you of every misdemeanour you ever misdemeaned and who'd then ram an eternal splintery stick up your arse, although being eight I didn't think of it quite in those terms exactly.

My dad had had a tiny genetic pre-disposition to not always be very good at interpreting the human imposed meaning of colours in relation to traffic lights. If he'd been born a couple of hundred years before, that pre-disposition wouldn't have caused him the slightest bother. If he'd been born fifty years in the future when the roads will be talking directly to the cars and traffic lights won't exist, he never would have known that they weren't his thing. As it was, he was born when he happened to be born, with the pre-disposition he happened to have, and without any intent or malice or any purpose whatsoever, an evolutionary force coded in his head in the form of sometimes forgetting what red meant, and an evolutionary force in the form of a bus, coincided at the same moment and had seen him off. And that I could deal with. That I could understand. If anything it was his own stupid fault for thinking taxi driving was somehow a good career choice for him. There and then I abandoned the nonsense of religion and decided to learn all I could about how things really were. I also decided to become far more selective when it came to believing things my Gran told me. After all, apart from helping steer me towards the bible for two confused years with all her God did this and God did that talk, this is the woman who always says that Kilmuir was founded by a naked shipwrecked sailor called Gask, who came from a Spanish Armada ship that went aground near Avoch, and who only escaped the pursuing the Avochies, who were cannibals at the time, by swimming across the mouth of Munlochy bay as the tide was going out, and then hiding up in the woods by the burn until some goat herding maiden came by with a hankering for the exotic. As if anyone could swim across the mouth of Munlochy bay when the tide's going out! My Gran also believes absolutely that witches were still being burned in Kilmuir in the point field until the late nineteen fifties, that the Cloutie Well grants wishes, that the cave at Cragiehowe contains a race of sleeping giants and cures deafness, and that somewhere in her house is a set of Bonnie Prince Charlie's personal silver spoons which were rescued by some other ancient Gask after the battle of Culloden. She even took me way along the shore to the deafness curing cave one weekend when I was about nine when I was staying at hers because mum was off somewhere else. All the way along the beach she was telling me crap like I should never go up to Loch Lundie in the winter because of the water bull that lives under the ice, or never to bring a trumpet if I was ever to come to Cragiehowe by myself, because a single blast was all the giants were waiting for to wake them up, and I might well get eaten if I woke them up because they'd be bound to be hungry. I asked her who ever goes for a stupid long hundred mile hike along a beach and takes a trumpet with them but she pretended not to hear. When we got there, Gran went into the cave and collected some water dripping from the ceiling to give to her friend who didn't want to get a hearing aid because it would make her look old. I informed Gran that all superstitions were rubbish and that's why we now had science instead. Gran replied that a lot of things had been believed true for a long time before science was invented, and just because science had shown up in the last five minutes and said otherwise was no reason why they couldn't all have been true in the first place. The old woman is clearly a nut.

Chapter 3

Friday April 12th, 11.10am

'Findo.'

'What?'

'Are you going to school today?'

'No.'

'Then come and visit your Mum in hospital.'

'Mnnn.'

Here's the geography bit. The Black Isle is a green peninsula about 20 miles long and 10 wide that sits just north of Inverness on the east coast of the highlands of Scotland. It's bounded by the sea in the shape of three firths. The Beauly firth which turns into the Moray firth along the South and South Eastern side, and the Cromarty firth along the North. You can go for a swim in any of these fine firths, the sandy beach at Rosemarkie being particularly popular for a day out, but even at the height of summer the water will freeze your bollocks off, it really will.

Unlike postcardy tourist Scotland, the Black Isle isn't mountainous, brooding, heather covered or tartan framed: it's mostly slopey arable land with forestry on the highest and slopiest bits and a scattering of villages, some of which pretend to be towns, lying mostly round the edges. There are exactly three kinds of people here. Firstly, there are the people who moved here because they think it's a fantastic place to bring up children or retire to or whatever, in other words, the white settlers; and there are lots and lots and lots of these. Secondly, there are the people who grow up here and are waiting to be old enough to escape as fast as they possibly can to somewhere proper – and just over the bridge to Inverness doesn't count. And thirdly, there are the people who grew up here and who didn't move away and who sit in the pub wondering why they never went when they had the chance, and while it's all very pretty here and all that, there's got to be more to life than this pissy village and these pissy people and why the hell didn't they go that time they had the chance?

Mum and Gran are in the third lot, and bugger me damned if I'm not going to be in the second. Show me the bus out of here, just show me the bus.

Now in my mind, and probably only there, the gorgeous Black Isle on the map looks like a side view of a cartoon head with its mouth open, a pointy nose and a big fifties quiff. So for the sake of argument let's say it is Elvis' head, and his mouth (Munlochy bay) is open, because he's saying 'Uh huh.' When I was born we lived near Tore, which on the map is inland at about the hinge of Elvis' jaw. Tore has a big roundabout and nothing else. Literally, nothing else. Nothing. Unless you count fields and trees and that, and I don't. We lived in a cottage on the farm that Dad's Dad, and then Dad's older brother Uncle Robert, owned. Mum always said that Dad never minded that Uncle Robert got the whole farm and the huge white Victorian farmhouse with the high bay windows looking down the hill on a forty mile view, and with the two sets of stairs (one for the servants), while he got a two bedroomed labourer's cottage infested throughout with damp, dry rot, wet rot and woodworm, painted a lovely shade of concrete and leaking in water in three directions when it was windy; because Dad had never been that into farming and wouldn't have taken it on even if he'd been left it. He could have sold it though, but Mum often insisted that Dad didn't mind.

A few weeks after dad died all his stuff vanished. Everything that was his wasn't there any more. Mum said it was for the best; clean break, no reminders. I disagreed. All I found was his athlete's foot powder that got left on the bathroom windowsill. I hid it from Mum and kept it. I hoped that one day when I was older I'd get athlete's foot myself and I'd be able to use the powder and get cured and it would be because of him. No sign of any foot fungus yet though I notice sometimes in the mornings now my armpits smell like I remember his did. We stayed in the cottage for three years after dad died as it rotted and sank into the field behind it, and one day after the doors wouldn't open any more because the roof had subsided a foot in one night, we left through Mum's bedroom window and moved to Avoch. Mum said she'd never liked living in Tore anyway and far preferred to be near the sea. Avoch, for those who don't know, is pronounced 'Och' like the Scottish stereotype, 'Och Aye the noo'. This is because Avochies are thick and five letters in a row are far too many for them to manage, so they leave the first two silent. On the map of Elvis' face, Avoch is just between the bottom of his nose and his upper lip. It used to be a fishing village and now it isn't one, but the Avochies are all very proud of their fishing heritage, which basically means that the unemployed Avochies are the most mouthy of the lot. I hated the Avochies and the Avochies hated me, and we were there so long that most people think I'm an Avochie, while only the Avochies and me know I'm not. Being called an Avochie is like being condemned for a crime you didn't commit. And now we don't even live in Avoch any more, now we live in Kilmuir with Gran. Kilmuir is a blackhead on Elvis' chin.

Kilmuir only gets to call itself a village because there's a church up the hill, but it's basically twenty houses in a line facing a crappy stone and mud beach at the end of a very, very long single track road that finishes at the last house. There's no pub, no shop, no nothing: unless for a shop you'd want to count the idiot down the end who sells home-made pottery to people who've got lost. Kilmuir is so pointless that it got to keep its old fashioned red phone box so someone might think it was quaint. But it's not quaint, it's shit. According to Gran, thirty odd years ago the whole place was almost derelict because no one wanted to travel miles up the hill and then round the back of the hill and then down the hill, and then back up the hill and back round the back of the hill and then all the way back down this side of the hill on a twisty narrow dangerous road, just to get a pint of milk and a packet of Benson's, and then add on to that a ferry trip to Inverness if you wanted anything more substantial than whatever you could get in the Kessock Spar. But then in the eighties they built a massive bridge from Kessock to Inverness and little abandoned Kilmuir suddenly became commutable. The ridiculous single track road that made all the sensible people leave, now made it a tranquil idyll that wasn't really too far from the office and would be a great place for the kids, and the schools are good, and it'll need

14

a new roof and an extension out the back, but we could have four bedrooms then and yes the single track road will be a bit of a pain, but there's no traffic on it and just look at that view over the water, and you could fish from the beach in front of the house if you wanted and yes I know you don't fish but you could if you wanted.

So new people moved in and Kilmuir didn't die, more's the pity as it means I've been living here the last two years in a bedroom the size of a cupboard in a house that smells of my granny. Gran's the only person left from before the original exodus. She's quite pleased that she has a tax accountant on one side and a restaurant owner on the other and everyone's polite to her because she's so authentic. I once heard some blond dyed old cow in one of those quilted I-have-a-horse-somewhere jackets, tell the friend she was walking along the street with that Kilmuir, 'Isn't really a village in the traditional sense, it's more of a boutique hamlet now'. Yet boutique hamlet or not, it didn't stop someone sticking a dog shit under your windscreen wiper, now did it.

'Findo, we're leaving for the hospital right now so get down those stairs before I kick you back up them.'

'That makes no sense.' I shout through the floor.

'Well it will soon enough if you don't get down here, and you better not be looking like a tink for your mother.'

I think maybe the other reason everyone in the village is so polite to Gran is because she's a little bit scary. Well, maybe not scary exactly, but certainly unhinged.

Gran is standing at the bottom of the stairs in the winter coat she'll wear till July and with her old lady rock solid sprayed hairdo like a grey bouffant crash helmet.

'You're wearing that?' she says.

'I am.'

'You couldn't wear your other one?'

'I couldn't.'

Gran snorts and fumbles in her bag at a glacial pace before she finally finds her keys and gets out the front door. I wait as she loads a couple of bags of stuff out into the boot and then she mumbles something as she goes back inside to get whatever she's forgotten. I step across the road to the beach. The tide is pretty well out so everything has the salty mud smell. Up the beach the two little home-school kids are throwing stones at a mound of something sticking out of the seaweed at the high tide line. I amble along the grass verge at the top of the shore to see what it is and I recognise the sound of a stone bouncing off a dead seal at near full inflation. I choose not to warn them that if they're ever curious enough to prod it really hard with a specially sharpened stick, they'll cover themselves in a smell so belief-defying that their parents will be forced to burn whatever clothes they're wearing and they'll be sent to live in the shed for the rest of the week. Instead, I shout down to the beach some friendly older kid advice for them, 'Try bursting it with a pointy stick'. I turn and amble back.

On the other side of the firth the clouds are doing a patchwork thing with the light down the mountains and fields as far along as Arderseir, and over Culloden to Inverness. On this side of the firth, Gran has found whatever it was she went looking for and is now standing by the car giving me a look for keeping her waiting. I consider telling her that I solved the universe earlier but judging by her face she wouldn't be that interested.

We pull away out of Kilmuir and up the hill past the churchyard that's full of all the old Gasks and on upwards into the woods.

'Why aren't you at school today?' asks Gran.

'I already know it all.'

'Must be nice for you.'

'It is.'

'When's your first exam?'

'A few weeks.'

'You'll be studying hard then.'

'Of course.'

Apart from I'm not. After five minutes of trying to read about crap that doesn't interest me, my mind wanders and I do something else instead. Gran pulls over to let an oncoming car pass and then complains about how busy the road has got and what a stupid big thing that is for someone to be driving along a road this narrow, and I tune out. Up through the forestry and along and down and past the old primary school that's a recording studio now, and down the steep burn valley and we're suddenly swept out of Victorian times and on to the dual carriageway, and out and over the bridge and high over the firth and descending into an Inverness traffic jam. Inverness, capital of the Highlands and the fastest growing city in Scotland is now reportedly growing so fast it doubles its size every two or three days. Soon Glasgow, Edinburgh and then even London will become mere suburbs of mighty Inverness. Already in my lifetime the Eastgate shopping centre has grown by a whole extra bit, political parties as important as the Scottish Liberal Democrats will occasionally hold a conference here to talk all their shite, and bands you've not only heard of, but might actually want to go and see, will sometimes come and play only a hundred and four miles away in Aberdeen. Life in the capital of the Highlands is truly sweet.

We avoid the throbbing heart of the city and peel off the A9 to Raigmore. At first Mum said she had a cold and then she thought she had flu and took to her bed. Then on Wednesday while I was at school, Gran called an ambulance. When we visited last night they said it was flu-like symptoms and they were doing tests and monitoring her closely for signs of change. Now call me a spakker on the Dingwall mini-bus if you like, but don't flu-like symptoms indicate a flu-like illness: something like, oh I don't know, flu? The doctors are just covering their backs and not wanting to say anything in case it turns out they missed some bullet holes and a couple of broken legs. Or should I say, some bullet-like cavities suspected to be of a gun-caused nature, accompanied by a strange backward bending of the shins giving a can't walk function and wrong way round appearance.

We go into the ward and Mum doesn't look well at all. Really not well. She's very white and looking all sunken and gaunt, which is pretty scary because she's far too fat to be looking sunken and gaunt. Gran takes a seat beside her and takes her hand and I stand near the end of the bed looking around for something else to do.

17

All the other sick people in the ward are looking at me like they want me to come and talk to them. I'm not going to. I don't know what to say to sick people. After 'how are you feeling', I don't know how the conversation's supposed to go. Sickness should be like in films. In the films if you're sick or wounded you either get better fast, or get cut out after a few minutes once you've made an important revelation or made the hero look good by showing everyone how much he cares, but he doesn't have to care every day through the whole film by showing up all the time. The sick person vanishes till the end when they might, might, get to show up in a wheelchair looking grateful, but in no way planning on being a burden to the hero after the credits.

'How are you feeling?' says Gran to Mum, nicking the only thing I had to say.

'Tired and sore everywhere but my feet. My feet feel fine, but that's all,' says Mum.

Her voice is raspy and quiet and her eyes are half shut and unfocused till she spots me and then fixes her bead on me.

'Why aren't you in school?' she half whispers, half rasps.

'I wanted to come and see you,' I lie.

I imagine for a second she'll believe me but she holds my gaze, reads the bullshit and unexpectedly gives up and looks off to the side. Gran is now giving me the exact same stare that Mum started and she stares me out no problem. That done, she starts quizzing a sleepy Mum on what the doctors have been saying, but Mum doesn't seem to know much. I have a look at Mum's chart and consider becoming a doctor, as they get all the nurses, then I think that maybe they have to spend most of their time dealing with sick people, so I decide against medicine and put the chart back. I grab a spare seat from beside the bed of a woman who's melted down one side and unlikely to complain and start flicking through a copy of The People's Friend, which they probably keep around for euthanasia purposes. An old nurse with a huge dangling chin wattle walks by and Gran assaults her with questions which all bounce straight off the nurse who says the doctor will be along in a minute.

18

After twenty minutes I'm so bored I feel like walking round the ward pulling out tubes and flicking switches, and now Gran is repeating the same stuff to Mum, for the third or fourth time, who's hardly even awake anyway. The doctor finally comes in and I think it might be his first day. He's all keen and helpful and he's an idiot who doesn't know anything. They don't know what's wrong with Mum, the tests they've done have been inconclusive and so they're doing more tests. At first they thought it was flu but now they're not sure and maybe it's something else, but until they've done the tests he can't say. He asks Gran about her own health and has she had a flu jab and how has she been feeling and has she been ill at all? Gran lists her usual complaints, and what she's on for them, and then he offers Gran a quick examination to check she isn't showing any symptoms of anything too and being an old woman she jumps at the chance of having a young doctor finger her.

'Well if you think it'll help doctor.' And the doctor takes her out of the ward somewhere and I'm left with Mum and I'm trying to think of something to say when I notice she's looking at me in a really strange way. Not like she's just sleepy or semi-conscious, it's more like she doesn't really know who I am, and she's trying to fix me into some memory. Then she seems to stop trying and her eyes drift a little and her mind isn't in the room any more. The thought that maybe she's not going to get better suddenly touches me inside like a block of ice.

'How are you feeling?' I ask.

She looks back at me with perfect recognition, but only for long enough to say, 'I'll be fine.'

She's going to die. I know it as surely as I know what day it is, and that I'm indoors and that the woman in the next bed is chewing on her plastic wrist band. Mum's closed her eyes again and I'm left sitting, alone. Mum's bulk under the covers, the embarrassment of almost everything about her and the icy feeling that, no, bollocks, she'll be fine. She'll be fine. And I keep convincing myself until Gran comes back in with the doctor.

'Findo, isn't it?' he says. 'I'd like to take a quick look at you too if you don't mind.' And like a zombie I follow him out.

He takes me into a little office on the other side of the corridor that's more like a storage cupboard and sits me down. He asks me how I've been feeling, any headaches or feeling hot, and he feels the sides of my neck and looks down my throat and takes an inside of my mouth sample with a swab on a stick thing. Just to be on the safe side, as because my Mum is quite ill, the immediate family should be tested for any infection, if it is an infection, and so if any symptoms should develop they can get right on it. And now a nurse is going to be here in a minute to take a small blood sample and then I can go back and join my Mum and Gran.

A blood sample? Well, I suppose if it helps. The doctor goes and a minute later, just as I've decided that Mum definitely isn't going to die and I'm going to steal that nice looking pen from the desk in front of me, a nurse comes in carrying some blood taking stuff. It's a happy, happy day indeed as my blood taking nurse is Polish. Of course it's not really a surprise, as most of the population of Poland lives in Inverness. In fact it's been predicted that in five years time the entire population of the Highlands will be Polish except for one Asian guy who's come on his holidays. They say we should welcome the Poles because they contribute so much to the economy and do the jobs that all the lazy Scottish arseholes won't, and that's perfectly true; but mostly we should welcome the Poles because the Polish girls are so much sexier with their big round faces and big round eyes than anything you'd otherwise get walking round Munlochy. Of course their lanky Polish boyfriends with their round heads and pointy faces can contribute to the economy or go back to Poland as they wish, as long as they bring their girlfriends and sisters with them and leave them behind when they go. Thank you, Poland.

Now my Polish nurse is no Mandy Duplin (but then who's Mandy Duplin but Mandy Duplin, and oh my God how I love Mandy Duplin). For starters this nurse is about twenty four so well past it, but still her eyes are big and Polish and her nose is lovely and tiny, and she even pretty well covered up the surprise that everyone gets when they first see my face, and now she's speaking to me in that sexy Polish I'd-probably-do-it-in-a-carpark accent. I roll up my sleeve and she wraps the inflatey thing round it and pumps. I'm concentrating hard on not getting an erection and yet looking at her tits every moment she's not looking at me. Girls, for some reason, hate it when they catch you staring at their tits, they think it's disrespectful or something, but as they've never been a boy they have no idea how seriously difficult it is for us to avoid looking at their lovely tits: and if they had the first clue I think they'd all be a lot less judgemental. Nurses' uniforms are crap for showing up tits well but my nurse has got fantastic ones. Well, pretty good. And now I'm going to have to be all manly testosterone itself and show no fear or pain as she's coming at me with the pointy needle. Ow! Shit-piss that's sore, don't they bloody train them? Fantastic, not a flicker, I can tell she's impressed. How could she not want me after such a display of bravery, or at least not mind too much if I tried to touch her up while she's popping the plaster on my wound. But up she gets and out she goes like I was just some ordinary patient whose blood she was taking. I steal the pen I had my eye on and go back to Mum and Gran on the ward.

Mum's asleep again and Gran's taking some of Mum's stuff out of a plastic bag, unfolding it, re-folding it and then putting it in the cupboard beside her bed, then she folds up the plastic bag and puts in a bag. There's only so much hospital visiting anyone can be expected to take and I'm miles past my limit, though Gran is a professional with the visiting stamina of a marathon-running nun getting paid by the hour. I indicate my desire to leave by pointing at the door and saying, 'Can we go now?'

Ten more minutes of needless rearranging and tidying the tidy and talking pointless mundane shite to an unconscious woman, and we finally step out of the ward and the endless corridors and into the sunlight. We head across towards the car park and just as it occurs to me to ask Gran if she thought it was weird that they took our blood and stuff when we were only visiting, I see a horribly familiar form gliding between the parked cars. I stick my head down and hope Gran doesn't spot him but he's heading straight towards us and he's exactly the kind of arsehole who'll always stop and say hello because he wants everyone to think he's charming.

'Hello there,' he says to Gran as soon as he's in range, all bright and breezy.

'Oh, Vincent, hello, how's it going?' says Gran, stopping to talk, all surprised and pleased to see him.

I'll tell you how Vincent Egger is, shall I Gran? He's an uptight smarmy twat, that's how he is. He's a fifty year-old or something, very tall, very skinny, sharp-faced, baldy-dick-bag in a geography teacher's jacket, that's how he is. He's a happy slappy Christian chappie who wants you to think he's just like Jesus, but nicer, when in fact he's just like Hitler, but worse. He's more like Hitler's older brother: the one who used to beat Hitler up and whose fault it all really is. So don't stand there and talk to the fraudulent arse-nut Gran, spit in his face, walk away and don't look back, but certainly don't stop and talk to the psudeo-pious bible-fanny.

'I'm just great, thanks,' says Vincent all cheesily to Gran. He looks at me and gives me an ineffective little fake smile entirely for Gran's benefit, and he says, 'Findo.' in his best pretend magnanimous voice, when really he's grinding his teeth and trying to swallow down his bile. Yes, it has been a long while, hasn't it Vincent.

'Mr Egger.' I respond, trying to un-nerve him with my politeness, but he ignores me and asks Gran about Mum as it seems the bastard's come to visit her.

'I heard she's been taken ill through the Monday Group, so I thought I'd pop in and pass on a card along with everyone's best wishes.'

Of course he's all oozing sympathy and concern and Gran's lapping it up so I walk on to the car and leave them to it. What bugs me most about Vincent Egger is how everyone thinks he's so lovely, or worse still, lovely and harmless and so well meaning. Oh, he's a little odd, they'll all agree, eccentric even, but then he's an evangelical or something isn't he and you have to respect a person's faith don't you, and he's always so friendly and he gives up so much of his time to do all sorts of good work with all kinds of people, so I hear. But no. No, no, no, no, no. Vincent Egger is a cold-hearted manipulative shit who wants everyone to believe exactly what he believes and he'll keep coming round uninvited and he'll listen and nod and 'Um' and 'Ah' and he'll eat all your crisps and he'll drink your diluting orange and he'll be your friend and he'll wear you down and he'll open your doubts and he'll pour his shite into the cracks; and he'll say he can help and he'll call his lies 'faith' and he'll invite you along, to a coffee with friends, and they'll gather you in and they'll make you feel safe, then one Saturday night, you'll announce to your son, that like it or not, oh yes, like it or not; he'll be going to church in the morning.

'Bollocks Mum I am not.'

'Yes you bloody well are.'

Is it any wonder I did what I did? I hate Vincent Egger.

Chapter 4

Primary 6

We'd not long moved to Avoch when Mum met the Eggers. I was nearly ten and being dropped into a new school wasn't going well. I didn't care that Mum wanted to live by the sea or that the old house had substantially collapsed two days after we left. I knew where I was with my old bullies, and as Avoch primary was so much bigger, my new bullies were less of a gang and more of a mob.

'Have you seen the ugly new boy? Come and look at him.'

'Where's he from?'

'He said he's from Tore.'

'Let's smash his feet.'

Avochies are as thick as shit. I tried to fight a couple of times but because everyone is everyone else's cousin, if not their uncle, it was like being a single goldfish in a bowl of illiterate piranhas. That Mum was making new friends, I didn't notice or care. Sometimes when I limped home from school she might be sitting in the kitchen drinking coffee with some woman or other, talking about some dreary grown-up's nonsense that hadn't saved me from that or any other day's torment. So some months later as I picked dried blood out of my ear, I didn't pay any more attention than usual to her or the departure of her smiley friends until she announced that we were both going to church that Sunday. Now to most recently turned ten year-olds who have to go to church, it's just a tedious, boring, droning waste of half a day to be endured pointlessly in smart clothes. But for me, not me, I wasn't having it. I'd already had my crazy religious phase and was more than a little embarrassed by the whole thing, as I had by now thoroughly investigated and rejected any notion of God. I also distinctly remembered explaining to Mum only the year before how God was an entirely surplus notion in a rationally observed universe, and I remembered how impressed she'd been with my argument and how at the time she'd nodded and smiled and agreed with me. So now what the very fuck was all this shit?

Wasn't it bad enough that I was suffering a school week of dead-eyed thugs playing Findoball with my carcass round the playground every lunchtime, and that every Saturday I had to follow Mum very slowly round the shops, or get dumped at Gran's and have to follow her, very, very slowly round the exact same shops. Sunday, God dammit, was the only day I had. What possible, plausible reason could she have for wanting to steal my only day from me? Where was the logic? Where was the reasoning? Where was the sense or the humanity? Why mother? Why?

'I've met some nice people so we're going.'

And bollocks to everything else, that was that. I protested, I swore, I argued, I had a tantrum, I rationalised with her, I had several more tantrums, I spoke reasonably and in measured tones, I slammed doors, I was silent, I was high pitched, I was sulky, I was rude, I chewed with my mouth open and yet despite all my flapping and my noise I was now a churchgoer. And a churchgoer under strict instructions to keep his atheism to himself.

Strict instructions be damned. 'I'm an Atheist.' I said to the smiling man the next day who asked me if I'd enjoyed the service. We were standing about afterwards outside the church and while I was itching to get back to the car and be gone, Mum was hanging about and chatting to people and being all smiley and friendly and nothing like herself at all and wasn't the service just so uplifting. Of course it wasn't uplifting, it was pish, they were all just saying it because everyone else was saying it and so if you wanted to fit in you had to say it too, which I didn't.

The man who I'd told I was an atheist looked at me like he couldn't decide whether I was joking or not, and then when he realised I wasn't, he decided to pretend that I was and he turned back to the group he'd just left, which contained my Mum, and said to them all with a fake laugh.

'Our new young friend here thinks he's an Atheist.'

And all of the recently uplifted people laughed along with the man, except Mum, who did a bit of laughing along for show and then told me with her eyes I was in the shit. The man turned back to me and went down on his haunches so his face was level with and close to mine and he said warmly: 'You're too young to understand what atheism really means in eternity, yet I think God has brought you to us here, because he doesn't want us to let you go down the path which risks you finding out what an Atheists eternity really is.'

And all the people watching murmured their approval and I was about to object on various grounds when Mum intervened and said:

'Thank you Vincent, I'm sure Findo will think about what you said.'

And that's how I met Vincent Egger. And I did think about what he'd said. He'd basically called me an idiot and had then casually assumed an intimate access to, and understanding of, the mind, plans and will of God indicating my certain eternal damnation. I'm never one to rush to judgement but I somehow found that I hadn't really taken to him at all. And I took to him a whole lot less a few weeks later, when him and his wife started inviting my Mum back to their house after church for coffee and tiny square cakes with 'a group of friends'. And of course because Mum went, I had to go too and watch all these people sucking up even more of my Sunday and sitting around talking about how God and Jesus helped them in whatever stupid topic was the stupid topic Vincent Egger had decided God would be interested in that day. The only people even approximately my age were the Eggers' two daughters, but they were a few years older and so docile, plain and lifeless that it was weeks before I could even remember one of their names. The only Egger who was alright was Mrs Egger. She always gave me extra cake and then when she could see that I was so bored I was about to pass out, she'd give me a conspiratorial smile and pass me even more cake. Yes, Mrs Egger was alright. Vincent on the other hand was a shitbag.

Vincent Egger wanted everyone to think exactly the same as he did, which was basically that Vincent Egger was the most Christian, most caring, and the most humble-while-still-getting-to-be-in-charge person in the world, who just wanted to help humanity be as good as him, and the more people who were looking at him while he did it the better. And if it ever so happened that someone's opinion differed from Vincent's on any particular issue, well, then he'd smile his smile and sit with them and pretend to listen and nod a lot and smile some more and give them a hearing and fully take their point on board. Then when he'd had enough of that, he'd start interrupting and making suggestions and then he'd just talk over them, usually invoking his superior understanding of the divine mind, until they'd either shut up or had agreed that God's will was essentially whatever Vincent said it was. And yet for some reason, they all sat there in that big living room full of beanbags and uncomfy chairs and they all thought Vincent was lovely.

One Sunday turned into weeks, turned into months, and Mum was still dragging me to church to pretend to sing and to fail to be uplifted, and then dragging me to the Eggers afterwards where I sat in a corner and bit my tongue and said nothing, or pretended I was elsewhere to wait out Vincent spreading Jesus' love in the form of his own ego. And why was I so silent? Not because Mum had made it clear she would kill me if I made a fuss about anything anyone said, but because I was waiting for Vincent, or anyone really, to question me on my beliefs; at which point I planned to argue their Christianity out from under them, shooting all their theological points down in flames and Mum wouldn't be able to say anything because I'd only be responding to what I'd been asked. Trouble was no one ever asked me anything. Once or twice Vincent referred to me as 'Our young atheist' but then he moved the conversation straight on past me and he never once tackled me on any of the many major and minor religious points which I could answer with the words, 'But there is no God you skinny, baldy old shitbag.' And so I sat eating cake and was ignored, because for whatever reason, Vincent didn't consider me worth talking to and everyone else followed Vincent's lead.

I mostly thought he wasn't trying to Jesusify me because he could sense that I could see right through him and that I was un-Jesusifiable. His crappy I-know-God-better-than-you stuff might work on everyone else, but I was sure he could tell that ten-year-old me was more than a match for him, so he didn't dare take me on. Then some other times, when the cake was all gone but they were still all talking, I thought that maybe he didn't bother with me because I was just some ugly fat child who'd sit in the corner saying nothing because he'd been dragged along unwillingly by his Mum, so why bother with the miserable little shit when all he wants to do is sulk and stuff his face with cake. But I only thought that sometimes. Mostly I thought he was scared of me.

Chapter 5

Friday 12th April, 12.45pm

'Well that's very nice of Vincent to visit your Mum,' says Gran as we pull out of the hospital car park.

I don't say anything for a while. Then I say,

'Mum will be alright, won't she?'

'Of course she will,' says Gran; though I'm not sure either of us entirely believe it.

Gran tries to interest me in what we're having for lunch but I'm not interested. It's cheese on toast. I text Diane to see if she's noticed I'm not at school and I text Alex to get him to tell her to text me back. By the time I've finished my cheese on toast and I still haven't heard from either of them, since it's now lunchtime at school I phone Diane.

'Findo you shagmonster, what's happening?'

Diane isn't one of those shy retiring girls from the olden days who sit in a drawing room doing embroidery, quietly hoping that some fine gentleman will one day pay a call, and perhaps six months after formal introductions, will be delighted when he remarks that he believes she has terribly dainty hands.

'Did you notice I'm not at school?'

"Course I noticed but I couldn't be arsed texting you back. You still coming out tomorrow night?'

Diane decided last year that I was her friend, I had absolutely no say in the matter. She'd worn some previous acquaintances in the ground and was casting her eye around the art room for some fresh amusement. And while many sets of eyes seeking amusement had fallen on me in the past, Diane's were the first to want to involve me in the fun rather than make me the butt of it. Of course when she first roared up to my potter's wheel, I was a little intimidated because physically she a bit of a discus thrower, although weirdly there's a significant section of boys at school, and according to Diane, any number of middle aged men, who find her bullish charms somewhat irresistible. I'm not one of these people though and if she thought I was she'd probably kick my head in with a bat. It occurred to me once that she might be some kind of mixed-up lesbian, so I asked her if she was, and she stuck a pencil into my wrist so hard that when it healed over she'd left a full stop tattoo. This didn't answer my question but it did teach me to be further away from her whenever I feel like tackling a thorny issue.

'Aye, I'm still coming, am I missing anything today?' I ask.

'No, you coming out tonight?'

'No cash, no transport.'

'So what, come anyway.'

'I really can't, I've only about enough cash for tomorrow. I'll get a lift over after town and see you about sixish.'

'Alright, tomorrow gorgeous.'

She hangs up before I remember to tell her I've solved the universe.

I call Alex but the randy little despoiler has his phone on voice mail. He's probably talking some very well brought up fourteen year old into becoming a single parent. God knows how he does it, he's nothing to look at, he's short and for Christ's sake he's ginger, but somehow, some way, he can convince almost any girl, for just long enough, that they fancy him. At first I naturally assumed that he was drugging them but I've since been through his pockets and watched him really closely, and it doesn't appear to be chemical. Alex says that he just likes to talk to girls and is genuinely interested in what they have to say, but I know there's no way it's that simple. And surely they all have eyes in their heads anyway: surely they can see he's a ginger. If it didn't give me some form of vicarious hope I probably couldn't stand to be in the same room as him, but whatever it is he's got, it's a mystery. If further proof were ever needed that there is no God, Alex's success with girls would be the absolute clincher. I've always known that in the unlikely event I don't die a virgin, it'll be because I settle for whatever I can get, rather than get anywhere near what I actually want. Namely, Mandy Duplin. Whereas Alex, who has no standards whatsoever, had slept with both Gillian

Melons and Sexy McDonald before either of them were sixteen. Unbefuckinglievable. There isn't a boy above third year who hasn't cry-wanked himself to sleep for the wanting of Gillian Melons or Sexy McDonald, yet Alex walked away from them both without a second thought and neither of them even seems to hold it against him. The little ginger shitehawk is made out of magic, while the rest of us and me in particular, are just made out of shite. I don't leave Alex a message, I'm too annoyed.

So now I'm stuck in Kilmuir on a Friday afternoon with nothing to do and nowhere to go and there's no one else who'd want to hear from me or who I'd want to phone. I probably should have gone to school, it's one thing skiving off if you live in a city and there's excitement round every corner, but here in Kilmuir there aren't even any corners. The most exciting thing likely to happen is the postman and he's already been. I could go outside and see if the tide's still coming in or if it's now going out, or I could walk up into the woods and be near some trees. I almost feel like phoning Cousin Dan. A few years ago he'd be the first person I'd call, the only person. But what would he say if I phoned him now? What would I say? It's not that I feel guilty or anything but he probably blames me for everything and he hasn't phoned me since either. No, I don't phone Cousin Dan any more. Might as well spend the afternoon on computer games with the sound up, and porn with the sound down.

The afternoon vanishes, mostly into a sock, and as I sit down to dinner I see Gran's already poured herself a whisky and ginger which means she's feeling talkative, or at least she will be in a minute. I eat quickly to try and make it upstairs before the reminiscing begins, but she's thought ahead and laid on some pudding so the 'When I was your age' chat begins before I'm half way through the ice cream. It seems that when Gran was my age, things were very different. Big news Gran, thanks for that. I rattle my empty bowl down by the sink and am about to disappear back upstairs when Gran asks me if I feel like playing a board game. No, of course I don't feel like playing a board game, computers were invented specifically so people wouldn't have to play board games any more. Then she says, 'And you can have a beer'.

'Scrabble or Risk?' I ask.

'You decide.'

Well, Risk takes much longer to play than Scrabble, but then again, without Mum stacking all her armies in Australia and sitting there defensively all night there may be a chance of an interesting game, even if it is only a two player. Then again, Scrabble is quicker.

'How many beers?'

'For as long as we play or until I say you've had enough.'

I get the Risk board out. Gran always wins at Scrabble anyway.

The board is set, the cards are drawn, my armies are poised. I'm sixteen and a half years-old, it's a Friday night and I'm about to spend it playing board games with my Gran. I really am living the dream. I bet Mandy Duplin isn't stuck in tonight. I bet she's at some party or successfully buying drinks in any club she feels like visiting. Or more likely having drinks bought for her by every lothario mechanic's apprentice or eighteen-year-old with a fancy haircut in town. It doesn't even matter that I know she's not interested in me and never, ever will be ever. It doesn't matter that the closest I'll ever get to her is breathing in when she walks past: there's a hole in my heart that's Mandy Duplin shaped and it won't fill up with anyone else. Definitely going to school on Monday because she's just in front of me in English. Her 1920s hair, her big sleepy eyelids, the front of her when she's walking towards me, the back of her when she's walking away and the shape of her which I've got to stop thinking about right now because I'm risking a stiffy and my saggy faced old Gran is looking at me funny.

'It's still your turn,' she says.

I have a swig from my tiny bottle of supermarket lager and try to concentrate on the game. As I make a move to sweep into South America, Gran who's well into the whisky now, starts banging on about herself when she was young and all the other stuff I've heard a million times before. Usually I ignore it but as she's obviously a bit worried about Mum I decide to indulge her a little bit.

'So is the village better now than it was or worse?' I ask her. That should keep her going for about a day or so.

'Oh I don't know Findo,' she muses, clinking the ice in her glass as she decides where to put down her fresh armies. Tonight I'm playing as pink for a joke. Gran always plays black.

'It's just different,' she says, and it looks like she's making a move to hold North America. 'Some things better, some things worse. I was seventeen when I married your grandfather and moved here, and in those days if you left your washing hanging out on the line past lunchtime on a washday, they'd whisper up and down the street that you were a slut and no-one would speak to you the next day in the queue for the fish van.'

She rattles back her glass and takes a deep breath. Here she goes, I should have passed on pudding and beer and bolted upstairs when I had the chance.

'You see most of the families here now, I don't know beyond saying hello and smiling and pretending not to mind when their dogs do their business in front of the house, but I much prefer that to everybody knowing every tiny little thing about everybody else. A community can be too close Findo, too close by far, and that's what Kilmuir used to be before everybody got cars and drove off in them. You couldn't sneak out a fart at one end of the street without people down the other end discussing what you'd had for breakfast.'

I smile and pretend I care about what she's saying and I go to the kitchen to get another tiny bottle of beer. Gran talking about farts is disturbing. The summer before last, just after me and Mum had to move in here, Mum got lots of duty-free booze from somewhere so Gran and her took it into the garden and tanked the lot. They made me sit out there with them and bring them crisps and dip on a tray while they were laughing about all kinds of crap like how Gask women were indestructible and Gask men were always enormous at birth and died before they were fifty. 'Long in the womb, but not in the room,' Gran said, and Mum almost pissed herself. Every time I got up to be somewhere else they shouted at me to stay, got all sentimental about how much they loved me and then said appalling things about their dead husbands. And that was long before the worst bit. The worst bit was when Mum accidentally farted. I'd never up till that point in my whole life ever heard a woman fart, I'd never even considered if they did or not, and then Gran decided to do an impersonation of a man in a pub, and she let one rip through her deckchair, that I swear, I not only felt through the ground at ten metres, but with my own two eyes, I actually saw. I still shiver down the inside of my spine at the thought.

Back in the living room she's talking about fish now, and how everyone used to stretch out their nets with a little curve in the end and how no one called it poaching and how good it used to be to have a huge fresh salmon in the house when there was precious little else to eat, and how the big ones, sometimes up to 40 pounds in weight and more Findo, would find their way in the back door of the Munlochy hotel and whoever caught it would emerge a day or so later out the front. Really Gran? Fascinating Gran. How long before you start telling the one about Bonnie Prince Charlie's spoons? I try to get her to concentrate on the game but my conquest of South America waits as she pours the nibbles into two small bowls rather than let me eat them from the bag, and then she wanders into the kitchen to get more dip. She comes back with another drink poured but no dip. When she finally sits down I mop her up in South America and then in a move I can scarcely believe, she shits all over me in Europe, sweeps straight down to take Africa and even breaches my South American fortress just to piss me off and deny me my extra armies. Two rounds later and she's won. I hate playing Risk with Gran, next time it's definitely Scrabble.

Gran packs the board away and I finish my tiny supermarket beer. I put the empty down on the table and make a satisfied 'ahhh' noise, to emphasise what a lovely beer that was and how I might accept another if offered, and wasn't I a good sport when I only swore once when she took out my last army in Peru. She takes the hint.

'You can have another beer if you promise to go to school on Monday.'

Thank you Gran. On Monday, Mandy Duplin will be in front of

me in English with her 1920s hair and her perfect neck and her body slipped inside whatever she happens to be wearing just inviting me in. Well, not inviting me in exactly, more like telling me to fuck off if I come within ten feet of her, but at least we'll be in the same room for an hour so of course I'll be going to school.

'Ok Gran, promise,' I concede to the old woman and I go and get my beery reward. Then as soon as I sit back down it starts.

'Now you'd better go in on Monday Findo, with your Mum as she is, she doesn't need to be worrying about your skiving as well as everything else.'

'I said I'm going in.'

'And what about the studying for your exams? Don't try and tell me you're studying when you're wasting the day on computer games or whatever else it is you do up there.'

I'd usually walk off at this point but as the deal seems to be, get a beer if you listen to the moaning, I decide to pretend to listen, drink it quickly and see if I get another if I promise to study too.

'Now I know you're more worried about your Mum than you're letting on, so the best thing you can do to help her is put a bit of focus into your school books, so when she comes home she can see you've done something productive.'

I wonder if she can see my eyes glazing over?

'You're such an intelligent boy and you're letting it all turn to shit because you think you already know it all, but you don't Findo, I can assure you of that.'

'Shit' is a very bad word Gran, naughty, naughty. I wonder when she's going to breathe in? By the looks of it, not soon.

'Your teachers used to tell us that you were capable of doing anything you wanted with your life, anything at all. Sky's the limit for Findo Gask. But now you don't bother and you think you've got an answer for everything because you've read a few books ...'

More than a few Gran, a fat bloody shitload.

'... you think it gives you licence to be rude to your teachers and to not even bother to learn what they're trying to teach you and we'll not even mention all that carry on with your Cousin Dan. Now, here's the thing and you'd better be listening boy. If you don't pull your finger out, I'm going to find it very hard to forgive you. If I'd had a quarter of your opportunities do you think I'd be living four miles from where I was born? Do you? I certainly would not. So if I see you keeping on wasting your chances like you are Findo Gask, I'll kick your arse so hard you'll choke on my sock. Understand?'

Charming language Gran, I'd probably laugh if I wasn't choking on the end of my tiny beer. So having taken Gran's stern talking at, and as there are no more tiny beers forthcoming, I head up the stairs. I might have chosen to say something back to her but she is sort of right. My educational track record over the last few years has been less than meteoric. Or rather, it has been meteoric, in the direction that meteors actually go. And yes I do feel I know it all, and no I can't actually be arsed learning anything that the school wants to teach me. I told Gran that I'll do my best but I'm not going to; why should I? Bollocks to it. Gran can worry about my exams all she likes but I'm not going to. I've given them all the thought they deserve and I've decided to cheat.

'Do it for your Mum's sake,' she said. Yeah, thanks Gran, twist the knife, use your dangerously ill daughter to try and get your only grandson to open a history book. It's almost enough to put me off having a wank. Almost, but not quite.

Chapter 6

Primary 7 to Secondary 1

Being ruthlessly honest, I suppose there were a few weeks back then, maybe even a couple of months or more, when I sort of stopped minding too much about having to go to church every week. It wasn't that I'd started believing again or anything like that, I'd just reached a kind of mental plateau. I quite liked how the church was perched on the edge on top of a crazily steep hill and how Mum always panicked that the car wouldn't make it to the top, and once there, all the slightly too happy people would be just a bit too polite to everyone else, and I used to wonder where they all went to get their grins painted on. The minister would preach the week's themed bag of shite and I'd sit simmering but quiet, undercutting in my mind everything that he said and slicing his pissy scriptures into shreds. It seemed that everyone in the church was made of a very agreeable kind of plasticy stuff, and as the only real person in the room I'd sit covered in a feeling of general superiority as all the idiots sucked up the gospel like it was gospel and amen'd away like a good little flock. The churchy people liked to use the flock metaphor as a metaphor but I always thought that the ministers and higher up professional God-botherers had invented it as an in-joke, because the people in the pews were such an easily led bunch of fucking sheep. Then like the sheep that Mum was, and me the lamb to the slaughter, we'd end up at the Eggers for the happening after-service, and I'd sit eating my cake and disappear into the wall. Sometimes I'd feel oddly drawn to one or two of the younger older women or I'd concentrate on tuning Vincent's biblical chat completely out of my head, as his charming arguments and self-godly attitude were so ridiculous and easy to see through, that the only source of constant surprise to me was that everyone else in the room seemed to hang on his every word. Once successfully ignoring the Jesus chat, I'd let my mind wander on to the real questions like, 'Why are people more keen on ornaments than newts?' or 'If you had a couple of rabbits, how hard would it be to make shoes out of them?' or 'Why do all women think that pillow covers have to match the duvet?' And after a long summer where I bothered no one and no one bothered me, and I'd mostly stopped caring about everything except what I was reading that day and what was for dinner, I was woken up one morning at a new un-godly hour and made to go and start secondary school.

Fortrose Academy, Academy Street, Fortrose. I had a plan and everything. I told myself it was going to be fine. I was going to keep my head down and not bother anyone, and then in a year or two if that went well, I might think about making a friend. On the first day it worked brilliantly, on the second I ran into my Cousin Dan.

Cousin Dan was nearly two years older than me and everyone knew he was a nutter. He was one of the people that the first years warned each other about. Before I saw him coming, he grabbed me as we passed in the corridor to show me to his friends. He was short, I was already as tall as him, he was classically ugly and he had hair like a dried out gorse bush which always seemed to have dust in it. Not dandruff. Dust. He wasn't quite thirteen yet but he had two cars and a crossbow and was known to have once taken the Rector's dog for a joyride to Balblair and back.

'This is my wee cousin Findo,' he said to a small group of big troubling faces. They were unimpressed.

'Brainy as anything my Cousin,' he said.

These people clearly didn't care for book learning.

'Goes to church and everything, don't you Findo.'

That sparked an interest, it meant I was dead.

'You a Christian?' asked one of the meatier ones.

'No.'

'What do you go to church for then?'

And with that he had me. I could hardly say, 'Because my Mum makes me go', these were third years: they'd all killed and eaten their own Mums long since. To admit even having a Mum would be bad enough, and I was about to be branded either a Christian or a Christian mummy's boy. Either way I was screwed. I looked to my Cousin Dan to see if he was going to step in and offer me any protection but it quickly became apparent he wasn't, and that his friends didn't really like him very much either.

It was stand up and be counted time. I knew that I already had a face that would attract all the bullies I'd ever need, if word got around that I was a Christian too they'd have to start making appointments.

'I'm not a Christian,' I said, adamantly and honestly.

'How are you not a Christian you weird looking Christian fucker? You go to church don't you?'

Again the logic was flawless. I may have considered myself the king of the pre-teen atheists and Darwin's champion on earth (except on Sundays when I wasn't allowed to be), but I was also a regular church-goer who also attended bible meetings with his Mum (a mum who he hadn't even killed and eaten yet). Oh shit, did Cousin Dan know I went to bible meetings at the Eggers? If he did, he didn't say, but by the time Cousin Dan and his friends let me escape down the corridor, my new name was Mongo Jesus Boy, and Mum and I were going to have to have a little talk that night because church and I were done.

So Mum and I had our little talk and that Sunday we went to church as usual. My arguments counted for nothing, my beliefs counted for nothing, my genuine desperation and the fact that it was going to get me beaten up counted for nothing too. Mum had made friends there and I wasn't going to spoil it for her, and if I tried I wouldn't get fed ever again and all my electrical goods would be seized. So I went and I simmered and I made comments under my breath and that earned me an elbow in the ribs.

During the weeks that followed I tried to avoid Cousin Dan's friends but the school that seemed so enormous during the first few days turned out to be not all that big. I'd successfully made no friends, which, added to the no friends I'd brought with me from primary school meant the safest option for me during break and lunchtimes was to try to give the appearance that I was on my way somewhere, while trying to avoid any groups that might look a bit … 'Hey you, Mongo Jesus. C'mere a minute.' … but the school just wasn't that big. And so they bullied me for my supposed Christianity, and after some months and considerable pain, when I'd convinced them that I wasn't a Christian, they bullied me on behalf of Jesus who must be very disappointed in me and who would, they believed, have certainly given me dead legs on top of dead legs if he was there to do it himself. And still I was pulled to church every week where I simmered and mumbled, and still I was pushed into the Eggers afterwards for a punishment dose of Vincent's oily crap. And sometimes life turns on a pinhead and sometimes it turns on some woman taking ages to get her pram on a bus.

One Saturday I was being sent over to Kessock on a bus where Gran was going to pick me up and take me to Kilmuir for the afternoon, as Mum was doing something, I can't remember what. The child in the pram was far too old to still be in it, and the woman taking so long was tiny, talkative and incapable of counting money. The skinny window shelf I was trying to lean my elbow on was vibrating up my arm, and I was looking out the window into the absolutely nothing happening on Munlochy High Street. Someone came out of one of the houses that had some garden and bushes in front of it and he turned to say goodbye to the other person who'd come to the doorway. It was Vincent Egger the lanky twat and the other person who stepped over the threshold was one of the younger older women from his church group. My cheek was against the window feeling the cool of the glass and the throb of the engine as Vincent Egger kissed the woman on the mouth and squeezed her boob, and as he turned and walked down the path he looked around and adjusted the lie of his cock inside his trousers. I was eleven and a half and didn't really know what it meant, but I sort of exactly knew what it meant at the same time. I knew that it wasn't Mrs Egger getting the tounge-boobing and I knew that I'd been right not to like Vincent all along. He wasn't a suspected fraudulent hypocritical shitbag any more, he was a proven fraudulent hypocritical shitbag.

The next morning as I sat simmering through church I already had my plan clear in my head. When Mum and I went to Vincent's

40

later, I wasn't going to blend into the wall eating cake. Instead, when everyone was sitting about nodding at Vincent's general marvellousness as he spouted forth on whatever was the pissy topic of the day; I was going to say,

'No Vincent, that's not true, and here's why …'

And then I'd out-argue him on science or diseased Africans or Fluffy Bunnies or whatever it was going to be, knowing all the time that when he tried to talk over me or ignore me, or do any of his other pious tactics on me, I would point at the younger older woman whose boob he felt and say:

'Vincent kissed her and felt her boob'.

And as I looked around the church all packed with its smiling thoughtful ignorance, and the minister was banging on about something, the gist being that everything in the bible must be true because it's written in the bible: which is basically the same as saying that everything in 'The Lord of the Rings' must have happened because it's written in 'The Lord of the Rings.' And it seemed that no one else in the whole church but me had any kind of problem with the concept. I suddenly found that my simmering in church days were behind me as I boiled over a couple of hours ahead of the plan. I rose from my pew and shouted in a voice that bounced back off the walls like someone else was joining in.

'Bollocks! Liar! No! That's all bollocks! Don't you see he's talking bollocks? It's all stupid shit what he's saying, but you all believe it because you must be spakkers or something!'

By which point my Mum was gripping my arm in anger and terror and trying to drag me down and back into my seat, as if that was somehow going to make the last ten seconds not have happened, but my lid was well off and I fought back heroically and struggled back to my feet and kept shouting.

'Darwin was right and everybody in here is an idiot to be in here!'

That was enough to set the elderly dear who'd been sitting on the other side of me into action and she said 'That's enough from you' and tried to put her scrawny old hand over my mouth. Meanwhile everyone in the church had turned to see, and a hubbub of 'disgusting behaviour' and 'must be on something' and 'get him out of here' was rising all around me. I found I was thoroughly enjoying it and managed a further quick,

'Jesus is bollocks and the bible's all bollocks and God is a c …'

before the old dear clamped her hand over my mouth with the strength of the queen vampire she clearly was, and then my Mum got a proper grip on me with her sweaty sausage fingers and I was shuffled through a nearby door into a side room, where there was a big desk and lots of crap posters with rainbows and a crap tapestry with a rainbow. Mum and the old queen vampire kept me silent with the power of their stares and the service went on with the minister sounding ruffled and the congregation murmuring to each other instead of letting the holy spirit fill them up with smileyness. Mum was bursting to give me a good shouting at, but instead, her and the old vampire discussed in whispers whether I should be taken out, or kept in here till the end of the service. Mum said 'Just you wait' quite a lot and the old vampire said 'Think of your poor mother' and some other stuff along the lines of 'disgraceful behaviour', 'never heard the like' and 'now in my day'. They decided they didn't want to walk me out through the church while the service was still on, so they kept me in the room sitting in the big round office chair. Afterwards, the minister came in and so did Vincent and so did some other people. They looked at me like I was a space monkey, and I answered 'I don't know' to all their questions as they alternately threatened, placated, cajoled, and even said they understood what I'd done, despite their dismay and disappointment they still had hopes for me and God had hopes for me too. I switched right off and they talked amongst themselves about whether I had a mental condition, maybe like Dustin Hoffman in that film. And they asked Mum if I was good at maths and she said I was and that seemed to settle something for them.

In the car on the way home Mum was switching between shaking her head, telling me she was too mortified to speak and making dire threats about how sorry I was going to be and how I just had to wait and I'd learn a lesson I'd never forget. And lots of 'How could you?

How could you? In front of all those people. That language. In a church. A church, Findo'. What must they all think of her and what must they all think of me? And how could she go back there now? How could she face anyone? What did I think I was thinking? In God's house. In a church. A church. And didn't I know what that means?

'What does it mean?'

'Shut your fucking mouth at me!'

So I shut my fucking mouth and she kept going on anyway, and wasn't I even sorry? Didn't I even feel remorse for what I'd done? And if I'd been allowed to open my fucking mouth I would have said 'No Mum, I'm not sorry, not even the tiniest bit, and for lots and lots of reasons'.

For one, this was the first Sunday in over a year that we were going straight home after church instead of going to Vincent's for some extra bland Jesus chat. For two, because I'd meant everything I said and anyway it was all true. And for three, because I enjoyed it. The sound of the collective intake of breath on the first 'Bollocks' and then the looks on all their swivelling faces as they turned in collective disbelief, burned themselves into a part of my mind that I found was making me very happy. How could I feel sorry for that? I couldn't. And how could Mum, uninventive, not really all that bright, and with no real advantage over me other than weight, really think she could come up with a punishment that might even begin to make me sorry? She had no chance.

Chapter 7

Saturday 13th April, 10.15am

Saturday morning. Even before I'm awake I know my head feels a little bit wrong. I'm drifting in and out of a dream about an underwater University where I can swim down and pick stuff off the floor. I open my eyes to see my unblinking computer screen pointing porn at me. I didn't even switch it off. How many of those mini-beers did I have? I could try and count them up but it's easier to roll back over and try to drop back into that dream, whatever it was. Maybe half an hour later there's a shout up the stairs saying there's breakfast if I want it. I don't. I doze back off.

Now Gran's shouting up that she's going into town and I wake up enough to ask for a lift over to Avoch later tonight. She says, 'No.' and that wakes me up a bit more.

'Why not?'

From the bottom of the stairs she goes into great detail about her plans for today and tonight, none of which involve either coming back to make me dinner or driving me anywhere I might want to go. She offers me a lift to Inverness if I want to get up right now and leave right now as she wants to visit Mum first before she goes to do whatever it was she said she was going to do with some other old woman or something. I decline and drop my head back on the pillow. 'Ok then,' she says in such a way as to send all the possible guilt vibes she can up the stairs and through the door, at the son who would rather have a lie in than get up and visit his ailing mother. Some of the guilt vibes work on me a bit so I make them go away by shouting back that I'll probably go and visit her this afternoon as I'm going into town anyway. As soon as I've said it I know I probably won't go because it's a long enough walk along the beach to Kessock just to get the bus into town without walking up to Raigmore or spending cash on another bus once I get there, as I need every penny I have for the booze tonight. I could tell Gran all that but she wouldn't understand. I continue to feel some residual guilt vibes until I hear the front door close and Gran drive off. I have another doze.

Living in the middle of nowhere is crap. If people in cities think they have it tough with all their urban squalor and people gang murdering each other all over the place, they should try living in a place where nothing ever happens ever. Nothing. Ever. The biggest thing ever to happen here was over 250 years ago and that was only about some stolen spoons. And so what if the spoons were Bonnie Prince Charlie's, he was just a tartaned-up Italian fanny. And the one thing that ever happened here didn't even happen here, it happened on the other side of the firth. It started as one mid-eighteenth century April morning dawned, and since my Gask ancestors and everyone else knew there was going to be a battle outside Inverness as the Hanoverians had finally caught up with the Jacobites, over the Gasks sailed to the opposite shore of the firth and they climbed the hill just as the battle of Culloden got under way. Canon roaring, highlanders charging and everyone getting mangled to shit, the Gasks, far too sensible to want to join in and run at any cannons waving a sword about, hung around just long enough to rob the corpses and the baggage train afterwards and then ran quickly back down the hill again with Hanoverian musket balls aimed at their arses. So back to Kilmuir they sailed, and the pick of the booty that was handed down untouched through the succeeding generations of poverty struck fishermen, was a silver set of monogrammed spoons, once belonging to Bonnie Prince-dress-up-as-a-woman-and-run-the-fuck-away-Charlie himself. However, did that really even happen just because Gran says so? I doubt it. And even if it did happen and we do have a priceless heirloom of the doomed '45 rebellion in the house; I'm pretty sure those would have been the spoons I borrowed to dig down in the mud with one low tide when I was six; and which I then threw into the sea because I didn't want to admit to anyone that I'd taken them outside and got them dirty. Anyway, even if that was them, Gran still seems to think they're somewhere in a cupboard somewhere and I'm not going to tell her otherwise.

I get up. Life might not be quite so shit if Kilmuir was at least on a bus route to anywhere, but it's not, so it is. A mile and a bit along the beach to Kessock just to get a bus. I might as well be living in one of the thirsty bits of Africa with a public transport service like that. And at least in Africa everyone else in the village would have to knacker their trainers out along the rocks to get anywhere too, whereas here, it's just me, because everyone else has a car and can drive out to civilisation up round the back of the hill.

Toast, shower and then make myself look as good as possible as I won't be back now before I'm out tonight. I look in the mirror. What to do with a face like that. Oh, my big brown eyes are universally acknowledged as gorgeous, but planted into the disaster of the rest of my head, they make what would otherwise be merely a very ugly face, both very ugly, and at the same time disconcertingly weird. It's like carefully placing a couple of daisies on a dog poo: it doesn't make the dog poo any prettier but it does make you wonder what the daisies are doing there. I squeeze my spots and blackheads and turn a mess into a catastrophe. Face destroyed I turn my attention to the hair and spend twenty minutes trying to get it to do what I want it to. I don't achieve anything approaching a hairstyle but eventually I get it to sit in a mostly inoffensive way. I get my stuff together, put on my coat and head out. I risk a glance in the hall mirror and for a moment I manage to delude myself that I like what I see.

I hate walking. Why no one ever built a road along the shore between Kilmuir and Kessock I'll never understand. Fuckwits. It's sunny between the fast little white clouds and the tide's half out. Fifty metres of road and Kilmuir-tropolis ends. My hair's already blown to shit by the time I step onto the beach. I jump the rotting high tide line and then nearly break my ankle on the stones below which are all exactly the wrong size for walking on. I negotiate my way over the biggest most stable looking ones, nearly breaking three more ankles before I reach the rocks, which at least aren't a problem to climb over when the tide's like this. Along past the shoulder high stone wall of what's left of the boat shed that used to be ours and now isn't anyone's, which is probably the place from where my ancestors set out to rob the twitching corpses after Culloden, and which is definitely the place, at least according to Gran, where my great great grandfather famously landed a mermaid. The incident is recorded in one of those local interest spooky-fable-history books that some interested local spooky-fable-historian wrote and that no one ever buys off the carousel in Munlochy post office. Well, no one but Gran bought one. It's filled with stuff like the cave at Cragiehowe that cures deafness, the Brahn Seer's future telling antics, fairy wells, fairy glens, monks that something happened to, witches that did things, and things that happened involving pixies on the way home from the eighteenth century pub. And in there too is how great great grandfather Gask caught a mermaid. The old boy was out in his boat fishing, gets a mermaid in his nets and pulls her aboard, whereupon she asks him to peel off her scaly skin (presumably in English rather than Mermaid). Great great granddad obliges, and she turns into a beautiful woman who he then marries. After many years of happy marriage she begins to pine for her old undersea life, so she asks great great granddad for her skin back, but he's long since forgotten where he put it. Eventually one of their children finds it and with great great granddad's blessing she puts her scaly skin back on and returns to the sea, promising before she goes that the Gasks would henceforth be the luckiest of all fishermen. Now Gran is very fond of this story, even though she married into the family, but if her and the book are to be believed, then the supernatural powers with fishing rod and net have been handed directly down to me. Yet the one and only time in my life I ever did go fishing, I was as bored as hell and caught bugger all. It's a bit like the story that's been going around school for years about Stevie Sutherland, whose parents kept goats in the house and Stevie successfully trained one to lick his balls. Now everyone knows Stevie Sutherland, and what he's like, but even though this only supposedly happened a couple of years ago, no one really has the slightest idea if there's a single word of truth in it. Stevie Sutherland is just one of those people you could hang any mad story on and it would seem to fit perfectly. My own theory about my great great granddad and the mermaid is: that once upon a time, many years ago, there was a fisherman in Kilmuir by the name of Gask. One day his wife left him and he had to tell the children something. As for Stevie Sutherland and the goat ball licking, I reckon that probably happened exactly as people tell it.

The sun has warmed me up inside my jacket so I take it off and stop for a minute at the little cliff bit with the really big rock against it which makes a passage through. This was the best bit of the shore to play at when I was a kid and I walk out to the edge and perch myself above the water. I've miles of time to get to the bus stop and I'd rather waste the extra time here than in a perspex bus shelter with 'fuck your cock in Gavin's bum hole' scratched on it. I don't know who Gavin is but it's one of those graffitis which has attracted lots of responses and addenda, and even a pie chart.

It's probably down to my mermaid ancestry but there's something that always gets me about sitting on a big rock above the sea. I prefer it when the tide's in as the low tide mud looks crappy, but with no one about and the sound of the wind through the forest up on Ord hill behind me, and the wave tops rolling along in blue rather than the usual grey, and the hills across the firth, and the size of the landscape stretched out around me; I feel like a tiny speck of nothing that's here on earth for less than a blip of time, and the nowness of everything fills me up. Then the act of realising my total insignificance tends to make me feel slightly significant again for having had the sense in the first place to realise it, and realising that in turn makes me feel a little bit self important. I lie back on my rock and flop into it for a while, feeling the sun and feeling the breeze and being nothing and being everything, until a thought of the Saturday bus timetable from North Kessock to Inverness creeps in at the edge of my mind. It's probably just as well too: whenever I lie on a rock by the edge of the sea I develop a terrible tendency to turn into a hippy.

Chapter 8

Secondary 1

After my youthful outburst in church, Mum spent most of the following week on the phone telling people she didn't know what to do with a son like me. My punishment for being honest and saying what I thought was to be in two parts. Firstly, anything Mum thought I might enjoy was seized and denied. This mostly meant that she took all my electrical stuff and I wasn't allowed out, not that there was anywhere to go, and as she didn't consider taking away any books, I was basically forced to stay in and read which is what I'd have been doing anyway: so the first part of the punishment wasn't really any kind of punishment at all. The second part was that I had to apologise to everyone in church the following Sunday. Apparently, atheist or not, I was to consider myself very lucky that if I made a sincere apology to everyone I'd so mortally offended, I would be allowed to remain a member of the congregation. And this, I was informed, was something I wanted whether I wanted it or not. Mum had somehow wangled it so that I wasn't the disturbed, foul-mouthed, blasphemous young troublemaker I'd seemed to be. I was in fact some sort of prodigal son, a living example of how cosy and smug-holy they would all get to feel about themselves if they let me back in. My penitent and humble re-appearance in the church that Sunday would confirm their own self image as magnanimous forgivers, and then despite the terrible provocation they'd received at my young hands, they could then morally lord it over me for all time. The second part of the punishment was punishment indeed.

Sunday church time rolled around all too quickly. I got out of the car and walked under close guard along the row of parked cars by the church wall like a condemned man facing execution, only a lot less willingly. I'd been drilled in what I had to say and I'd even been allocated a little slot in the sermon, when the minister would give us the nod and I'd stand up and display my very very sorryness for what I'd said last week. The only trouble was, as we entered the churchyard and the conversations politely quietened around me so they could bore at me with their eyes, and as Mum elbow nudged me towards the door where God lived, I had the distinct feeling that, although I knew I was supposed to be feeling humble and repentant, I wasn't sure I knew what humble was supposed to feel like at all, and as for repentance, well I certainly wasn't feeling that. And so in I went, and all the kindly old dears were throwing me the sort of looks they usually reserved for the backs of Muslim women who dress up as ninjas.

Mum steered me to a pew quite near the back and told me where to sit, and she tried to make small talk with the people who came and sat next to her. And as the rest of the congregation filed in I caught more murmurs and glances and Mum tried to smile despite her obvious shame and she hissed at me that I'd better remember to say it right.

'I'm very sorry for what I said last week, I didn't mean it, I hope you can all forgive me.'

I was also supposed to add, 'With God's help and yours, I hope to turn my anger into something positive before it's too late for me'. But there was no way I was going to say that bit, as I was sure the words had come from Vincent. I looked down the front for his skinny baldy skull but the church was busier than usual and I couldn't see him.

Minister, prayers, songs, the usual shit, and it occurred to me that maybe church was busier this week because they'd all come to see a young repenter repent, and that thought made me simmer a little. The minister started the sermon and at first I wasn't listening but as I felt some eyes up the pew sneaking in my direction I started to pay attention. He was talking about Jesus ordering unclean spirits out of people, and how these people said and did terrible things when the spirits were in them, but how it was the unclean spirit in control of the person and not the person who was really responsible; and that faith in Christ alone could remove the unclean spirit from the body. And as more eyes surreptitiously creaked towards me I was overwhelmed by the distinct sense that the bugger of a minister was trying to imply that I was possessed. Then he started on about some bible guy who was taken over by a huge horde of demons and he couldn't be subdued by ropes or chains or anything, until Jesus wandered up, and as there happened to be an enormous herd of two thousand pigs nearby, Jesus sent all the demons out of the man and into the pigs, and the pigs didn't like having demons up them and were driven mad, and all two thousand of them ran over a cliff and drowned themselves in the sea. Splash, splash, splash, two thousand dead pigs but the man who did have the demons in him is feeling a lot better. And it wasn't even that I was particularly angry, and it wasn't that I'd planned anything at all, but the bible story had raised a small query in my mind so I voiced it. Clearly, but not so loudly that the minister couldn't have ignored it if he wanted, I said,

'But what about the poor fucker who owned the pigs?'

And that was it, my feet didn't touch. Even before the uproar of tutting began, I was grabbed from behind, lifted straight over the back of the pew and bundled outside. I was landed just about still standing on the gravel by the main door, and only then saw that it was Vincent Egger who'd picked me up and dragged me out. The skinny bastard had placed himself right behind me and must have been waiting for me to breathe wrong. He was really mad too, he had white gunky stuff in the corners of his mouth and he was looking all glinty, like a shitty teacher who can't handle it when his class all ask if his wife has a big-bucket-man-fanny. And then before anyone else had time to come outside to gawp and murmur at my pre-teen insolence, he slapped me so hard across the side of my head that the inside of my eyes flashed white and I felt my brain rebounding twice. I was stunned. Involuntarily my eyes filled up and before I could blink back the tears, he stuck his face into mine and furiously hissed, 'You'll go to a special room in hell and nothing you can ever do will save you from it'. And some of his white mouth gunk went on my cheek. My equilibrium was as far off centre as it could be. I was terrified. As he straightened up and towered over me I thought he might hit me again or strangle me or I didn't know what. It didn't occur to me to say that I'd seen him kissing a woman that wasn't his wife. It didn't occur to me to point out that hell wasn't real, special rooms or not. All my shocked eleven year-old self could think to squeak was, 'You can't hit me'. Which of course was nonsense because he already had.

The main church door turned on its hinges, and Mum and one or two others came out. Mum's face was threatening murder. She thanked Vincent, actually thanked him, then she grabbed my arm and started hauling me away. 'Vincent hit me,' I complained as I was shoved towards the gate, keen to deflect her anger to where it should be. She stopped in her tracks, swung me round to face her and said, 'Where did he hit you?' I pointed to the side of my head and Mum instantly responded with an open handed whack on the same spot that made Vincent's effort feel like an autumn leaf wafting past a sleeping baby. 'Anything like that was it?' she said at my traumatised face, and not expecting an answer she dragged me to the car.

Every child knows that adults aren't allowed to hit them, even the ones whose parents beat them up all the time know it, but the shock I felt wasn't that Mum had hit me; or even that so much of her great big fat arm turned out to be muscle: it was that she had taken Vincent's side, when he was clearly far further over the line than I was. I thought I'd just asked an honest question, someone in biblical times was out two thousand pigs, which was probably a lot of pigs in those days, and there was no mention whatsoever of Jesus compensating the poor owner for filling his innocent pigs with someone else's demons and making them suicidal. Was it really that unreasonable a question, or was it because I used the word 'fucker'? Either way, no one called Social Services and I was still tasting blood two days later. I didn't blame Mum for hitting me really, I knew she never would have done it if Vincent hadn't done it first and given her the idea. And why hadn't I thought to tell anyone what I knew about him and the woman he kissed? I was sure Mum would decide not to believe me if I told her now, but if I waited till next week, perhaps someone with a developing habit of speaking up in church, might just speak up again. And the more I thought about it the more my indignation turned revengy. It soon stopped mattering what I might deserve and what I might not, I decided I wanted justice. A justice that suited me and what I thought. Perhaps people should know that he hit me, and perhaps he did it because he found out I knew about the woman he kissed and he wanted to stop me saying anything. Perhaps that's what happened. And perhaps he even sometimes touched my willy. A vindictive eleven and a half year-old never plotted a more diabolical plot.

Then on the Wednesday it was suggested to Mum by one or two well-meaning people, very politely of course, that she might consider never ever bringing me back to church ever again. I wasn't a prodigal son any more, I was now suspected of being possessed by the devil, or at the very least a few demons. And while it was obvious to most of the congregation that an exorcism would be the best way to deal with me and my fledgling case of possession, it turned out that some of them had friends in the real world where if you talk about exorcising demons from an eleven year-old you end up looking like a dick. And anyway, if you let the demons out you never can tell where the demons might end up, so wouldn't it be better simply to leave the demons where they were, make sure I was kept far away from everybody who wasn't full of demons, and then forget about me. So they cast me out, expelled me from the body of the kirk and officially shunned me. I was no longer welcome. What lovely paranoid crazy-arsed people they were. I was absolutely delighted. Meanwhile my reputation at school had soared. I'd told my Cousin Dan what I'd done and by the time he told his friends, it turned out that I'd told the minister to 'go and fuck his mother with his brother'. And Cousin Dan's cronies began to look on me so favourably I could tell they were only beating me up and robbing me out of habit, rather than any real desire.

Cousin Dan also told me I was going to his on Sunday, which was news to me, but it turned out he was right. Despite my expulsion, Mum was going to continue to go, and I'd be dropped off at Uncle Robert's and Auntie Roberta's farm every Sunday, while Mum went off to sing flat, drink coffee and pray for my soul. The first Sunday she drove me up, she told me Uncle Robert and Auntie Roberta were only taking me because she had promised them that I would be helping out with whatever work needed doing and that a bit of hard work might knock some sense into me. I saw Cousin Dan was already waiting outside as we pulled off the road and headed up the long straight drive to the farm. Mum didn't stay to speak to Uncle Robert or Auntie Roberta because she didn't like them much, and she spun the tyres on the gravel as she headed off to spend the day with Jesus and his pals.

'Mum said I'm supposed to help out on the farm,' I said to Cousin Dan.

Cousin Dan, dressed in a boiler suit, dust in his mad hair, and looking every inch the working farmer's son, looked me up and down then summed up his attitude to rural life and farm labour in particular.

'Bollocks to that,' he said.

When Cousin Dan was at home, he didn't really care about anything except pretending he wasn't a farmer's son on a farm. Auntie Roberta said Cousin Dan was trying to avoid the inevitable and Uncle Robert said Cousin Dan was a lazy useless waste of spunk, and Cousin Dan said he didn't care what either of them said, he wasn't ever going to be a farmer and that was an end to it. Cousin Dan said that cattle were shit on legs and growing stuff was dickish, so growing whole fields of stuff was super-dickish, and as soon as he left school he was going to form his own rally team or hunt impala in South Africa. Uncle Robert was wrong about Cousin Dan, Cousin Dan wasn't lazy and he was only mostly useless, he was far more of a nutter than anything else. Like when he took one of his cars into school when he was twelve and then kidnapped the Rector's dog and drove it to Balblair and back, or when he put his head through a window in metalwork for a bet, even though the bet was only that someone said he wouldn't. And I've heard it said he once did a shit in one of the chemistry cupboards. I don't know if he did, but Mum thinks he's like what he's like because of when he killed his twin sister, Cousin Pam. And even though it was an accident, and even though they were only seven, he still did totally kill her. Maybe that's why he really doesn't like farming: because of the combine harvesters.

It's just as well for me that my Mum never married my Dad as otherwise I'd have been a Paterson like Cousin Dan and people might have thought I was his brother, but as long as you weren't involved in farming in any way, Cousin Dan's farm was the best place in the world. I mean apart from the fact that Cousin Dan owned a crossbow and two cars, the farmhouse was so big it had two sets of stairs, because there used to be servants who had their own skinny set that went up from the kitchen that was like a secret passage. And there were loads of joined up barns and sheds outside, and most of them were never used and full of all kinds of brilliant junk and stuff to smash or burn, as the farm didn't have nearly as much land as it used to so Uncle Robert didn't need them all. I asked Cousin Dan where the land went, and he said that most of it was up the hill and got sold for forestry after world war one, and then more on the far side of Tore roundabout got sold for houses about fifteen years ago, but Uncle Robert said that it didn't matter, because of all the big glacial erratics and because the access had always been shit.

I hardly saw Uncle Robert the first Sunday, he was going off somewhere to do something farmy and when he passed by he just nodded and didn't mention anything about me being expected to move bales, or learn to plough, or shovel anything anywhere. So that morning Cousin Dan taught me to drive and we did time trials round a field. After lunch we tried to get Cousin Dan's other car going so we could do car jousting, but he couldn't get it to start because he'd lost some bits he'd taken out. So we towed it up to the field and towed each other round doing towing time trials and I didn't even mind a bit that I went home that afternoon with severe whiplash.

Chapter 9

Saturday 13th April, 12.36pm

The bus delivers me into the heart of Inverness. The bus station, one of the great bus stations of the world and the place where most of the pivotal world events over the last thousand years have occurred, is pretty busy this early Saturday afternoon. Tourist season seems to be kicking off, as there are a couple of groups of Spanish or Italian backpackers pouring over a map and arguing amongst themselves as to whose stupid idea it was to come to Scotland in the first place. They'll probably go down to Loch Ness to be conned, or perhaps the west coast where the midges will eat them, or to the far north west where the midges will eat them, or maybe even to John O'Groats where there is absolutely bugger all to see and even less to do. One of the backpackers looks at me and I spot the flash of mild horror at her first sighting of a pure-bred highland freak before she collects herself and glances away. Charming.

I have a few hours to kill, so I wander up Academy Street towards the Eastgate, daydreaming that there may be some pretty girl in there, and she doesn't even have to be that pretty, one who doesn't recoil when she sees me and maybe even thinks I look quirky rather than car-crashy, and who possibly needs my help reaching something down from a high shelf. And while I'm daydreaming, she'll also need to have a massively overly developed sense of gratitude and no fear of what her friends would say if she was ever seen with me.

'He's tall and dark,' she could say. 'Two out of three's not bad,' she could explain.

But tall and dark counts for nothing when instead of being tall, dark and handsome; you're tall, dark and oh my God what's going on with his face? Mum would always try to tell me, 'There's always someone worse off than yourself.' And while that may well be true mother, it's absolutely no use whatsoever to me unless somebody can tell me where she lives.

The Eastgate is packed and the Inverness young are out in force with their girlfriends and their haircuts. Little groups of haircuts chat and text while other haircuts saunter past sneering at the first group for their ridiculous haircuts. Other haircuts lean on the railings checking out the haircuts coming up the escalators, while those who can't control their haircuts shrink inside themselves and walk past as anonymously as they can, wishing to themselves they had the kind of face to support a better haircut. I am a youth sub-culture of one. No one gives a shit what I do with my hair, or where I buy my clothes, or who or what I say I'm into, and no one wants me to join their sub-culture either, because I scare away the girls.

I do a couple of circuits of the Eastgate, I look at some clothes that I'd get laughed at for attempting and I consider buying some music that's so far outside my haircut league I'm sure the assistant wouldn't even sell it to me. I wander out of the shop and hang around at the top of the escalators for a bit, trying to look as if I'm waiting for someone. I recognise a couple of fourth years but don't know their names and they don't look at me. City or not, Inverness isn't nearly big enough to spend a whole afternoon in, I should have come on a later bus. I walk down the High Street and go up to the museum and art gallery so I can look cultured and sit down for bit. There's an exhibition of paintings by local artists which guarantees it will be crap, which it mostly is, except for a couple of paintings of really bad weather which I quite like. I sit down for as long as I think I can get away with without looking homeless then I walk back down the hill. I might as well head to the Eastgate again and I'm crossing the road between the town hall and McDonald's when I see her. She's with Lyndsey Jack, who she's always with at school, and they're sharing some joke or other and she looks absolutely incredible. Every other girl in town can go home, their efforts have been wasted, they've come a distant second best. Because they're not Mandy Duplin. Only Mandy Duplin is Mandy Duplin, and there she is. There she walks. God how she walks.

I notice I've stopped in the middle of the street and there's a car about to get angry with me so I start walking again and get on to the pedestrianised bit. Mandy's on the other side of the street and of course she doesn't see me, and even if she did she wouldn't. Her and Lyndsey are heading up the High Street in the same direction as me in no particular hurry, so I have to ask myself; to stalk or not to stalk? That is the question. I quickly reckon that if I keep my distance and don't follow for too long, but just long enough to see where she's going, then that could hardly be called stalking, and if I do happen to get into a conversation with her at school on Monday I could mention that I happened to see her in town and we'd have something to talk about. Not that I've ever been in a conversation with her before, but you never know, so that's that decided. I'm definitely not going to stalk her, but I am going to follow her for a bit.

Mandy Duplin, Mandy Duplin, Mandy Duplin. I've only ever seen her in Inverness once before now, and other than in Biology and English our worlds don't intersect at all. She's not going out with anyone that I know of, but then I haven't a clue what she does outside school, though I do know there are plenty of others exactly like me who are all happily risking blindness every night on her account. Mandy Duplin, Mandy Duplin. She's not all tits and lips like the ones Alex usually goes for, or like that vacuous cow Lyndsey Jack who's nothing like Mandy so God knows why she hangs out with her. I mean Mandy Duplin wears a bit of make-up, though not that much really; whereas Lyndsey Jack bases her look on the trowel-faced creatures who work behind the beauty counter in Debenhams, who'd love to put on just a little bit more make-up except their necks won't take the weight.

Mandy Duplin is small and quite slim and she moves with grace and does everything in a considered and precise way, and she's also a little too frightened of germs. But best of all, Mandy Duplin has two laughs. She has her everyday one which is polite and short and she laughs it a lot with nearly everyone she speaks to. And she has her other one which is loud and dirty and her eyes sparkle when she's doing it and that's her real laugh. I can see she's laughing her real laugh now, but I'm not jealous as it's only the orange wall of make-up Lyndsey Jack that's caused it. Usually at school it's some idiot who's all lower jaw and eyebrows that makes her laugh like that, and then I seethe like an albino on the sun.

I cross to the same side of the street as them at an innocent ambling pace and follow the loveliest bum I've ever seen in my life till it turns into some woman's shop. I slow down as I pass the doors and glance in, but they've already disappeared into the racks of clothes. I could wait further up the street or double back a few times till they come out, but now that those are my only options I really am into the realms of the stalker, so I abandon that lifestyle choice for the comparative dignity of an eternal hopeless wanker, and wander on up towards the Eastgate for another pointless circuit.

I need some new kind of outlet for it all, all my pent up frustration, the loneliness that doesn't go away, all of that. Where do I put it, what can I do with it all? I've an empty feeling that keeps growing emptier with every step away from Mandy Duplin and my entirely unrealistic hope. Ugly hopeless cases such as me should find some positive thing to do with all the energy that the rest of the population get to use on rubbing up and down against each other. Maybe I need a healthy hobby, something outdoorsy and athletic like all those fit young Germans had, running around the woods, throwing balls and canoeing and stuff in all those 1930s black and white film clips.

Another circuit of the Eastgate and time's getting on at last. Half an hour till my bus comes, so I can go and buy the booze now. My rule for booze buying in the supermarket booze section is very simple: divide the price per litre by the alcoholic content and the lower the resulting number the better. Sherry scores well and has the advantage of tasting exactly same in both directions, though today I think I'm going to opt for the more discreet quarter bottle of cooking vodka, as being the easier to smuggle into the pub. I also pick up a bottle of vermouth as ordered by Diane and head to the checkout looking as old as I possibly can. I choose the queue with the most gormless looking Saturday girl and as she beeps my stuff through the till she asks me if I've brought my own bag, if I want a hand with my packing, if I'm collecting vouchers for schools and if I have a loyalty card. She doesn't however ask me my age and I don't even have to get out my fake ID (my name is Brian McGee). Being tall and a bit frightful to look at doesn't have many advantages but buying booze under-age is definitely one of them.

Carry-out in the bag I head for the bus station. Not just back to Kessock and the long walk along the beach for me tonight; but all the way to metropolitan Avoch for a grand night out. I should be there around the time Diane finishes her dinner, so straight to the pub and lots and lots and lots of booze till the money runs out, then crash at Diane's and Gran can come and collect my carcass sometime tomorrow. Just remembered, I didn't go and visit Mum. Perhaps I should have. Nah, she'll be fine. I'll go tomorrow when Gran'll make me anyway.

Chapter 10

Secondary 2 to 3

Sundays at Cousin Dan's were the best. When the ground was hard enough we'd drive round a field, when it wasn't, we'd build contraptions in the farm sheds or we'd try to put crossbow bolts through crows. Occasionally we'd make a zip line in the woods and Cousin Dan might break his rib on it, as it was a little on the fast side, and the only time Uncle Robert ever shouted at me was once when Cousin Dan drove me through the yard surfing on the bonnet of his car. We hardly ever had to actually help on the farm, because when we did, Cousin Dan made such a deliberate hash of it, or took so long to do anything that it was pointless to ask us. Uncle Robert wouldn't say much about it; he'd look at whatever Cousin Dan and I had or hadn't done, and he'd give Cousin Dan a look of 'later', and he'd walk off. Cousin Dan would stare at his Dad's back till he'd gone and curse him, because it usually meant Uncle Robert was probably going to give him a few slaps later. Cousin Dan's reaction to the de-motivational effects of domestic violence was to be even lazier. But then that stuff never happened when I was around and Cousin Dan said he was used to it and it didn't bother him, so as far as I was concerned Sundays at the farm were the best and were all about the fun.

A year and more went past and I hardly even noticed except that I'd mastered handbrake turns in all kinds of muddy conditions, could sometimes crossbow a rabbit or crow, though it was usually more luck than judgement, and we were finalising plans to build full size trebuchet. At school I was doing well, but not so well as to make myself any more visible as a target than I already was, and at home I was reading a lot of ancient history and teaching myself Esperanto, kvankam mi ne scii kial. It was a simpler time.

Then one Sunday towards the end of October, just as Mum was about to drive me up to the farm for the day, Auntie Roberta phoned to say I wouldn't be able to go up. It turned out that Cousin Dan had gone a bit mad in the house when Uncle Robert and Auntie Roberta told him Auntie Roberta was pregnant. Cousin Dan assumed they'd done it on purpose to replace him and he'd smashed some stuff up, and Uncle Robert went a bit mad too because it was some stuff he'd really liked. I didn't find out any of that till later; at the time it just meant that Mum was stuck for something to do with me while she was at church, and she was going to phone Gran to take me and then remembered that Gran had gone long line fishing off the west coast.

'You could just leave me here.'

'Hardly.'

'I'm old enough, I'll be fine.'

'No way, anything could happen.'

'No it couldn't, not anything. There are plenty of things that couldn't happen. If you like, you can leave me here, and while you're gone I'll write a list of all the things that couldn't happen while you're gone, which will keep me out of trouble as well as prove you wrong.'

'Cocky won't get you anywhere, you're coming with me.'

'To church?'

'Well not into the church Findo, obviously not into the church. You'll have to wait in the car outside.'

'Aw Mum.'

'Don't you "Aw Mum", you know very well why you can't "Aw Mum" this one. Now we're leaving in half an hour so go and sulk in your room if you want, but no more "Aw Mums".

I brought a book to read in the car. I brought 'On the Origin of Species', which I read as ostentatiously as possible on the way, but she either didn't notice or she didn't get my point. Usually on a Sunday, she had to do a huge out of the way detour to drop me off at the farm, which she liked to complain about, then another huge out of the way detour after Vincent's bible thing to come and pick me up again, and she liked to complain about that too. This Sunday however was a quick along the shore to Fortrose, through the back of the town and then up the really steep hill through the trees where Mum's crappy car could hardly make it, then over the lip and out of the woods to where the stupid church stood in fields overlooking the town and firth and everything else. Mum parked on the verge at the nearest end of the line of churchgoers' cars, told me to stay in the car, then got out, put on her special smiley face that she used for other women who she thought were better than she was, and joined the other deluded fools to talk shite and walk into the church with. For the next ten minutes or so, other cars parked up and other fools got out and walked past me towards the church. I half expected them to see me sitting in the car and point and stare because they all thought I was possessed, but none of them noticed me, or my book. Then once everyone was inside it was just me on my own in the car on a silent country lane.

I got out and knocked around the churchyard for a bit. Near the windows I could hear the singing and I briefly considered nipping in to shout something unholy, but thought better of it and went to sit on a wall instead. The view was pretty spectacular. It was built, I had once learned during a sermon when I was still considered unpossessed, a couple of hundred years ago by farmers who didn't want to descend all the way to the coast every Sunday just to have to sit next to fishermen (who are smelly and unpleasant people). And then in the nineteen sixties or seventies, when the farmers had sensibly started avoiding the ministers as well as the fishermen, the church was about to go out of use when the bearded Evangelicals came along and bought it, so they could clap along like mad in their very best jumpers, and yet not have to be in the middle of a town where they'd have to face other people who might question their foolish beliefs and their equally foolish jumpers. But it is a spectacular place. The church is perched right on the edge of the high ridge above Fortrose and Rosemarkie, overlooking Chanonry point which sticks straight out a mile into the many miles of Moray firth stretching on either side. Opposite the point on the far side, Fort George sits squat and hard looking, built after Culloden and still there making sure no Jacobites get any fancy ideas about wearing kilts, or speaking in tartan, or rising up to try and put Catholic Italians where Protestant Germans apparently so obviously rightly belong. So well done there Fort George.

A rain shower was coming in so I got off my wall and went back to the car. It was then that I noticed that we were parked right behind Vincent Egger's car. It was one of those ones with a fish symbol on the back.

Half the cars parked along the verge had the fish symbol on them, but of course it was Vincent Egger's that annoyed me most, smartarse early Christian bollocks that it was. Oh, look at the fish on my car Mr Driver behind me, it means that I love Jesus very much, and I'm letting you know with a symbol that's much smugger than a cross, as that's the kind of self-satisfied twat that I am. And of course smug twat Egger wouldn't ever see any problem with the fact that his little fish symbol is a graven image, or that God was very specific to his beardy jumper wearing friend, Moses, when he said, 'Don't use graven images, I'm really not keen'. But Vincent Egger knows the mind of God better than Moses ever did, so Vincent Egger can do what he likes. And as I sat there, Vincent's little fish symbol made me more and more pissed off and I found myself simmering like I used to in church or in Vincent's far-holier-than-thou living room.

I remembered I'd once seen a fish like this,

on the back of someone's car, and I was thinking how it would be fun to swap a Darwin-fish one for the Jesus-fish on the back of

64

Vincent's car, and would he ever even notice and if he did, how much it would annoy him. And it occurred to me it was perfectly possible to evolve Vincent's Jesus-fish into a Darwin-fish with a marker pen, so I scrabbled about in the glove compartment and under the seats but Mum didn't keep a marker pen handy. So I looked around for something to scratch into his paintwork with, but Mum didn't carry penknives or compasses either, so I got back out of the car and looked up and down the road till I found a rusted old U-shaped nail from a fence post. Everyone was still in church and there was no one else around, so I set about my evolving task, but after a few tentative scratches and before I'd even finished the 'D' it was apparent that the finished result was going to look like crap and wasn't even going to be very obvious. There was only one thing for it: if I was going to annoy this devout Jesuser and cause him as much upset as possible, though in a subtle way which he might not even notice for ages, then I was going to have to do the job properly. A well made stencil shaped like this,

and a can of spray paint were called for. Vandalising Vincent's car was going to be a little art project. So I found a stubby pencil and ripped out a page from one of Mum's magazines and I carefully traced the exact size and outline of Vincent's Jesus fish on to my bit of paper, and by the time the singing inside the church reached a clappy crescendo that frightened the pigeons in the trees, I had the makings of a template for Jesus-fish evolution.

I called Cousin Dan later that day and I tried to start telling him about my idea but he was in a funny mood and wasn't listening and was all mumbly, and then he blurted out that his Mum, my Auntie Roberta, was going to be having a baby, which was pretty disgusting because she was ancient. Cousin Dan, though disgusted because of her age, was even more concerned with how they'd done it on purpose to get at him, and how if it was a boy they'd train it to like farming, and then leave the farm to the baby and not him, even though he was by miles the oldest because the baby wasn't even born yet. He was convinced that because of all the stuff he always said to them about selling the farm as soon as they were both dead and starting a rally team, they were bound to leave the farm to the baby so what was he supposed to do, because he couldn't hardly start liking farming just because they were going to have a baby, and he knew it was going to be a boy, he just knew it.

I didn't really know what to say to any of it as I was trying not to think of what people as ancient as Uncle Robert and Auntie Roberta did to make babies, so I told Cousin Dan again of how I was going to make a stencil to vandalise a Christian's car.

'A stencil of what?'

'The bits you need to spray paint a Jesus-fish into a Darwin-fish.'

'A what? Eh?'

So I explained to Cousin Dan the significance of the fish symbol to early Christians, and how some modern Christians thought using it made them cool, and then I explained what evolution was exactly, and how it worked, and where Charles Darwin came into it all. Cousin Dan had heard of Darwin but he'd thought he was a fighter pilot from World War 2 with no arms. Then I explained why Vincent Egger didn't believe in evolution and how enormously pissed off it would make him if we evolved the fish on the back of his car with a can of spray paint and a stencil. And in the end, Cousin Dan seemed mostly cheered up by the idea of pissing someone else off.

'Scan a copy of the thing and send it over and I'll make the stencil', he said, not grasping that I'd already said I'd make it myself, but as he wouldn't bother anyway, I scanned the drawing, sent it, and set about making it myself. Cousin Dan may have been useful when it came to skinning a rabbit with a hacksaw, but fine letter work with a craft knife was another matter. So I took a bit of grey cardboard from the back of a sketch pad and copied the fish shape on to it, then I pencilled in the 'DARWIN' text and the shape of the feet, and after a bit of rubbing out and a few more goes I'd managed to get all the text to fit in and the feet looked more amphibian than elephanty. So I biro'd over the pencil marks and put a new blade in my craft knife. I then cut slowly and carefully to the lines I'd made, and when I was done it looked both precise and artistically fantastic, and even though I had big holes in the middle of the D the A and the R because I hadn't considered how to keep the middle bits of the letters in place, it still looked great. Then in art class that week I stole a can of silver spray paint, and with that I was ready to evolve Vincent's Jesusy superstitious bollocks car badge into an indisputable scientific fact car badge, and that would learn him to mess with me, yes that would learn him good.

That Sunday as soon as I was dropped off at Cousin Dan's I showed him my handiwork and frankly expected him to be a lot more impressed than he was.

'That's total shit, Cousin Findo', he said, and he led me round the back of the farm outbuildings to the big corrugated iron shed at the end where he kept his cars and all his mechanical stuff and where Uncle Robert never bothered him. On the big wooden work bench that ran down one side among the piles of twisted metal and half dismantled oily stuff, he pointed to a tin biscuit box and told me to open it. I did. And inside glinted perfection.

There may not be much on the Black Isle in terms of civilisation or things to do, but there is on the far side of Tore roundabout from Cousin Dan's, a sheet metal laser cutting facility, and Cousin Dan knew the old guy who ran it and said he owed him a favour. Cousin Dan had taken the tracing of the Jesus-fish I'd scanned for him and then had his stencil professionally designed and crisply laser cut through a highly polished aluminium sheet. And not only that; he'd had a stack of twenty of them done in a range of sizes to accommodate not only Vincent Egger's car, but any Christian transport with any sized fish symbol we might ever encounter. And not only that; on his stencils he'd left tiny supporting struts so the middle of all the Ds, As and Rs were still in place and weren't going to fall out. And if that wasn't enough, the feet he'd done looked perfectly amphibian without being too overcomplicated or webby. In short, they were every young Darwinist vandal's dream. I didn't know whether to congratulate Cousin Dan for exceeding my expectations of him by a thousand times, or whether to be a bit annoyed that he'd made my cardboard effort look like bin luggage.

Truth was I did feel a bit pissed off even if I'd accidentally said 'Wow' when I opened the box. It was one thing for Cousin Dan to be better than me at the farming stuff we did like shooting at crows or playing tractor chicken, because he'd had far more practice at shooting stuff and driving tractors, and he had access to lots of chickens: but when he was better than me at anything else it felt wrong. He was the one who was going to leave school with no qualifications and spend the rest of his life on this farm whether he liked it or not, whereas I was the one, who at least within the family, still had the whiff of child prodigy about him, and so was probably destined to go on and do great things, even if I didn't have a clue what those things might be. So basically, when Cousin Dan who was well known as a nutter, appeared to have talents I didn't know about; I didn't exactly like it very much. It even briefly occurred to me that Cousin Dan may not be as thick as he looked, acted or continually demonstrated, but it was only a brief thought, and it was overtaken as he gave me the complete boxed set of Darwinist stencils as a gift as he'd had another set made for himself at the same time. I was almost overawed. I even said thank you.

'Right, let's go and use them,' said Cousin Dan.

'What on?' I asked, looking around the shed for a bit of wood or wall to test them on.

'That Egger guy's car obviously.'

'Eh?' I replied, as it was Sunday morning and that Egger guy and his car would be ten odd miles away up at the Evangelical Church on the hill above Fortrose. So I explained this to my simple Cousin.

'Not a problem, we'll drive there,' he said, smirking.

Most of the time when I was with Cousin Dan, I found it was best if I was in charge, and this was going to be one of those times. We couldn't drive anywhere, and not because Cousin Dan was fourteen and I was twelve, but because in order to get Cousin Dan's car out of the farm, we'd have to go right past the kitchen window that Auntie Roberta lived behind, and down the long straight drive that was overlooked in its entire length by the farmhouse and that a hedgehog couldn't cross at night without Auntie Roberta commenting on it from the kitchen sink.

'Your Mum will see us,' was all the explanation I felt I needed to give to bring him back to his senses.

'Not a problem,' he said, still smirking like a gypsy's dog, 'We'll go out the back way'. And he grabbed his own set of stencils and a bag that clinked like spray paint cans and threw them into the back of his one car that worked, then he slid back the high shed door on its runners till it was wide enough to let the car out.

'There is no back way,' I said, getting into the car anyway. Cousin Dan, still being all enigmatic and twinkly got in to the driver's seat, hooked his door shut with the bit of wire, and fired up the un-taxed, un-insured, un-MOT'd, semi-lethal heap of junk in his usual unlicensed way, then we pulled out of the shed at a stately pace. He took the track up the hill towards the top fields where a couple of months before we'd tried to hold our own sheep car trials, till Uncle Robert spotted us and let us know he disapproved by firing a warning shotgun from the upstairs bathroom window. Through a gate, Cousin Dan drove us up the side of the field towards the top, where the farm ended and miles of forestry began. He stopped at a point where the farm below dipped of sight and he got out and removed a fake bit of fencing between the field and the forest. He drove slowly through and over a section of deep ditch that had been filled in with big logs. He got out again and went back to put the fake fence back in place. I looked into the forest in front of us. It was old forestry so the trunks were quite well spaced, the solid canopy above let no light down and the forest floor was made up entirely of dead brown pine needles. Ahead it looked like some smaller trees might have been recently removed, cut very close to the ground. Cousin Dan returned and he set off into the forest picking his route slowly over the ground cut stumps and along what might almost be taken for a track, and which even looked to have some previous rut marks. At one point he headed between a couple of big trees which were so close together there was clearly no way the car was going to get through, until notches appeared, newly chainsawed into the sides of the trees at a height which miraculously allowed the wing mirrors to pass through undamaged, even as the wheels jolted over the roots. After another couple of minutes we emerged into the light across another log-filled ditch, and out onto a legitimate forestry track that the forestry commission had put there themselves. I looked at Cousin Dan and Cousin Dan smiled, as he put his foot down and the speed picked up and the sitka spruce canyon we were in began to move past like matches in a wind tunnel. I knew then that I'd shortly be found dead in a car wrapped round a tree, it was just a question of which tree.

'Don't worry, I've driven this tons of times,' he lied.

By the time we came out of the forest my bum was so clenched it was unlikely I'd ever poo again, and it turned out that the speed he could do in the forest was nothing compared to what he could do on the back roads we were now on. The car only had a small engine which took a while to build up speed, so Cousin Dan was unwilling to lose any momentum by using the brakes, or maybe they'd just stopped working, I never found out. He drove like a procrastinating kamikaze. 'Shall I kill myself on that wall? Oh no, there's a bigger one along there. Perhaps I should wrap myself around that post? No, I'll go off at the next corner instead, that'll be far more fatal.' He paid no attention to any customs relating to national preferences for driving on a particular side of the road, and at blind corners it appeared to be enough to assume that there'd be nothing coming the other way, rather than do something so foolish as slow down and check. My fingers were crossed, my toes were crossed and my arse was crossed, but I knew I was going to die anyway.

Fields flashed by the passenger window so fast that the fence posts blurred out of existence and the free floating wires bobbed and jigged above the ground as the few remaining seconds of my life counted down. A blind crescent, the sensation of flying, the crunch of landing on ancient suspension and a few out of control wobbles, not helped by even Cousin Dan screaming, but still no sign of brakes. A long straight building up even more speed towards an impossible corner. An impossible corner rounded on the racing line and an extra minute of life for Findo and his now grinning again Cousin Dan, the thinks-he's-in-formula 1 dickhead. Which tree were we going to eat? Which corner was going to have the lorry coming round it? Could I hope for another minute? Could I dream of two? When a full ten shit-clenching minutes later we raced to a T-junction and left the back roads, Cousin Dan did a strange thing, and then a ridiculous thing. Firstly he started obeying the speed limit, then he made me hand him from the glove compartment, a baseball cap, a pair of old man's thick rimmed glasses with the lenses missing, and a crappy false moustache from the joke shop in the Inverness market.

'Villages coming up,' he said. 'Need my disguise so we don't get reported.'

And he put on the baseball cap, the old man's glasses and his crappy moustache joke shop and he looked completely ludicrous.

'That's not going to fool anyone,' I told him. 'You just look like a dick.'

'I already know it works,' he replied unfazed. 'People only glance for a second as you pass and they'll only see the glasses and the 'tash. Internet says they won't notice my face at all.'

'What about my face?'

'You're not driving.'

We'd come the long back way round and were descending to go through Rosemarkie before we could go back along to Fortrose, and as Cousin Dan cruised at a legal pace up Rosemarkie High Street his internet bullshit theory seemed to be proving accurate. The few people who did glance as we passed seemed to flicker for a moment at the sight of him, but then their brains seemed unwilling to register the evidence of their eyes, which said a fourteen year-old Groucho

Marx was at the wheel, so their faces went passive again and they drifted by.

Out of Rosemarkie, into Fortrose, then up the very steep hill at the back through the beech trees. Just before we came out of the woods at the top, where we started to see the steeple and church roof poking above the brow of the hill, Cousin Dan stopped the car, did about a fifteen point turn on the single track road, and eventually got us facing back the way we'd come: in order to make our getaway all the quicker. Cousin Dan ditched his disguise and we gathered up our stencils and spray cans, got out of the car, and walked over the brow of the hill where the church was in full view. It had been over a year since I'd last been inside, being dragged away as a demon-possessed disgrace, and as far as I could see, nothing about the place had changed: a long line of parked Evangelical cars stretched out ahead of us along the verge and there was no one else about.

My original thought had been to vandalise Vincent Egger's car, but Cousin Dan had just assumed that we were going to do them all – or at least every one that had a Jesus-fish on it. My fear of death from the drive had worn off and been replaced with a fear of being caught. Why was I doing this? Oh yeah: because I was taking a stand against Christianity as it was untrue made-up nonsense, and because the people who believed in it needed their heads pulling out of their arses. And because evolving a Jesus-fish into a Darwin-fish had a certain poetic justice about it. And because we'd come all this way and gone to all this effort and if I backed out now Cousin Dan would laugh at me and do it anyway. And so it wasn't just some petty vandalism we were doing, there was clearly a far larger cause at stake here. We were fighting for the truth in the face of two thousand years of lies; we were fighting to turn the tide of religious ignorance back up its own superstitious bum-hole, and we had right and science and Mr Charles Darwin on our side. We weren't just Darwinian vandals, we were far more than that, we were the first ever Darwinian Terrorists, fighting the ignorance of blind faith by whatever means necessary, in this case with stencils and spray paint.

Oh, and also because Vincent Egger was a twat who'd hit me and because I was a vindictive little shit.

I took charge. 'Try to walk more casually.'

'I am walking casually.'

'No you're not, you look like you're up to something.'

'No I don't.'

'You do, you look furtive.'

'Well you look like you're shitting yourself.'

'No I don't, shut up.'

'You shut up.'

'No you shut up.'

'Shut up, there's one with a fish on it, keep a look out, I'll do it.'

'No, no, not yet. We should go to the far end first and work our way back.'

'Why?'

'So the more we do, the nearer the getaway car we'll be.'

'Okay then, casual walking casually to the far end.'

'Okay, casual. That's not casual.'

We walked, more or less casually, along the line of cars, casually scanning to see if anyone was about and casually noting which cars had Jesus-fish stickers on them and which didn't. As we got alongside the church we instinctively started to duck down behind the churchyard wall a little bit and quickened our pace just a touch until the casual observer would have seen our mad crouching sprint and assumed we were escaped convicts who'd heard the bloodhounds in the distance. When we popped our heads up like meerkats for a look around, we were behind the last car at the far end of the line, and there was still not a soul to be seen.

It was a beautiful thing. About a dozen of the cars were sporting Jesus-fishes of various sizes and Cousin Dan's bespoke laser cut stencil sets had a size to fit them all. Working our way down the line we took turns, one on lookout, one spraying, then move on and swap. Size the right stencil over the target, spray a couple of even strokes of paint (not so much that it runs), and an ignorant Jesus-fish is evolved into an enlightened Darwin-fish. Vincent Egger's car was parked near the gate and his fish coincided with my turn to spray. We could hear singing from inside the church, and as the voices rose I placed my stencil and prepared to revenge myself. The voices inside lifted to a crescendo praising the wonder of creation as I sprayed, and I lifted off the stencil unveiling a crisp, clean-edged beauty of an evolutionary paint-job. Perfect moments don't come by often but the flawlessness of the paint, the irony of the hymn in the background, and how mental I imagined Vincent going when he discovered my immaculate desecration; these things all melted into a glowing ball of pure happiness that I'll be able to look back on in my old age when I need to cheer myself up, as it's unlikely there'll be any sexual experiences in my memory for me to call on instead.

I may have felt a tinge of guilt as we passed by Mum's car towards the next target, but it was only a tiny tinge and it was gone by the time we saw the Jesus-fish a couple of cars further on, as it was such a great big shiny one. Job done, we scuttled back to Cousin Dan's car, checking over our shoulders as we went. We piled into the car, threw the stuff in the back and then I had to wait as Cousin Dan re-applied his ridiculous driving disguise before we finally made good our getaway. No one had driven past, no one had seen us. I wasn't a prodigal anything any more and I certainly wasn't possessed; I was the world's first Darwinian Terrorist. We were so flushed with success and chatty, Cousin Dan almost drove like a sensible person as we imagined the holy outrage that kicking out time at the church was about to bring. We imagined Vincent's head exploding with rage and the other Churchies having to pick bits of his brain out of their finest washed clothes as Vincent's headless body continued to stomp about in a mad tantrum, before the Minister comes out and has to beat his body to the ground with a big crucifix. It was the happiest day of my life.

We got the car back to the farm through the forest, and even had time before lunch for a few high-speed turns around the field we were pretending we'd spent the whole morning in. Uncle Robert didn't show up for lunch, he rarely did, and I noted for the first time that Auntie Roberta was starting to look a bit pregnant, which really was pretty disgusting in someone so old. Cousin Dan spotted me looking and drew what looked like a coat hanger in the air and then pretended to brandish it. I didn't get what he meant but I smiled along with him as if I did, in case I was missing something obvious and was being stupid. In the afternoon we shot the crossbow at an old car door in Cousin Dan's shed and made plans as to who we could Darwin-fish next. We weren't just vandals, there was no question that our motives were higher than that now. We were fighting for a cause, and the cause was truth. We were Darwinian Terrorists and anyone who didn't like it would end up with paint on their car.

Mind you, Darwinian Terrorists or not, I was slightly concerned as to how Mum was going to be when she came to pick me up that afternoon. Would she suspect me? Would she accuse me? Would she call the police on me? I knew everyone in the church would think that it was me, even if I could prove I was miles away at the time. My past actions in God denouncing would be enough for most of them to jump to the conclusion that Darwinising their cars was exactly the sort of thing I'd do. And leaving aside for a minute the fact that it was me that did it, I decided I had every right to be annoyed if Mum's churchy friends were going to assume the worst about me without any evidence whatsoever. So if Mum did happen to mention that a terrible thing had happened outside the church that day, and if she did happen to ask me any probing questions: then I would take the dual paths of moral indignation, and of having been miles away at the time.

When Mum rolled up a couple of hours later, she took a different tack than expected. She pretended everything was perfectly normal, but she spent some time chatting to Auntie Roberta, which she never did, while I waited outside in the car. Then on the way home she asked me what might have been perfectly normal questions, but in a bit more detail than usual. How had I spent the day? And what had I done, where, and in what order did I do it all? Of course Cousin Dan and I already had our story straight, though later, once we were home and dinner was cooking, she unexpectedly took my hands and looked at them closely, ostensibly to check if they were clean for dinner, which she never usually did, but in fact to check for any lingering evidence of spray paint (which we'd washed off with petrol and a nail brush earlier on). And as she didn't find anything, she didn't say anything. And finally, during our perfectly normal, nothing unusual going on here dinner, she happened to mention that some damage had been done to some cars outside the church that afternoon, and I didn't take any particular interest in what she said, and so that was that.

Chapter 11

Saturday 13th April, 4.44pm

Inverness Bus Station truly is one of the world's great bus stations, because Mandy Duplin's at my bus stop. Her and Lyndsey Jack are perched on the skinny red plastic seats with some fancy wee shopping bags at their feet, which say, 'Look at me, I was in a fancy wee shop'. The bus stop is pretty busy and I have to pass right by her to get to the end of the queue, and as I do I breathe in. There are only three kinds of girls in the world: ones who make you breathe in as you pass, ones who you don't think about your breathing as you pass, and ones who you hold your breath or breathe out as you pass, to avoid any chance of contamination. As I fill my nose and lungs with Mandy Duplin I listen. They're talking about some girl who said something that they can't believe she said it, the bitch. They don't look up or see me. There are no seats left so I have to stand at the far end where I can't hear them. Some mutton dressed as pig plods up and blocks my view of Mandy. I move a pace and casually re-establish my line of sight. She's quite animated with her hands as she talks, but weirdly she hardly moves her arms at all. I try to work out what she's talking about by lip reading and watching what her hands do, but I can't lip read and her hands are just very flappy. There's probably a lip reading course on the internet; it may be worth looking into.

Mandy Duplin, Mandy Duplin, Mandy Duplin. Even her eyelids do it for me. I can see under her jacket she's wearing quite a low neckline. If she were only to turn around a little I could maybe see the beginning of the top of her cleavage, and as it's really quite warm, maybe she'll want to take her jacket off. If she were then to turn back around a little the other way and see me, you never know, she might give me a little smile. Bollocks Findo, back in the real world there's no chance of that, but take the opportunity to stare a little at those thighs. Who wouldn't I kill for the chance to run my hands up those. All the way up. And leaving the real world once again, if she were to turn around, notice me, get up and slowly saunter over, shedding her clothes as she did so, I'd slide my hands around her and quickly think of something else, as the bus is here and it's a very bad time to be getting a stiffy as there's usually a bit of a crush getting on. Oh but look at her arse and the curve of her back as she stands up. Perfection. No Findo, getting on the bus is no time for a stiffy, look at the mutton dressed as pig woman, her face would wilt steel. But then look at the shape of the back of Mandy's neck. To hell with it, I'll drink in the sight of her while I have the chance and I'll carry my bag in front of me. Don't worry mister, that's just my friend Diane's bottle of vermouth in a plastic bag knocking into the back of you there, nothing in any way more disturbing than that.

The bus is a single decker and I get the first of the raised seats, only a couple of rows back and on the other side from Mandy and Lyndsey. People tend not to sit beside me on buses but this one fills up and I get a middle aged waster with two lazy eyes and long grey I-used-to-be-a-roadie-for-a-rock-band hair. He's sweating whisky and Indian food. On the back of the seat in front of me, in red marker pen, someone's written, 'Gavin and his poo hole are available to sailors.' I find I can now quite safely take my carry out bag off my lap and put it on the floor.

The bus moves off. Usually I'd be off at Kessock and get Gran to pick me up or maybe have to walk back along the beach, but as tonight I'm going all the way to Avoch, I'll be able to gaze at Mandy Duplin till she gets off at Munlochy. She's texting someone. I managed to get hold of her number last year but I've never had the nerve to use it. I contemplate texting her now, but then she'd want to know how the hell I got her number and what would I write anyway? Perhaps, 'Someone on this bus would like to go out with you.' But then she'd probably end up with the stinking old rock casualty who's started coughing up gunk into his hand, before she'd end up with me.

As the bus grinds out of town and up the bridge, the view opens up for twenty miles on either side, and is said to compare with any of the best in Scotland. Bollocks. The best view in Scotland is the back of Mandy Duplin's neck. She's laughing her real laugh, the dirty one, at some text she's just got. Now she's whispering something giggly to Lindsey and my heart drops into my gut as I decide it's probably a text from some arsehole who doesn't want her nearly as much as me, but from the look I can see on the side of her face, whoever he is, I think he's already got her. As the bus goes down into Kessock my mood goes with it. It doesn't matter how much I want her, it doesn't matter how happy I know I could make her: she doesn't want me making her anything. I have to accept that the time she smiled at me in the corridor was to make me get out of her way, and the time she asked me for a pen was because she needed a pen. Of course I know I should aim lower but I can't. Of course I should aim lower, I should. Not even towards the bottom of the barrel, I shouldn't aim as high as that, I should move the barrel out of the way and dig a deep well under where the barrel stood, then perhaps someone suitable will ooze up out of the mud.

The grey roadie smell beside me gets off in Kessock so at least now I can wallow in my hopeless longing in a little more comfort. I delude myself with the idea that she might turn round and see me and maybe happen to wonder why I'm still on the bus, having passed my usual stop. Perhaps she might wonder what exciting place I'm off to or what exciting people I'm meeting, though in reality she neither knows nor cares which bus stop I get off at, or where I go, or what I do, or with whom. I'll just try not to think about any of that and concentrate on the shape of her neck goddammit, the incredible shape of her neck. I'm going to need that carry-out bag back on my lap.

My phone rings and it's Gran. I answer it because I'm only a few seats away from Mandy Duplin so I want to look like the kind of person who gets phone calls, but then I don't want to appear to be the kind of person who gets phone calls from his Gran, so I'll try and adopt a tone of voice that'll make Mandy think I'm talking to a friend. And maybe I'll talk quite loudly to make sure she listens.

'It's me Findo, your Gran.'

'Uh, huh.'

'Did you see your Mum this afternoon?'

'Eh, No, I didn't have time.'

That was exactly the wrong tone of voice. It sounded like I couldn't give a shit. Gran doesn't get that my offhand tone isn't for her benefit and she expresses her pissedoffness at me by going silent till I ask after Mum. Sorry Gran, can't help you. There is a loooong pause at the other end as Gran steams up.

'Well don't you even want to know how she is?'

'Yes.'

'Well, the nurse said she didn't have a good night last night, and she's not doing as well as they'd hoped with her temperature. She said they're doing more tests and the vet was in.'

'A vet?'

'Yes, no. I didn't know what she meant either. I thought it was maybe some kind of injection or something and maybe you'd know. I mean I'm sure she didn't mean a vet, vet. It'll be something else but I didn't want to ask. Do you know what it might be?'

'I don't know, a vet's a vet. Maybe it's a term for something.'

'Oh yes, that'll be it, it'll be a term for something.'

'Or more likely you misheard.'

'No, I'm pretty sure she said, vet.'

'Then maybe it was a vet.'

'Don't be stupid Findo, of course it's not a vet, that's only what I heard her say it was. Now are you coming home tonight?'

Here's my chance, I can raise my voice for this in case Mandy's having trouble hearing me over the engine.

'No, I'm staying at Diane's tonight.'

I try to add just enough implication into my tone so that Mandy might feel jealous, if she was so inclined.

'Oh, I see,' says Gran. Oh shit, the old woman's picked up on my implication.

'Well then, you be sure and be, you know, careful. You know.'

'We're not ...' I stop myself because I once read somewhere that girls are more likely to fancy you if they think another girl already fancies you. Doesn't matter what Gran thinks, more important that Mandy Duplin gets the idea I'm desirable. So I say, 'ok,' to Gran and let her think what she wants.

'So you'll be home tomorrow then,' she says, with something in between disbelief and tentative respect in her voice.

'Yes.'

No point trying to explain the true nature of my relationship with Diane to Gran. Girlfriend/boyfriend – never in a million years. It's more like owner and pet.

'And where are you going tonight?' she asks.

'Avoch, maybe Fortrose, maybe. Don't know yet.' I try and make it sound like I'm talking to one of my multitude of fictitious clubbing acquaintances.

'Well if you get stuck later on, don't bother me for a lift, I can't help you. I'm taking some pills now as I'm feeling a bit, you know, with everything.'

'Ok, I'll see you tomorrow sometime then.'

'Ok, and you, you be careful Findo. She's quite a spirited girl, that Diane.'

'Yes ok, bye.'

I hang up and glance over to see if Mandy Duplin's been listening and she quite plainly hasn't. Lyndsey Jack is in the middle of telling her loudly about something she thought about buying once, but then she didn't because of some other thing she did buy, though it wasn't the same, and then in the end she didn't like it anyway, and now she's gone off the first thing too. Lyndsey Jack is a moron.

We roll on to Munlochy. Mandy gets up to get off here, and her and Lyndsey say their goodbyes like a pair of drug stimulated gerbils. They get this over-excited girly shit from all the TV American girly shit they watch. It's a pity that Mandy goes along with it as she's obviously better than that, but Lyndsey Jack isn't, the malign orange bitch. The bus pulls off and Mandy is waving at Lyndsey. I follow Mandy surreptitiously with my eyes until the bus passes her and till I can't bend my neck round any further. As I turn back I accidentally make eye contact with Lyndsey Jack who's just finished all her waving. Did she see me staring at Mandy? She narrows her eyelids into a sneer at me and turns back into her seat. That'll be a yes then.

A handful of countryside miles later and we roll into Avoch, and as I prepare to stand for my stop I'm annoyed to see Lyndsey getting to her feet too. Back when I was nine and me and Mum first moved to Avoch, Lyndsey Jack was in the same primary class as me. She was a sulky thick stuck-up bitch cow even then. We get off the bus and it roars away and for a few strides we're alone on the street together and walking in the same direction. The bitch-cow can't help herself, she turns as she starts to cross the street and sneers,

'Like Mandy would ever be interested in you.'

'Don't know what you're talking about,' I say back, not kidding anyone.

'Aye, whatever, Bigfishpoo.'

She's used a nickname I'd almost forgotten about. Bigfishpoo was what a few of the more loathsome sharp-faced girls, who the boys all fancied, used to call me. They had a song which went 'Findo Gask is a Bigfishpoo' and they repeated the line till they either pissed themselves laughing, or encouraged some of the feral mob of boys that hung around them to hit my legs with sticks, because Findo Gask is such a Bigfishpoo. Well I'm not taking that shit from this bitch any more, and as the bile rises in my throat I call after her.

'I hope your step dad gives you syphilis.'

I remember she used to be not very keen on her step dad and even from behind I can see I've scored a hit. One nil to me I think. She turns her head and throws back over her shoulder,

'Aye, well it's more than anyone will ever give you.'

Ouch. Perhaps that'll be one-all then. I try to think of something else to insult her with, but now she's over the road and away, and just shouting 'bitch' after her wouldn't really cut it. I head for the chippie.

Bag of chips in hand and Mars bar in pocket I head down to the harbour to eat, cutting down James Street on purpose to walk past our old house. I must be getting nostalgic or something in my old age. We'd probably still be there, instead of at bloody Gran's, if Mum hadn't fancied herself as an online gambling genius. The curtains are different and the outside of the house looks cleaner. Mum said she was going to buy it at one point until the bingo madness got her; but then authentic former fishermen's cottages in authentic terraced streets in an authentic fishing village, are highly desirable. So she probably could never have afforded it anyway, particularly when the fishing industry's gone and so there are no actual fishermen living there any more to spoil the ambience of all that authenticness.

At the harbour I walk out to the end, sit on the edge, text Diane to let her know I've arrived and she should shift her arse. I dig into my chips.

Chapter 12

Secondary 3

Our Darwinian-terrorist-Darwin-fish-stencil-paint-spray-attack made the local paper; but they called it 'Vandalism at Fortrose Church'. They didn't even get, or mention, the anti-religious ideology behind it, though it did give Cousin Dan an idea. Or rather, it gave Cousin Dan's friend Maxwell an idea. Not that Maxwell was Cousin Dan's friend, Maxwell wasn't even one of the ones who Cousin Dan told people were his friends, but who in reality only vaguely tolerated him hanging around until he ran out of money, drugs or shotgun cartridges. Maxwell was a nutter too, everyone knew that, but he wasn't a nutter in the same way Cousin Dan was. If you asked people who was the biggest nutter, half of the boys and all of the girls would say, Maxwell. Cousin Dan was a run-through-a-plate-glass-door-to-see-if-I can-do-it, kind of nutter; whereas Maxwell was a throw-a-bag-of-puppies-through-a-plate-glass-door-to-see-how-many-puppies-are-left-while-telling-everyone-he's-descended-from-aristocrats-even-though-he's-from-Cromarty, kind of nutter. In primary school Maxwell had punctured the left eardrum of each of the Bell triplets with a propelling pencil; he really had got rid of a litter of puppies, but no one could agree how he'd done it; and one of his eyes was a bit wrong where he'd once tried to dye it red in order to make himself look fierce. So, nutter that Cousin Dan was, in an attempt to show off and win some nutter points, he decided to show Maxwell our vandalism newspaper article and tell him it was us, and it was Maxwell who had the idea Cousin Dan told me.

'T-shirts.'

'What?'

'And mugs maybe too, but definitely get more of the stencils made, so we can sell them to other people who want to fuck up Christians' cars 'n all.'

'Don't be a dick,' I said. 'We can't go drawing attention when the police are looking for us.'

'Balls.' reasoned Cousin Dan. 'The police don't give a shit about us, and even if they did, if we sell all stencils and that to other people, and then they all go about spraying cars too, then how can the police pin anything on us when lots of other people are doing it too, so it might as easily have been them?'

And I couldn't argue with that.

The first meeting of the new, slightly enlarged Darwinian Terrorist Organisation, as I'd decided we were now called, took place on the steps to the assembly hall by the tuck shop. Present, were me, Findo Gask, President and Founder; Cousin Dan, Chief Terrorist; and Maxwell, Marketing and Publicity Officer; on the condition he made us some money, otherwise he could fuck off. The result of the first meeting was that:

The Darwin-fish was our logo, with the words Darwinian Terrorist Organisation around it.

T-shirts with the logo would be made at Maxwell's expense, Cousin Dan would get lots more stencils made at the sheet metal laser cutting facility near Tore at Maxwell's expense, and all profits from everything would be split three ways.

If Maxwell told anyone what we were doing, or that it was us who'd Darwinified the cars at the church up the hill, then we were allowed to kick him in and he had to agree.

Not that Cousin Dan or I would ever probably actually kick Maxwell in because he was a bit of an odd one. No one at school thought that Maxwell was hard or anything – he was quite stocky but podgy too and wore big square cheapest-frames-in-the-shop glasses, and you could call him pretty well anything you liked to his face and he didn't seem to care. So on the face of it he was placid, fat and as soft as shite, but then no one ever really tried to get into a fight with him, because there was always the feeling that if you did, he'd probably wait a week, put on a cravat, then walk up behind you and gouge out your eye with his thumb. And standing in front of the Rector before the police arrived, he'd probably argue that the eye was probably loose to begin with. And the Rector would ask him why he then also ate the eye that he'd gouged out, and Maxwell would probably say, 'Don't know sir'. Of course Maxwell had never to my knowledge actually gouged out anything and eaten it, but if you ever heard he had, you wouldn't be all that surprised.

Anyway, in exchange for Maxwell investing in stencils, and sorting out t-shirts to sell, Cousin Dan and I agreed that once all the stuff was ready, we'd do an attack on another church car park to get in the paper again, and we'd use the publicity to promote the website Maxwell was going to build to sell the stuff on. As a plan it was more or less flawless.

Chapter 13

Saturday 13th April, 6.40pm

'Findo you bloody great blowjob, get your arse over here!'

Diane's voice has no trouble whatsoever carrying over the harbour. In fact, if Findo was a more common name, Findos up and down the north east coast of Scotland would be looking around them right now to see who it was who was calling them a blowjob.

As usual I've waited ages for Diane to show up. She doesn't really bother with make-up or hair-dos and she doesn't look any different than she does at school but she's still taken so long to get here that boats which were afloat in the harbour when I got here are now resting in mud. My legs are stiff and my arse has passed out the other side of numb, yet as instructed, I shift it back along the harbour wall to where Diane is already impatient at having been forced to linger for almost a minute.

'Did you get my vermouth?'

'Lovely to see you too Diane, and yes, I've been waiting a very long time, it's only a pity it isn't raining so I could be all wet too.'

'Stop complaining and hand it over.'

I give Diane her bottle, she cracks open the cap and gulps it from the neck as we walk slowly towards the pub.

'What did you get?'

'Quarter bottle of vodka. If they don't serve me I can sneak it into my coke.'

'That all? Want some of this?'

'Does the Pope get wood?'

She hands me the bottle and I take a big swig of the disgusting, strong, cheap filth. It poisons my taste buds, burns its way down my throat and warms up my stomach as it dissolves the lining.

'That's really grim,' I tell her. 'Why can't you drink cider like the other delinquents?'

'Because the other delinquents are wimps and because this gives my street drinking an air of sophistication. So give us the bottle back before I stick it up your Kilmuiry arse.'

Diane has a lovely way with words. Some guy at school once told her that he wouldn't piss on her if she was on fire. Diane replied, that she would piss on him if he was on fire, but not on any of the burning bits. I still wish the image in my mind wasn't there. I hand her the bottle back. She takes it and asks, 'So are you on the pull tonight or what?' I sigh.

'Are we going to start this again?'

'We are.'

'Are we?'

'We are.'

'Must we?'

'We must.'

'Then no, I'm not on the pull tonight.'

'Of course you're on the pull Findo, of course you are. We'll find some brazen little bitch for you and maybe she'll even have all her faculties. Have a bit of faith, stop going for the overly attractive sober ones, and we'll have your bin bags emptied in no time.

I strongly suspect – no, I believe – that I'm probably little more to her than some challenge she's decided to set for herself. A little project to keep her amused in this armpit of the earth till she goes off to lay waste to continents or maybe do a degree. Take the ugliest, lumbering no-hoper, get him drunk, point him at some girl with a cauliflower ear and a rib cage that goes the wrong way, having first pumped into him just enough self esteem to carry him across the floor. Then keep on doing it because it was so funny the last time.

Diane has drained almost half the bottle in the hundred yards before the pub and she caps what's left and sticks in her bag for later. We reach and step through the door of The Railway Hotel. The place looks pretty empty as it's still early. The people who are sitting around are all old and look like they've been there all day. I concentrate on looking confident and nonchalant like I'm legally entitled to walk into pubs and I do it all the time, but I feel it's coming across like I'm nervous and shifty, so I step into Diane's wake as she struts up to the bar like Queen Victoria on cocaine. A few of the local heads turn towards us and I concentrate on generating an aura of eighteenness around me.

'What do you want?' she asks.

'A pint of Guinness.'

She looks at me like I've asked for a pint of old lady wee, but I'm thinking that no sixteen year old would ever drink Guinness, so if I'm ordering it I must be going on thirty. The barman finishes with an old guy at the far end and comes over to us.

'A vodka and coke and a pint of Guinness, please Alan,' says Diane.

'He got ID does he?' says the barman, looking at me.

'Eh, yeah.' I say.

I fumble in my pocket for my fake card, and hand it over. The barman looks at it and looks at me and I can feel my forehead cracking into sweat like in the films.

'Was yours the Guinness?' He asks.

I nod.

'Well I can't serve you that. Pick a soft drink and be thankful I don't kick you out,' he says, handing my fake ID back.

I'm about to protest that the card is genuine and of course I'm eighteen and I'm Brian McGee just like it says, but I don't. I crumble. 'A coke please.' The barman pours two cokes and puts vodka in one of them and puts the good one in front of Diane. I'm almost tempted to point out that Diane's two months younger than I am but then just because I'm annoyed at not getting served it doesn't mean I'm suicidal. We take an empty table by the wall. I say to Diane that it would be best if we went over to Fortrose immediately and met Alex there, as if I can't get served in here I'll go through my half bottle far too quickly. She disagrees in two words, so I decide to work on Alex as soon as he gets here.

I don't add any of my vodka to my first coke as I'm worried the barman might be watching and it's still pretty empty in here. But gradually people start to arrive in ones and twos, and by the time my second coke's in front of me it's busy enough to sneak in a large measure of vodka under the table, and Diane, in a goodwill gesture, and a lot less surreptitiously, loads it up to the top with vermouth.

'How is it?' she asks, while the shock of drinking it is still causing post-traumatic stress.

'It's like Satan's burning filth; but not as nice,' I reply, as the power of movement slowly returns to my upper body.

'Do you want some of my ice?'

'Probably best.'

Diane fingers some ice cubes from her glass into mine, and as I breathe deeply to recover my equilibrium and to work up the courage to take another sip, she engages a middle aged couple a few tables over in a conversation about their escaped pet bird, and she does it at such a volume that it draws in the people at the tables in between, whether they wanted drawn in or not. Everyone in here seems to know her, so they must know she's under age, but they all let it slide because she's the kind of presence that can lift the mood of the whole room, and she'll be relentlessly loud, sociable and upbeat till she's satisfied that everyone's having a good time. In the five years I lived in this dump of a village I made no impression on anyone except the people who used to chase me through the Seatown for sport, with bats. Diane's been here less than two years and she knows absolutely everybody and their cousin, and the guy their cousin went to school with and his friend from Dingwall who got done for stealing people's lawns; you know the one, the one who has a tattoo of a hand on his hand; that's him, the one who's brother sold his girlfriend's mum to the Chinese brothel in Alness. By the time Diane turns back to me a few minutes later, the conversational fuses she's lit have spread over and between several tables, and the atmosphere of a Saturday night has begun to take root.

Well, the atmosphere of Saturday night has begun to take root in everybody but me. I was going to use my vodka to top up, and off, the night, but if Diane decides to get comfy here then within an hour my cokes are going to have nothing but coke in them. So as Alex the ginger lothario finally slinks in through the door, my chance to influence events arrives. Not that Alex really slinks in, he actually walks in like any other normal human, but I know I'd be a lot happier if he looked more like the slinky greasy git that he is, as then the girls might see him for what he is and steer clear. As it is, he's infinitely more successful than any looks-like-nothing-special-shortish-ginger-shitbag ought to be, and his very God-knows-how-he-does-it-charm only serves to constantly remind me exactly how far down the food chain of sex I really am. The ginger fucker.

'Alright Findo, how's it going?' he asks, as he comes over and hangs his coat on the back of a spare chair.

'No bad, yourself?'

'Aye, no bad. How's it going Diane?'

'No bad,' says Diane.

'Now, which one of you lucky beasts wants to buy me a pint?'

'In your scabby dreams McLeod,' says Diane, draining her glass in one and clunking it empty in front of him. 'I'll have a vodka and coke, and why not make it a double because you love me, and they're not serving Findo so he'll have a coke.'

I interrupt. 'And since I'm not getting served, we should go over to Fortrose now. I don't want to be on cokes all night while you two get pissed.'

'Bollocks Gask, you've got your wee bottle under the table, you'll be cool as beans.'

'No I won't be anything to do with beans, my wee bottle's already half empty already.'

'Come on man,' says Alex 'I'm only here, we'll get a couple in this dump first before we move on to the big city.' Then he drops his voice and adds, 'Unless they don't serve me either, in which case we can fire over now like.'

A grinning Alex heads for the bar casting his eye about for somewhere to stick his cock later. I notice his glance lingering on a couple of girls who look about twelve but who seem to have been served nevertheless. Diane starts chatting to some woman on the next table and I wonder whether I should have even bothered coming out. Mum is dangerously ill in hospital and I'm pretty sure any half-decent son would probably be by her side. But then again it's past visiting hours now anyway. I need to get served otherwise it

91

looks like I'm going to spend all my money on not getting pissed and having a pointless shit night watching pissed people being pissed. And doubtless Alex will pull and vanish, and doubtless Diane will spend most of the night talking to dodgy looking randoms. I maybe should have gone to see Mum this afternoon, I could have got a bus up instead of pissing away the day following Mandy Duplin about and making myself even more depressed at the sight of her perfectly out-of-reach tits. I'll go and see Mum tomorrow, definitely. I can't not go tomorrow, Gran would skin me. She'll be alright though. 'Course she will.

'Findo you miserable-faced shite, what's the matter with you?'

That'll be Diane finished her conversation then. She's looking at me and waiting for some witty back-chat. Instead I decide to bring her down to the level of my real mood.

'My Mum's in hospital.'

'Jesus taking a shit boy, why didn't you say earlier? What's the matter with her?'

'They don't know. Flu they think but they don't know.'

'But flu's not serious is it?'

'Don't know, she's all dripped up and they're doing tests.'

'Shit Findo, I'm sure she'll be fine though, she comes from hardy stock. Tell her I was asking for her when you see her. And what you need to do is finish that drink and then drink some more. Your Mum wouldn't want you to be a gloomy-faced fanny-boy all night. Now where's Alex with those dr … I don't believe it.'

On his way back from the bar Alex has already coerced three girls into having a conversation with him. A little frizzy haired one is trying to monopolise him and he's all attention and smiles as she tells him something that involves her hands a lot. Diane draws in a breath of suitable size.

'ALEX!'

The whole bar skips a heartbeat, except Alex, who in his own time glances over to let Diane know he's heard her, then he's all smiles and attention again as he lets the frizzy haired girl finish whatever she was saying, before he excuses himself from all three and saunters back over with the drinks.

'Who are they?' I ask.

'Dunno, only met them, I got some crisps too if you want.'

He fishes a couple of crushed crisp bags for somewhere up the back of his shirt, chucks them on the table, sits down and says generally.

'So what's happening in the world?'

And I remember I solved the Universe yesterday, so I tell them.

'I solved the Universe.'

'Did you?' says Alex, 'That's very nice for it.'

'Aye,' says Diane. 'All the scientists will be pleased.'

And Alex tells Diane that he saw someone earlier who Diane hates, and Diane details what she'd like to do to him if he ever tried to walk up her dark alley again. I'm suspecting they don't believe me. I try again.

'I really have solved the Universe.'

Diane asks me if I've been hanging out with any notorious Cromarty drug dealers.

'I've told you before,' she says. 'They all have experimental labs in their garages over there and they'll sell you it cheap just to see what it does. So Findo, whatever you've taken, it's all in your mind, it isn't real and don't try and fly off anything tall: you're not a hippy and it's not the nineteen sixties.'

'Thanks for the advice. Very kind. Now do you want to know the solution of the Universe or not?'

'Not really.' says Diane.

'Universe doesn't bother me, so I don't bother it.' says Alex.

I get up and go to the bog. I can hear them laughing behind me. Pair of fuckers. I push through the gents door and enter another world. There are many unwritten and unspoken rules that govern you when you're in a public bog that you just sort of have to learn as you go, and as soon as I stand in front of the urinal and start fishing it out, I realise I'm in danger of breaking one of them. One of the rules; which has never been agreed or discussed but which has been in place ever since men started standing in rows and peeing indoors; says that once you start to pee, if there is anyone else in the bog who started to pee first then your peeing must outlast his peeing, because otherwise that means you've got a tiny bladder and you've lost. And while competitive bladder capacity testing is far too ridiculous a thing to ever mention openly, let alone knowingly enter into competition over with every stranger who ever happens to stand near you in a bog, it is, regardless, exactly the competition you're in anyway, like it or not. Whenever you start peeing at nearly the same time as someone else, you have to outlast them if they started before you, it's as simple as that.

My problem is that I came in here more for the change of scenery than for actually needing to go, and some other guy has just started before me. I need to control the flow and make it last. Control, Findo, control, that's the key. I stare at the wall directly in front of me and try to make a little go a long way. Someone's written on the wall 'Try Gavin's poo hole for all your man-fun needs.' Someone's really got it in for poor Gavin and his poo hole but my own problems are far more urgent. After only a few short seconds I'm already losing pressure and I can sense the guy next to me's still going off like he's putting out forest fires. Now I'm squeezing for all I'm worth, trying to hurry my kidneys into rapid over production, but that's it, I'm done, an embarrassingly tiny amount of pee made all the worse because the other guy's clearly plumbed into the taps. I shake and tuck it away and try to pretend that there is no competition really and that it's only in my mind, but of course I know differently, and can sense through the ether that the other guy is silently fully aware of his victory. I wash my hands and as I chuck the paper towel in the bin, the other guy is still peeing. For fuck's sake, that's just unnatural.

'Ok, you can tell us how you solved the Universe now,' says Alex as I return to my seat.

'Stick it up your bollocks, you don't deserve to know. I'm leaving humanity in its ignorance.'

'Suit yourself.'

'Ok I'll tell you. But this really is the solution of the Universe, no messing about. It's the how and the why of the big bang, the answer to the ultimate quest of all humanity. So no taking the piss till I've finished. What are you doing?'

Alex stops craning his neck around the room and says, 'I was checking Steven Hawking wasn't lurking somewhere in the room with a notepad. And it's ok, he's not. Go ahead.'

'Ok then, I mean bollocks to you both, but ok then. I had hoped for a slightly grander platform for the most important announcement in history, perhaps an assemblage of the world's press on the steps of the Parthenon, but if it's got to be an assemblage of you two idiots at not even the best table in the Railway Hotel, Avoch, then so be it. Here is where they'll build the monument to me and you can tell your grand kids you were here. Ahem. The solution of the Universe. Well you know how they can't figure out what caused the big bang.'

'Aye,' says Alex.

'No,' says Diane.

'Well,' I explain to Diane, 'They can figure out what happened after the big bang, and they can get really, really close to the start of it, like nanoseconds and closer, but they can't get right back to the moment itself because the maths goes crazy; and they certainly can't tell you what caused it because there's no space, time, energy, mass or anything at all to do any maths with, so they're fucked.'

I give this a moment to sink into their heads so they can begin to grasp the enormity of what I'm about to tell them. I notice that they don't look particularly in awe, or even in anticipation of the awe to come so I continue before their minds wander on to more genital things.

'Anyway, so yesterday, while I was just having a little think, and without even really meaning to, I totally figured out what caused the big bang.'

'Were you stoned?' asks Alex.

'That's not relevant, but anyway …' and I pause again to wait for the suspense and awe to build.

'Have you forgotten?' asks Diane, through a mouthful of crisps.

'No, I haven't. Right. Well, do you agree that you can't have the word 'yes' without the word 'no'?'

'Eh?'

'What?'

'I mean, the one has no meaning without the other. If there was no word 'no', then the word 'yes' would have no meaning. The word 'yes' needs its opposite to exist in order to exist itself. Without 'yes' there can be no, 'no'. You see?'

'Yeah.'

'So?'

'So the same thing goes for existence. A thing can either exist or not exist. If something exists, then it must also be possible for it not to exist. You can't have existence without non-existence. So although pre-big bang the universe didn't exist, for its non-existence to have even been possible, it had to have also been possible that it could exist – and so because its existence was possible, as simple as that, it did exist. And that's what caused the big bang. The universe came into existence because it can, because when it didn't exist, it still could, so it did. No God required, no match, no fuse. The whole universe is just an infinite puff of logic.'

I'm being stared at by a pair of blank faces as they take in the enormity of being the first human beings in all of history, to have the actual actuality of the origin of the universe, succinctly and entirely explained to them without any need for religion or maths. The Nobel prize will be the least of my future honours.

'What a load of pish,' says Diane.

'I can't believe you called the universe a poof,' says Alex.

I look at them, and they look back, and I realise how Galileo must have felt when he'd got really excited about all the stuff he'd seen through his telescope and decided to share the obvious conclusions down the pub with his friend, Pope Urban VIII. At least these two forward thinkers don't have the power to burn me at the stake – at least not legally. Would-be Pope Diane notices that I was perhaps expecting a slightly more enthusiastic response and attempts to console me.

'I mean it's a very nice idea and all,' she says. Slowing in her thoughts, 'Except ...' And she looks up into her brain for a diplomatic end to the sentence, which Alex quickly supplies for her.

'Except it's bollocks and you're a dickhead.'

'Yeah, except that,' she says, smiling and satisfied in her mind that I couldn't possibly be offended by such supportive words of kindness. And as it happens I'm not offended. It was probably the same for Einstein at the Patent Office when he spent his lunch hours doing sums instead of hanging out in the staff room. Diane looks at Alex whose attention has already wandered to the small group of girls he was talking to earlier. He always comes out with us but he equally always finds someone else to finish the night with, and now he's scanning the room, already getting itchy feet; or more precisely, a twitchy cock. The dirty ginger fuckmonger.

Chapter 14

Secondary 3

Darwinian terrorist attack number two was under way. Cousin Dan had scoped out the car park of an evangelical church in Inverness and said that it was full of cars with Jesus-fish on them, and it was secluded too, so we could evolve the whole car park no problem. This wasn't mere vandalism, we were fighting for a cause and it was right and it was just. We were freedom fighters for evolution over ignorance, and we were toppling the first domino that would eventually bring down all religion. There was, however, no way I was getting back into a car on the open road with Cousin Dan at the wheel, so despite all his moaning, this time we went on bikes. Initially he'd refused to cycle anywhere because he had a car so what's the point: we could be there and do it and be back within an hour, and he'd even drive slowly if it was because I was frightened of going a bit faster than elderly people like. I explained that of course I wasn't frightened of going fast, but that his stupid hat, glasses and moustache disguise might get us through the odd village unnoticed, but sitting at traffic lights in the middle of Inverness he wasn't going to fool anyone he was anything other than not quite fifteen yet. Unfortunately Cousin Dan was convinced that his disguise was impenetrable, so I pointed out that a good terrorist organisation would mix up its travel methods so as not to establish a detectable pattern, and then I refused point blank to do any terrorism at all that day unless he agreed to go on bikes.

So Darwinian terrorist attack number two set off a bit later than planned because of the arguing about the car, and then the arguing about whether Cousin Dan needed to bring his crossbow. The six or seven miles into Inverness took a bit longer than we thought it would because Auntie Roberta's bike, which I was riding, was complete rusted crap which was the main reason I couldn't keep up. Even so, there were long downhill stretches and the service was still going on when we free-wheeled, me a bit puffed out, the last few yards to our target. The church Cousin Dan had chosen was by the river and had a car park behind it, so we wheeled the bikes round towards the back looking as innocent as any sweating teenager, backpack clinking, pushing an ancient woman's bike and followed by his mad haired cousin in full camouflage gear, can. But Cousin Dan was right, it was a big car park, and rounding the corner hidden from the street by the church, I could already see more than a handful of cars with Jesus-fish simply begging to be evolved.

'Shitsticks,' said Cousin Dan.

'What?'

'Over there.'

I looked. It wasn't just us in the car park. Some old guy was sitting in one of the cars with the window open, smoking a fag, and not looking like he was planning on driving anywhere until his wife or whatever came out after the church service ended.

'What'll we do?'

'Should have let me bring the crossbow, shouldn't you.'

We waited. The guy glanced at us once but paid us no more attention, as we pretended to be waiting for someone too. After five minutes we agreed to do what we could here and then find another church. As it was, there were a few cars parked further round where the guy wouldn't be able to see us, but only one of those had a Jesus-fish on it, and that was a sticker inside the back window. As I was placing the stencil over the window, there was chatter from the street as church was coming out. I quickly spray painted it but my speedy work didn't go well. On lifting the stencil, rather than a clear and bold statement of evolution on top of a sham symbol of a sham religion, it looked more like a giant seagull had passed overhead. I stuffed the stuff back into my backpack and we pedalled out past the chatting Sunday best. There was another church further up, but it was out too, and so on up to the cathedral, but no service and no cover, then over the river and up through the town to find the place entirely abandoned by Christianity and its associated motor cars.

It was mostly uphill on the way back to Cousin Dan's and we didn't talk much after falling out near Halfords. We still needed to be back before Mum came to pick me up after she'd been to the Egger's church group thing, and the wind was against us and Auntie Roberta's crappy bike was crappy and my legs were too stumpy for cycling fast, and Cousin Dan was back to being pissed off we'd cycled in the first place. Not that I could admit he was right, I clearly wasn't built for cycling and when it started to rain as we passed Halfords I was starting to prefer the idea of dying in a car with Cousin Dan at the wheel to ever pushing down on another pedal. Sheltering at the BP garage while seeing if the rain would stop, Cousin Dan lost the plot a bit and got mad when I wouldn't agree to try and do a car-jack with him on anyone who might leave their keys in the ignition when they went inside to pay. It didn't stop and before we were even on the Black Isle, as we cycled the uphill mile up the bridge, and high over the firth into the horizontal sheeting rain, as far as we were both concerned, Darwinian Terrorism was extinct. We were now just a couple of soaked through crappy vandals whose vandalism looked like seagull crap on the longest most pointless cycle home in history. It was all a load of bollocks, so bollocks to it. Next Sunday we'd go back to trying to kill things in trees or maybe get round to building that trebuchet we'd been talking about.

'Tell him it went good.'

'What?'

'The Darwin thing yesterday, tell him it went good, he's made a shitload of t-shirts.'

Cousin Dan had got to me moments before a wide-eyed and slightly too intense Maxwell bore down on us in the school corridor at lunchtime the next day. He was very keen to hear from me exactly how well our terrorist attack had gone, even though he'd already heard from Cousin Dan that it had apparently gone fantastically well. And so when did I think it would be in the newspapers? Because Maxwell hadn't seen anything anywhere yet, but then it was probably too soon for that wasn't it. It would probably be tomorrow, but then he'd been checking online all day in case it went up on one of the local news sites first, but it was bound to be in tomorrow's wasn't it. He'd printed two hundred t-shirts with the Darwin-fish logo and the statement 'Doing it for Darwin' on the back, in a variety of colours and sizes to cash in quickly on all the publicity we'd be getting for the thing we hadn't done.

'Bound to be in tomorrow,' I said.

'Bound to be,' said Cousin Dan.

And we both nodded and told Maxwell how we'd sprayed every car in the car park with a Darwin-fish and how we'd only just got away without being spotted, although maybe we had been spotted, you know, by that guy in the car, but not so much that we'd be recognised or anything. And Maxwell was suitably very pleased, and he started to tell us about the website he was building and how we should trademark the Darwin-fish if no one else already had, but he didn't think anyone had, and his research was telling him we totally had a USP. I could see why Cousin Dan had decided it was best to lie to Maxwell. Maxwell was a different flavour of nutter to Cousin Dan, with possible reactions to bad news that ranged into the 'best not to think about it' category. He'd gone at this like it was the only thing in his life and if we were to suddenly cut his tightrope from under him, there was no way of knowing how he'd come down. Like when they made him leave the Cromarty Boy's Brigade for putting a tent peg through Thingy Bell's foot.

'What's a USP?'

'Unique Selling Point.'

Maxwell explained that we were the only Darwinian terrorists in the marketplace, and whereas with all the other terrorists you had to be in their religion or country or whatever to sign up, and even then none of them were really trying to sell anything to anybody. But with us, we could really focus on down on our products.

'Products?'

'The t-shirts, obviously,' said Maxwell. 'They're ready to go as soon as the story hits the papers tomorrow, we can link into our site from all the comments pages on the newspapers' pages and rile people up and make them hate us, which will make other people love us and that. I've got all the screen-printing gear from when my dad was protesting about the GM crops or something that got poisoned or something, or was it from when someone shot a dolphin? Did someone shoot a dolphin? Anyhow, we can screen-print up anything we like, more t-shirts, flags, pillowcases, and we can get posters and mugs and pens and stuff like that. You know, stuff tourists and people buy. Oh, and we need to get lots more stencils and that made at the laser place, and sell them in kits with cans of spray paint and balaclavas, and probably a free t-shirt too, so anyone can go out and spray cars, and that'll get publicity too and make it into a marketing snowball and that.'

It was definitely best to let Maxwell imagine he was a big part of what we were doing, until eventually he realised we weren't doing it any more. But in the meantime there was one little thing bothering me.

'It's not about selling stuff,' I said. 'It's about confronting religion and telling them creationism is wrong. It's about pointing out that you can explain things without the need for God and Jesus and all them. It's about challenging the idea that religious beliefs shouldn't be challenged just because they're religious beliefs; and so breaking the bonds that keep people in ignorance from one generation to the next. That's what it's about.'

'Aye, well, aye,' said Maxwell. 'I mean, that's true, aye, but until I can pay back the marketing budget I took off my Uncle's credit card, it's also about shifting some t-shirts and that n'all. But write down all that stuff you said so I can stick it on the website: give people even more reason to buy the stuff. Doin' it for the cause.'

I wasn't sure that Maxwell was fully into the ideology behind Darwinian terrorism, but then we weren't going to bother with it any more so it didn't really matter.

'Do you think he'll be mad when there's nothing in the papers tomorrow; or ever?' I asked Cousin Dan after Maxwell had rushed off bubbling with plans.

'Dunno,' said Cousin Dan. 'How much do you think two hundred and fourteen t-shirts cost him?'

'Dunno,' I replied. 'Quite a lot probably.'

'Do you think we should maybe do something to get in the paper?

'Cos if we do, then he's got nothing to complain about and it's not our fault if he's robbing his uncle to buy shite.'

'Yeah, maybe better had. Just a little terrorism, just to get into the paper.'

It wasn't that we were scared of Maxwell or anything, I might have been two years below him but I was already bigger than him, and Cousin Dan wasn't frightened of anything but farm work. Maxwell wasn't scary, Maxwell just had a reputation as being a bit tricky to predict. Most of the time you could prod him with a pointy stick till your arm got sore and he'd just stand there looking at you like someone's cow. But then everyone knew how he'd poured a litre of acid into Morag McLean's bag and melted it, after she said she wouldn't go out with him, even after he offered her all his dinner money; and everyone knew that Maxwell's the reason Adam Reeve has teeth marks all the way round one kneecap. So given the choice between maybe putting Maxwell in an unpredictable mood, or doing some more terrorism; doing some more terrorism seemed to be the more sensible option.

Chapter 15

Saturday 13th April, 8pm

'Have you chosen tonight's poor unfortunate cow?' Diane asks Alex, as his gaze wanders to the clique of girls he was talking to earlier.

'No,' he replies. 'I haven't decided who I should offer the gift of ultimate pleasure to yet. There are a couple in here who'd go for me, though it's still early so we'll have to see.'

'What about the frizzy one you were talking to? I ask him.

'Aye, possibly her, or her friend with the nose. What about you? Are you on the pull tonight or what?'

I'm always on the pull and simultaneously never on the pull. Always, because given the opportunity wouldn't I just love to. And never, because the girl who would give me the opportunity, either doesn't exist or is a heavily drugged in-patient behind a good deal of security. Alex is waiting for a response but his face isn't giving away if he's messing with me or not. He may not be much of a physical specimen but the little shit has some way of talking to girls which totally disarms them, and he doesn't understand why everyone else can't do it too. One minute they're chatting to a charming but harmless individual, well he's got red hair and he's kind of short and nothingy looking, so of course they wouldn't with a barge pole; but then he seems to understand them so well and there's a real connection there, and the next thing they know they're waking up with unwanted teenage pregnancy concerns. Any sane person would suspect he drugs them, but these poor girls all come out of the Alex roller coaster with their memories intact and the disturbing knowledge that the whole thing seemed to have been their own idea.

I, however, am not Alex. When a girl sees me lumbering at her trying to affect a casual smile; she goes rigid with fear while nervously fumbling in her bag for the rape alarm or a stabbing weapon. As my attempts to cover up my desperation with a laid-back and unconcerned manner, give me the exact appearance of a drooling bug-eyed sex offender. And according to Diane, this puts women off.

'Be yourself,' she says. 'Give a girl a chance to get to know you,' she counsels. 'And most importantly, Findo. Lower your sights.'

'No,' I tell Alex. 'I'm not on the pull tonight.'

The trouble is, I can't help who I like and I can't help who I don't like either. If I ever took Diane's advice and lowered my sights to an appropriate level, I wouldn't be making myself happy and I wouldn't be doing any favours for my new girlfriend either, as I'd be taking her away from the bridge she lives under with the rest of the family of trolls.

'What about her?' asks Diane, breaking my train of thought and directing my eyes to the far end of the bar where now sits Nancy Blas, Scotland's most perfectly spherical girl and the owner of a black moustache thick enough to wax at the ends into a Victorian military style. Diane had better be joking. I mean of course she is, but what if she's not? What if she really thinks that that's the best I can hope for in life. Nancy Blas, a name everyone always pronounces in their deepest and slowest voice to emphasise the true horror of the girl, and which thinking about it, is basically the exact same way most people pronounce my name when they think I'm not standing behind them.

I turn back and Diane's got an evil little glint in her eye. Well at least she was joking.

'Yes, ha, ha. Good to know you think so much of me.'

'Now don't get all touchy on me Gask.' she says. 'I'm not suggesting you marry the Nancy Blaster, I'm suggesting you go and get some practice on her. You know, say hello, ask her how she is, take an interest. Go on man, see, she's looking over.'

'Only one of her eyes is looking over. And as fun as it might be for you two if I went and chatted up the gorilla lady, I think instead I'll maybe just not. Perhaps Alex might like a go,' I add, trying to deflect attention from myself.

'Alex might well like a go,' says Alex. 'As I'm sure there's a lovely human being inside all of that problem area. Maybe even two lovely human beings. However, I've only this minute discovered the need to go and talk to someone else. Back in a bit.'

And off Alex prowls, straight over to the little frizzy girl who he taps on the shoulder and who looks really pleased to see him. Damn his eyes, the freakish lucky ginger bastard.

Diane proceeds to spout forth about this and that and she lays into the booze as I try to work out whether I should ration out what's left of my vodka into the cokes, or drink the lot quickly through a straw while exercising, and then hope that whatever level of drunkenness that gets me to, lasts the rest of the night. Then just as Diane's starting to look like a crowbar won't get her out of this pub tonight, Twiglet, Diane's ex, comes into the bar, and I feel the night start to swing in my favour. There's no way she'll want to hang around here if Twiglet's about. I indicate his presence to her with my eyes.

'Ah shit, no. Shit it,' she says as she spots him. 'If that arsehole comes over here I'm going to punch his lights out.'

For once I don't think Diane means it. Twiglet is a massive scary man and mostly entirely brainless. I'd never even dare call him 'Twiglet' to his face, and since I don't know what his real name is, I wouldn't call him anything. I'd just never speak to Twiglet. Diane went out with him for ages from when she was fourteen. Twiglet was about twenty three or something at the time so it raised eyebrows even in Avoch. It then took a long time for Diane to convince him that she wasn't going to marry him the minute she turned sixteen, and an even longer time after she dumped him, to get him to stop disintegrating in her front garden after the pubs had shut. Twiglet spots Diane and isn't sure what to do, then he follows his friends to the bar so he can make a decision with a beer in his hand. I've always meant to ask her what she saw in him but I'm also reasonably sure I don't want to know.

'What did you ever see in him?' I ask anyway.

'He made me laugh.' she says.

That surprises me. I'd no idea he could finish a sentence without forgetting why he'd started it. The answer I was expecting was 'big cock'.

106

Twiglet's lurking at the bar like a sub-post office in a bad mood and I'm starting to feel a bit uneasy. If he thinks I'm going out with Diane I might be in trouble, and Diane might tell him as much just to wind him up. She's also now adamant that we're not going anywhere, as since we were here first, he's the one who can piss off if he's not happy. Oh shit, he's coming over. The smell of all day drinking arrives just before him.

'Hi Diane,' he says in a voice a lot higher than you'd expect from a guy who broke Diane's back door off its hinges with his head.

'Twig,' says Diane, pitching her voice to be emotionless.

'I saw your Mum last week,' he says to her.

'Did you?'

'Aye, in the shop. You alright?'

'Aye. You?'

'No bad. Got new alloys.'

'Have you?'

'Aye. You still got the scooter?'

'Aye.'

'I used to see you on it a lot. Not seen you on it for a while.'

'No?'

'No.'

'I've still got it.'

'Have you?'

'Aye.'

Good God in his shiny house, this man is dull. Is this the dazzling wit that kept Diane laughing for almost two years? Perhaps it was a simpler time back then, when alloys and mums in shops were funny. Oh shit, I just amused myself and I think I made a noise. Yes I did, Twiglet's looking at me. He looks like he's deciding whether I'm worth the small effort of breaking into tiny jellied pieces. Now he's opening his mouth at me and I think I'm in trouble.

'Are you Foreskin's wee cousin?' he asks.

Maybe he isn't going to kill me. 'Yeah,' I say. Cousin Dan's had his own share of nicknames.

Twiglet's curiosity seems satisfied and thankfully I'm not worth bothering about. He turns his hydraulic neck back towards Diane and he tries to wear her down with a story about how he's got new jeans on, because his old ones wore out and does she remember the old ones and how they were the best ones he ever had, and he's not sure about these new ones but he'd sewed up the holes in the pockets of old ones till he couldn't fit his keys in them any more. Now there may be some deep emotional connection between Diane and Twiglet and his old pair of jeans or perhaps Twiglet was just unusually attached to them, and he goes on and on about the demise of the greatest pair of jeans that ever graced the earth for what feels like about a week. He finally ends his sophisticated buttering up by asking Diane, 'What're you doin' later?' He'd tried his Neanderthal best to make it sound like an innocent question but it came out all psycho-stalker and Diane's cold toleration of him up to now, freezes right over.

'It's none of yours what we're doing. We might stay here, we might not.'

'We're going over to Fortrose,' says Alex appearing from nowhere. 'I've sorted us a lift with the girls, we're going now.'

Diane instantly flashes Alex a filthy look which says 'For buggery-bollock's sake Alex Milton McLeod, why are you telling my enormous compulsive ex-boyfriend where to find me later when he's paralytically drunk and as lonely as a horny bear that's been stuck on an island?' Alex misses the look and is already grabbing his coat, 'Hey Twiglet, how's it hanging?' he says casually to the enormous man who's blocking out most of the light, then to Diane, 'Come on, down that drink, they're not going to hang about.' Alex heads for the door saying, 'Later Twigs, good to see you.' And for once, Diane does as she's told and empties her glass in a one second gulp. She and I slip out from behind our table leaving Twiglet standing alone, and for a moment as I'm passing him, he looks like a tiny little lost boy: albeit one who'll smash your back door in with his head if you ever dump him.

Chapter 16

Secondary 4

A church door with a six foot Darwin-fish painted on it in shiny white gloss paint. Two miles down the road, three Darwinfish on churches in Cromarty and six around Beauly. When there had been nothing in the papers about our highly successful attack that never happened in the church car park in Inverness, we had to convince Maxwell it must have been some sort of conspiracy not to report it, as the Highland News and the P&J and all of them must be owned by Christians, probably a federation of Evangelicals and Wee Frees, we decided, who are probably trying to suppress the truth for their own ends or something. Maxwell seemed happy to accept this explanation, and then when we considered the manifest injustice of it ourselves, and even though we'd made it all up, it made us determined to break the strangle hold that the Christians had over all the Highland's media, by committing some Darwinian Terrorist acts that they wouldn't be able to ignore.

I overcame my reluctance to let Cousin Dan drive me anywhere by taking up smoking, and occasionally Maxwell would come on our expeditions too, and we'd all wear moustaches and glasses and baseball caps, though I got quite pissed off they made me sit in the back even though I was in charge.

Church notice boards usually have stupid little home-printed A4 posters with rainbows on them that say stuff like, 'Jesus died for your sins', 'Mother and toddler group Wednesdays 11am' or 'Come to our Alpha course and we'll fix up your shit life'. After we'd been by, they said stuff like, 'Jesus has never heard of you.' or, 'God hasn't evolved yet' or, 'This church wants your money, everything else we say is bollocks and purely designed to make you give us your money, you dick'. It was Cousin Dan's idea to paint the enormous Darwin-fish on the church doors and that got us straight into the papers with photos and everything. Cousin Dan and Maxwell were bouncing off the walls with happiness.

One newspaper article had called us 'Disgusting Godless Hooligans' and so we quickly made some t-shirts with the words 'Disgusting Godless Hooligan' and the Darwin-fish logo, and a few of those started to sell off the website, and so did the DIY Darwinist Terror Kits consisting of stencils, latex gloves and a balaclava (we decided against including a free t-shirt). We spent most Saturdays for the next year or so over at Maxwell's Uncle's, where Maxwell lived because his Mum had issues, though we never saw anyone but Maxwell in the place. We screen printed t-shirts and designed posters and packed up orders for distribution. We weren't making any money because Maxwell had had to outlay a lot on materials and equipment and stuff, and as he said, 'It takes time to build a brand', but we knew that once we got going it'd be one of those snowball effect things and then we'd be coining it. In the meantime we agreed it would be best to separate out the sales and marketing part of the terrorist organisation from the terrorist part of the terrorist organisation. As Maxwell pointed out, it would be easier for the police to find the website and so find us that way, than it would be for them to catch us red-handed or anything, so all the stuff we could deny as having anything to do with anything, we kept at Maxwell's Uncle's, and everything slightly more criminal went into a water tank at the back of Cousin Dan's big shed. That way, as long as we didn't ever tell anyone what we were doing, there was pretty much no way we could ever get caught. And just because Maxwell might appear to the police to be running a terrorist website and selling things off it, that didn't mean he, or anyone else he knew, not that he knew anyone else, was doing any of the more newsworthy lock-em-up-for-it stuff.

So security was good, and Maxwell's Uncle wasn't a problem either because Maxwell said he never even looked in the spare room where we'd set up the t-shirt printing, because he worked on an oil rig, and wouldn't say anything even if he knew because he knew all about advertising so would understand what we were doing. Because according to Maxwell, fifteen years ago, Maxwell's Uncle had been the person who'd compiled the definitive list of the sexiest letters in the alphabet, in order of sexiness, which was worth millions to all the big advertising companies who'd been chasing it for years. But Maxwell's Uncle got his list ripped off by some big advertising company who'd been using it to sell cars and phones and tennis rackets ever since, so Maxwell's uncle had gone to work offshore instead. Maxwell said he knew what the sexy letter order alphabet was too, but he wouldn't ever tell us because he'd been sworn to secrecy as it was too valuable a trade secret to tell to anybody. So I had a go at compiling the list myself, and from sexiest letter to least sexy, I came up with: XSTVZAREFNYMOLPKBIUGQWHCDJ. Maxwell told me I was miles off, I wasn't so sure.

Cousin Dan and I reckoned that the big advertising agency had probably put Maxwell's Uncle in prison, or maybe up in the same mental hospital where Maxwell's mum spent lots of her time, because he was never around, ever. Not that we cared where he was, his house was out past Culbokie and used to be the gate house for some estate that wasn't there any more, so there were just these two enormous gate posts in a field and then Maxwell's Uncle's house hidden behind one of them. So as well as being able to do what we liked at Cousin Dan's every Sunday, on a Saturday, I could get a bus over to Maxwell's (when Cousin Dan could be persuaded not to come over and offer to drive me) and we could do what we liked there too. If we didn't have a Darwinist Terrorist attack on, we'd usually spend a few hours or more making t-shirts and filling orders, and after that we might play our own slightly violent version of lawn bowls down the hall and through to the living room, while smoking cigars and talking in English accents. It was Maxwell's idea that we start videoing the Darwinist attacks and sticking them up on the website too, to make the brand edgier and realer, and to get the marketing snowball properly going.

Chapter 17

Saturday 13th April, 8.25pm

The car Alex has got us a lift in is tiny, and has the three girls Alex has chatted up plus the three of us to fit in it. And I'm not small. I can already sense that the girls would rather I didn't even try to get in the car with them, as apart from being far too big, I'm not very nice to look at. However, Alex is buoying them along and is offering to sit with the little frizzy one on his knee in the front, so that at least satisfies the one he's picked, if not the other two. So we pack in like refugees and I find myself wedged in the back between Diane and the least attractive of Alex's three. Alex is keeping the driver and the one on his knee amused, as the suspension complains underneath us along the road. In an effort to make light-hearted conversation, I ask the one next to me what they're going to Fortrose for. She looks at me like I'm something that floats but won't flush, and answers 'To get pissed'. Then despite me taking up more than all the space between her and Diane, she starts taking to Diane across my back and cuts me out. Diane quickly establishes common ground with her, and they talk about a mutual friend who's gone right up herself since she got a boyfriend who works in H&M. I decide to say something clever to the girl whose thigh is, albeit involuntarily, warmly pressed up against mine, to see if cleverness will get me somewhere light heartedness won't. So I lean backwards into the conversation and mention to her that everyone in the world would probably get on a lot better, except for the fact that we tend to judge ourselves by our internal ideals, and everyone else by their external actions. Diane tells me to stop talking such shite and tells the girl to ignore me, which she was doing already. It's as well it's only a few minutes drive to Fortrose: the sooner I get to a pub that's going to serve me, the better.

Once into Fortrose the hair dryer of an engine only just makes it up the hill and we pull over outside The Inn. I've decided I don't like the girl sitting next to me, hot thigh or not. I think she probably thinks she's bubbly and has a great personality, but in reality I think that just means that she's annoying when she's sober and intolerable when she's drunk. We escape the crush inside the car and pile into the pub which is even busier than the car was. We find a tiny space to stand near the toilets and crowd into it, as Diane volunteers me to go and get the drinks, which it seems I'm buying for everyone. The bar is three deep with people and it takes me a slow age to get to the front and another significant era before either of the staff even notice me with my best 'I'm eighteen, maybe even nineteen' face on. When then barman does eventually get to me, my size and ugliness at last do the trick, and he takes the order without a second glance. Trapped at the bar with more drinks than I can carry I make faces over the crowd till Diane spots me, takes the hint, and comes over to give me a hand.

Back in the tiny space by the toilets I take a big sip of my first precious pint. The head start Diane and Alex got while I was rationing my vodka means they're already in the first stages of rowdiness, and the fact I've noticed means I must have already slipped well behind. I take another, much bigger sip of my pint and look around. I don't know why we're drinking in here. Of the two pubs in town, this one attracts the people who leave school in fourth year. We should have gone to The Crown. I prefer the Crown, and not the public bar either, the lounge. Looking around there are quite a few faces from past years above me at school, and any number of them would have been likely to give me abuse if I ever passed them in the techie corridor.

Alex has effectively commandeered all three of the car girls for himself and they are now actually competing for his attention, all flicking hair and laughing at everything he says. There's arm touching going on too, and everything else the internet's taught me about recognising flirty girl body language. And it's all, as usual, happening to Alex. Good bloody God in the sky, can't they even see he's got red hair?

'He's a jammy shit bastard,' I mutter to Diane.

'You could be a jammy shit bastard if you wanted,' she replies quietly. 'What about Suzanne? You talked some crap at her in the car but you could still redeem yourself. I happen to know she's single and I also happen to know she's a bit of a slag.'

I look with new eyes at the bubbly Suzanne, and try to filter out the fact that I really don't like her at all.

'I'm going to need more drink.'

'So is she,' Diane replies. 'Now you talk to her and don't try and be charming or intelligent or impressive or any of that shite. Just take an interest. Ask her about herself and then follow up on what she says so it looks like you're listening. I'll ply you both with drink and then let you know if I think she gets drunk enough to go with you willingly. Sound like a plan?'

'That actually does sound like a plan.'

'Then let's call it "The Plan". Now give me your pint and I'll nip into the bog and make it into a Vermouth tops for you.'

Diane takes my pint from my hand and vanishes with it into the toilets. I try to think of something to say to this Suzanne girl. What might this Suzanne girl be interested in? Maybe we have something in common I could ask her about and it'll make her desperately want to lick my glans. Now what might that be? Judging from her outward appearance, she looks like she enjoys being thick and talking loudly about nothing. So what the hell do I say to her? The king of Swaziland doesn't have these problems. The king of Swaziland is too busy having the best job in the world. No wondering what to say to a girl for the king of Swaziland. Instead, for him, every year on his birthday, all the finest eligible virgins in the country come and do a bare breasted dance for him en masse, then the king of Swaziland picks the bare breasted virgin he likes the look of the most and she becomes his latest wife. Every birthday another mass tits out dance, and every year another wife for the collection. No standing about like a self-conscious twat for him, just a few hundred virgins jiggling about and which one's tits does he like the best. I suppose I could tell Suzanne about the king of Swaziland.

'Why aren't you talking to her?' hisses Diane, who's back. 'Take that and drink it and get in there.'

She shoves my pint of Vermouthed lager into my hand. I try it. It tastes likes tramp's piss. She's taken my lovely first pint of the night and made it into tramp's piss.

'It doesn't taste very nice,' I tell Diane.

'Balls,' she replies. 'It's a sophisticated cocktail that fancy people drink in cities and that, so suck it down you.'

I take a big swig and while not feeling very sophisticated, at least I avoid the urge to throw it back up. And within moments I'm feeling the first flush of early onset drunkenness spreading across my cheeks. Now if only I could think of a single thing to say to this girl. I turn to Diane and she reads my vacant look.

'Tell her you like her hair or her necklace or something and take it from there. Now by the time I get back I expect you to have stinky fingers at the very least.'

Diane slips away into the throng and I'm left with my mission and an opening line. I wait till Alex is concentrating on the little frizzy one, and now the one who was driving is talking to them both and Suzanne is briefly out of the conversation. I swoop like a pterodactyl. At least I think about swooping like a pterodactyl. It's definitely now or never. Am I going to open my mouth? Am I? Can I? Does the thing even work any more? My heart is in my mouth and my balls have re-ascended, but Diane will kill me if I do nothing; so I'm swooping like a pterodactyl.

'I like your necklace,' I blurt.

'What?'

Oh shit, she hasn't heard me but at least she's turned around. I suppose I shouldn't have tried talking to her back.

'I like your necklace.'

'Oh thanks,' she says and even smiles a little. 'I got it from an ex.'

'So you preferred the necklace to him?'

She laughs and says, 'Aye, right enough, 'spose I do.'

I feel it's going very well, but now she's looking at me like I'm supposed to say something else, and I've got nothing. Absolutely nothing, not a thought in my head. She's still looking at me and I've got to say something really quickly before she loses interest, which is starting to happen. King of Swaziland? No, not that, something else, something about me, anything at all, shit she's going to turn away.

'My great great granddad married a mermaid.' I say.

No idea where the hell that came from but at least it's got her attention. She's still not saying anything though, she's just looking at me funny. Perhaps I should add something or clarify what I mean.

'Anything like that in your family?'

What the hell did I say that for? Now she definitely thinks I'm mental.

'No, not really,' she says, and she turns back to the girl who was driving and mutters something to her, and that wins me a glance of disdain and now I'm being actively ignored. I spend the next half hour, eyes wandering around the pub, overhearing snaps of conversation and standing cramped by the wall and far nearer the toilet door than is fashionable. I'm now trying to perfect the look of having just finished talking in a fascinating manner to someone, and being about to start another sparkling conversation with someone else any second. Alex is starting to entwine with the little frizzy one and Diane is at the far end of the pub chatting to a couple of people who have hated me since first year. My pint of lager-vermouth is empty and no-one I bought a drink for earlier is showing any indication of even looking at me, let alone returning the favour. I've now been squeezed so near the gents door that every time someone goes in or out I have to move aside. Fantastic Saturday night this is. I squeeze further aside than usual to let some big under bred animal past, and it's not till he comes back out that I realise it's Twiglet.

Diane's bull-headed suitor ploughs through the crowd towards her, meandering slightly into some guy who would probably definitely say something about his spilt pint, if Twiglet wasn't so clearly the kind of gentleman who would bite his nose off if he did. Twiglet slows as he gets towards the table Diane is now sitting at and when she spots him, he says something to her, then she says something to him and whatever it is she said, the jaws of the people at her table have dropped a little with astonishment. Twiglet's gestures suddenly looks all placatory but Diane's having none of it, and she's getting quite animated and pointing at him, the sense of it being, 'What the shit are you doing here? Piss off now and never ever stop pissing off.' I move past Alex and the car girls to get a better view. Twiglet's trying to communicate his appearance in this pub is entirely coincidental and he's all shrugging and palms out, and then he starts getting annoyed Diane isn't buying it, so he starts to get a bit pointy and bullish. At this, Diane picks herself and her drink up, jabs a parting comment at Twiglet and heads back through the crowd straight towards me. Good God woman, don't bring him over here. Diane swiftly elbows her way through, draining her drink and discarding the glass as she approaches.

'We're going. Where's Alex?'

I look round to where Alex is and he isn't, and neither are any of the car girls. I look back at Diane blankly.

'And where's Suzanne? You're supposed to be chatting her up.'

I look even blanker. Diane rolls her eyes, tuts and heads for the door pulling me in her wake. I risk a sideways glance to see if Twiglet's bearing down on us but it looks like Diane's put him off for now as he's joining the crush at the bar; or rather the crush at the bar is getting out of his way. I scuttle outside after Diane.

The High Street's dead quiet and cold and the stars are out. Diane phones Alex while I decide to text him. It's no surprise that he's skipped out on us but that he's taken all three girls with him is just greedy. The car we arrived in isn't where it was and Alex isn't answering Diane's call.

'The bastard's voice-mailed me,' she says to the street in general and then she leaves a message.

'Alex you whore, you could have said goodbye you impolite crust of penis cheese. Twiglet showed up and I'm blaming you, so next time I see you I'm going to staple your bollocks to your feet. Me and Findo are going up to The Crown so if you're not already there and you get bored of your horny women we'll maybe see you there later. Anyhow, try and not give them AIDS, try and not get AIDS off them, and don't let on that you dye your pubes. Later darling.'

117

My text to him is a bit more succinct. It reads 'You are a fanny.'

We walk up towards the Crown.

'What was that about Alex dyeing his pubes?'

'Nothing. Decided to accuse him of it, that's all.'

'Does he dye his pubes?'

'I wouldn't know, but I think it would be pretty sound advice for such a very ginger young man.'

'I'm going to start telling people he dyes his pubes.'

'It's the least he deserves.'

Chapter 18

Secondary 4

In our defence, we had no idea. At least I didn't and Cousin Dan didn't, and I'm really pretty sure Maxwell didn't either because he would have said. But then why would I know? Just because I'd spent half my life up to that point reading and was pretty sure I knew twice as much as every other fourteen year-old, didn't mean that one or two things hadn't slipped past me. And as I never gave a crap about America or anything that went on there, how was I supposed to know anyway? Cousin Dan was far more likely to know than I was, given the dodgy websites he lived in and all the endless crap he watched. And if Maxwell did know, and I don't think he did, but if he did; he maybe wouldn't have thought it mattered, because at the time it was such a good, simple and straightforward idea. Or at least it would have been a good idea if those Americans hadn't got there before us and ruined it for everyone else who wanted to try.

The Darwin Terrorist Organisation wasn't making any money at all, even though we were spending most weekends at Maxwell's screen-printing t-shirts and packing up orders. Our marketing snowball wasn't snowballing yet and although we seemed busy enough and none of us was taking any money out, our materials and production costs were higher than expected, and the spreadsheet showed how Maxwell was having to make up an operational shortfall with his own cash. He hadn't said anything about it for ages because he had faith in the brand and was sure that when it established itself, when it 'made its marketing mark,' so much cash would roll in we wouldn't have time to count it. In the meantime we just had to work like foreigners and for nothing. I'd suggested that if it was costing him cash then we could pack the whole thing in and go back to graffiting Christians' cars and churches for fun, but both Maxwell and Cousin Dan were adamant that we'd turn a profit eventually. Of course I reminded them that we weren't doing it for money, but for the principles, for the ideology, for the truth; and while they both agreed they also said it would be nice to make some cash on it as well.

Cousin Dan was about to leave school, which meant he was expected to go full time on the farm, no matter how much he didn't fucking like it. So what with his total lack of qualifications and a world view which meant prospective employers would invariably tick the box marked 'Watch closely till off the premises', his employment options beyond the farm were limited to the idea that bringing down Christianity with a spray can could somehow be turned into a business. As for Maxwell, he'd stopped going to school the year before and the school hadn't tried very hard to make him come back. He lived in his Uncle's house which his Uncle didn't live in, and though he said he had lots of friends and claimed to be at the centre of some kind of cosmopolitan social whirl, where he was lauded as a marketing genius and always being invited to openings; whenever we came round he'd be sitting in a granddad chair in the living room with the TV off. I think he was only keen to keep going with the Darwinian Terrorist business model in order to get back some of the money he'd spent on it, and God knows where he got that from. And since Cousin Dan and I were the only real life people who ever came round to see him, if we gave up on the terrorism then Maxwell would probably be pretty lonely. Of course Maxwell wasn't really my problem, but then I kind of knew how he felt. I longed for intelligent, sophisticated and mentally stimulating company too, but as no one else ever spoke to me, I was hanging out instead with a pair of knob-heads who thought they were tycoons. It was Maxwell's idea that we do something a bit more impressive than spraying cars and church doors, and it was Cousin Dan's idea as to what it should be. And at the time it really did seem like a good idea. It really did.

It was on the Tuesday after the Sunday night we did it, that we learned the thing that none of us knew. We learned that far from being a simple and clever anti-Christian statement, the huge cross we'd planted in a churchyard out past Balblair, and then set fire to, had a certain other symbolism and associated implications we'd never even suspected. That the minister of the church in question turned out to be Nigerian, well that was just unlucky as fuck.

120

Chapter 19

Saturday 13th April, 9.10pm

I've been served no problem whatsoever. The lounge bar of the Crown is now my favourite bit of pub in the world, and the dozy barmaid who didn't even think of asking me for ID, is my nominee for the Nobel prize for selling beer to the people who need it the most. Diane doesn't like the lounge bar as much as the public one, but as Twiglet isn't lounge material, he's less likely to stick his pining and confused big drunk head round this door, so for once Diane's letting me drink where I want to.

It's sedate in here by Diane's usual standards, mostly middle aged Volvo people who like to cycle and play instruments. The kind of people who think they're going to stabilise the earth's weather systems by taking their own bags into Tescos. It's only the wide variety of whiskies and the strawberry beer she's chasing them down with that's stopping her complaining loudly that it's far too quiet. For once she doesn't seem to know anyone in the place and though the bar is small it's only about half full so we get a table with some elbow room. So with my beer in front of me, and no one looking like they want to inform the authorities, I set about making up for lost time. For at this time on a Saturday night I should be a lot drunker, so I down my pint like a Glaswegian on holiday and get a round of banana beers in to add a spot of tropical excitement to the evening.

'So what did Twiglet want that you left the pub so quick?' I ask her after savouring my first taste of alcoholic bananay goodness. I get a half suspicious eye from her before she says,

'What the hell do you think he wanted? He misses my tits but he can't quite grasp that there's another part of me that isn't my tits, and that part of me has free will, and has had more than e-bloody-nough of him.'

I put on my best most innocent face and ask. 'Is the part of you you're talking about your bottom?'

Diane cracks a grin and threatens to boot me up mine. For a fleeting moment I wonder what would happen if I made a move on her, and as she's just been talking about them, I'm finding it suddenly hard to resist taking a long glance at her tits. These are super dangerous thoughts. If she catches me staring she'll tear my balls out through my throat, but now the thought's in my head I'm feeling compelled to choose a moment and take the risk. Diane isn't unattractive exactly, and compared to me she's an Italian film-nymph, though if I do have a type; she isn't it. Discus thrower built as she is, it's one throwing event too far up the ladder for me. I lose interest somewhere around the javelin type, and even then that's only if it's as part of a decathlon or something, javelin couldn't be her only event. And Diane doesn't exactly bring out a man's protective instincts, unless you're a farm animal like Twiglet. In fact, that's maybe Diane's problem: the force of her gob scares the living shit out of most guys, me included, and so she has this reputation as a man-eater despite only ever having been with Twiglet, and I'm not even sure about that. What she needs is a man who likes to bend iron bars with his hands and has a Ph.D. in arguing at volume. Now she's turned to see who's just come in so I take my chance and stare at her tits. I manage a full couple of seconds of leering, and I can kind of see why Twiglet's so persistent. It's because they're big. As Diane turns back round my eyes are staring into the middle distance somewhere near the bar in a perfectly ordinary and everyday way.

Two hours of uninterrupted drinking and talking shite. I've mostly stuck with the banana beers but that set of cherry liqueurs we veered off into in a foolish moment has made my face go numb. The other problem with Diane is that she'll talk to anybody. I'm just trying to explain to her about toilet etiquette and how some old guy broke it by talking to me in the bog just now about some football match or other, while I was in mid-pee, and how that's a flagrant 'do not do' in the gents thing, and how I should be able to issue him with some kind of ticket or something and I should get the money from the fine for having my human rights so horribly breached. But Diane's all chatting to the next table over who are in their twenties for God's sake so what can they possibly have to say that's interesting? So because she's distracted, as the door opens and Twiglet comes in, the beer fumes rising from his eyes, I'm the first to see him. He doesn't look so much like a lost little boy any more, he looks like a steamed up fuck-gorilla. His swivelly beery eye sweeps the room and falls on Diane. The right thing to do from a chivalric point of view would be to quietly intervene on Diane's behalf and gently but firmly remind him of her expressed desire not to see him, and though I am finally feeling quite drunk now, it turns out that drunk and brave are by no means the same thing. Twiglet hasn't said anything yet but because he's the major gravitational object in the room, eyes and heads swirl towards him of their own accord. Diane notices the lull in background chat and spotting him lets go an exasperated, 'What now motherfucker?'

'You can't say that to me,' says Twiglet in his weird high voice while still standing half way across the small room which is feeling smaller by the second.

'I can Twig, I can say whatever I like, and because you're still following me despite what I said earlier, I'm going to say piss off, piss a long way off and keep pissing off for all time. I've totally had it with you now and you're making me angry. Go away Twig, I don't want to see you.'

Twiglet comes over to the table like a death star which isn't in a very happy place and all the middle aged Volvo people go silent and decide they're not going to intervene in what are obviously working class matters. Should I break the tension with a quip? Nope, don't think I should.

'You can't call me that,' he says.

'What?' says Diane, sparkling defiance.

'You know what.'

'Oh, you mean mother fucker you mother fucker? Because she's dead you mean, is that it you mother fucker? Well if you stopped humping away in her ashes all the time I wouldn't have to would I? Now why are you still here?'

Even I felt myself breathe in at that one and the Volvo people have started shitting themselves. Someone at the bar just whispered, 'Should we call the police?' Lucky for them Twiglet's oblivious to everything but Diane. He looks at her like he might rip her head off and says, 'Because I love you,' in a surprisingly genuinely almost touching way. Diane is less than impressed.

'Heard it before, changes nothing, don't care. Still here?'

'I'll kill myself.'

'Heard that one before too, what, about a million times now would you say? Yet here you still are.'

'I will, I'll kill myself.'

'Go on then.'

'I will.'

'I'm asking you to.'

'I will.'

'Then please do.'

'I'm serious.'

'I'm glad.'

'I will.'

'I look forward to it.'

'You'll be sorry.'

'I'll be relieved.'

The unstoppable force stares at the immovable object. The immovable object stares back. Somewhere over near the bar I think I hear someone dialling. I'm not going to look over to check as if I move even the tiniest bit the enormous scary man might notice me and decide that the reason she doesn't love him any more is me.

'I will do it,' says the unstoppable force to her.

'Then do it,' says the immovable object.

The unstoppable force straightens up leaving absolutely no space in the bar for any of the rest of us, turns on his heel, wobbles a little and goes, leaving the door open for the air to rush back in behind him. There are about fifteen audible sighs of relief, not least my own, and I'm on my beer before the last one dies away. I look at Diane. She smiles at me.

'Really?' I say, 'Humping his Mum's ashes? Is that not a little …?'

'I know, I know, it's an outrageous thing to say to an orphan, and yet still he thinks I'm God's gift. Normal person reasoning doesn't work on him so you've got to be cruel to be cruel.'

'Do you think he'll kill himself?'

'I don't.'

'Do you think he'll come back?'

There's no time for Diane to answer as a couple of Volvo women come over from other tables and start clucking round Diane, asking if she's alright and how terrible that big man was and how brave she is and is she sure she's alright and would she like anything and how terrible it was. I'm draining the rest of my bottle and to celebrate still being alive I consider more of those cherry liqueur things as I've decided my face could be more numb than it is. Diane is assuring the women that it was really quite low level behaviour for Twiglet and the women go on being concerned and nice and isn't it all terrible, but nevertheless are looking at us like perhaps we should be round in the public bar, or better still down the road in the Inn.

I wonder if in all the commotion I can possibly risk another look at Diane's tits. Seems I can.

Chapter 20

Secondary 4

Scottish regional TV news programmes are invariably total shite, and that's not just because of the presenters, it's because interesting or important things almost never happen in Scotland. The regional news is always full of inconsequential wankage dressed up as heavyweight journalism, or worse, it's morons in the street being asked moronic questions on moronic subjects by a moron. Then on the rare occasion that something major actually does happen in this stupid country, it's already been reported on the national news a few minutes earlier so by the time the Scottish reporters get to tell anyone about it, it's no longer news. Not that they care. They get so excited by a big Scottish story you can see the gleam of pleasure in their eyes when they're supposed to be being serious, but since they're getting to say stuff like 'worldwide' and 'foreign TV crews' it makes them feel all sexy in their chairs and they can't help themselves. Then of course they take a good hold of their big story, and long after nobody cares any more they'll still be dragging out its corpse and flogging it. They'll flog off the skin and then get all that muscle flogged off while they're there, then they'll hold up the rotting innards and flog them off from all directions till they're entirely gone and then they'll stand around on location flogging away at the bones. Then when nothing else big happens in the meantime in this piss-arse country, they'll flog the dust that's left and ask some morons in the street how it makes them feel.

So there you have it, Scottish regional TV news programmes: total shite. But regardless of my arguments, Mum always had them on in the background while we ate our dinner. And during one meal on a Tuesday night, when I was half way through a mouthful of chips which weren't even cooked all the way through, the name of a familiar place was mentioned on the regional news programme and what had been background blah, blah, came into very sharp focus as I turned to watch. Less than a minute later I'd learned I was a member of the Ku Klux Klan and was being hunted by the police.

According to the TV programme, a small Highland community was reeling and shocked and sickened by a racist attack on a black clergyman. The reporter was on location, expressing the disgust that was being felt throughout the highlands at the Ku Klux Klan style cross burning attack which had been perpetrated by the clergyman hating racists. As I recognised the church in the background of the shot I slowly froze in my seat. A half-cooked half-eaten chip may even have fallen out of my mouth as connections in my brain which had previously gone unmade, clicked into place. The reporter informed me that the Nigerian minister, who had been welcomed into the community only two weeks before, had given a statement to the police but had declined to be interviewed: however the policeman in charge of the case was very keen to appear and he put the shits up me even further.

'We are taking this matter extremely seriously and are currently following a number of leads. We intend to send a very strong message that racism will not be tolerated in Scotland and that people who engage in cowardly attacks such as this will be rooted out and dealt with in an extremely robust manner. There is no place for the Ku Klux Klan in the Highlands and Islands and my officers and I intend to apprehend the culprit or culprits and prosecute them to the fullest extent of the law.'

By the time the policeman finished talking, my hands were shaking so much I couldn't keep my sweetcorn on my fork. I wasn't a Darwinian Terrorist any more, I was a member of a racist gang.

'That's terrible,' Mum said towards the telly. 'Imagine the Ku Klux Klan being around here, them and their silly hoods. You wouldn't have thought that would catch on round here, but then nobody thought mobile phones would catch on so it just goes to show. Still, the police should spot them easily enough if they're all wearing those silly hoods.'

As she turned from the TV to look directly at me I was sure my guilt must be as obvious to her as a tattoo on my forehead. I tried to look as innocent of a major race-hate crime as possible and to

127

stem the panic rising up my frozen corpse. I was convinced she could tell it was me, and while I tried to keep my face blank on the off chance she couldn't, I knew that she must know and could see and could tell. I was caught. I was dead. A questioning look came over her and for a split second I considered confessing before she asked. Maybe she'd go easy, maybe she wouldn't tell the police if I could convince her I hadn't meant to be in the Ku Klux Klan, that in fact I wasn't in the Ku Klux Klan because I was a terrorist and not a racist. But before I could figure out how I'd then explain that one, the question in her mind took form and she asked me, 'Don't you want your sweetcorn?'

No Mum, no, I didn't want my sweetcorn. I wanted to not get arrested for the hate crime I committed that was totally different from the one I intended to commit.

When dinner was over and my shaking limbs had calmed to the point I could leave the table without falling over on to my terrified knees, I bolted jelly-legged up the stairs, dived under the bed covers and phoned Cousin Dan.

'Did you see it?'

'What?'

'Didn't you see it?'

'What?'

'On the news, the whole of Scotland Scottish TV news. What we did was on the news, just now. The guy was a black guy and what we did is the Ku Klux Klan Dan. They're totally looking for us and we're totally in the shit 'cos of who they think we are, the police, we're totally fucking fucked.'

I thought I'd explained it pretty thoroughly, but maybe I was talking a bit fast as Cousin Dan wasn't quite following.

'Who thinks we're a what?' he said. 'Have you taken some of the stuff that made those third years get artistic in the quadrangle?'

It took a few minutes to persuade him I hadn't taken anything and another few to calm down enough to explain a bit more rationally what had happened. Then, when he was finally convinced I was un-drugged and telling him the truth, the idiot dick-shit was delighted.

'Are you totally off your head?' I whisper-shrieked down the phone, trying not to panic, trying not to be heard downstairs, and completely failing to make Cousin Dan understand that we were up to our balls in shark infested shit. If we opened our mouths to anyone, or said anything, or did anything, or even breathed wrong, there'd be more shit and worse shit and falling on us from higher up shit, than any shit that'd ever been shat on anyone before.

'Nah,' said Cousin Dan. 'They'll never find us, and even if they do, we just deny it. Anyhow Maxwell will be totally chuffed too, this is way far better than getting in the papers.'

Somewhere in my head a safety valve popped, and the fear and frustration that'd been piling up behind my eyes burst forth into the single thought that I was talking to an unredeemable fuckwit. Cousin Dan was nothing less than the most dangerous idiot I'd ever met, and the shit storm, when it came, would be directed to my door by him. And then, for a beautiful empty moment, the inevitability of my doom almost took away the fear.

'My dear Cousin Dan,' I said, thinking clearly and calmly. 'Do you really, really think that Maxwell will be pleased? We went out on Sunday as Darwinian Fundamentalists, promoting the absolute truth of evolution in the face of thousands of years of superstitious ignorance, and tonight we're members of the Ku Klux Klan and the most wanted racists in the country. Why the hairy cock sticks do you think he'll be pleased?'

There was a thinking pause on the other end of the phone, but it wasn't real thinking and it wasn't for as long as I might have hoped.

'Well it's publicity isn't it. The marketing snowball. Branding and that. And you know there's no such thing as bad ...'

I hung up.

Five minutes later when the panic had fully returned, I phoned him back and told him to start taking it seriously, to burn anything remotely incriminating and to keep his mouth shut and that was it, no more terrorism, no more Darwin-fish, no more painting cars or churches. As far as I was concerned, as long as the police didn't come round, Jesus could win. Fuck it.

Chapter 21

We've been ignoring the plaintive shouts of love occasionally wafting in from the street and some people who've just been out for a look are saying that the giant man outside is half naked now. Top half I hope. The police were called, he went away quietly, the police went away and now he's back.

'I'm sure he'll go again soon,' I say, noticing my face is now totally numb from the extra cherry liqueurs.

'Nah,' says Diane, 'If clothes are coming off, that'll be him out there till they show up with a Tazer. When he put in our back door with his head he only had his work boots on.'

Diane's getting a look in her eye and I don't like it even a little bit.

'You're not thinking of going out there are you?'

'Course not, that would be both stupid and dangerous, though that being said, the fucker's putting a real downer on your night and I've had enough of it. I think he's needing properly told. I think it's time to go all fishwife on his arse.'

She's getting up. Don't get up Diane. Sit back down and keep pretending you're not bothered like you've been doing so well for the last half hour.

'No need to look so shitey Gask, you don't have to come. I'm only going to shout at him in the street for a bit in the ancient Avochie manner, let off a bit of steam and call the fucker some names.'

She goes out. I'm left sitting here and now I'm gathering looks from the Volvo people. I feel them silently questioning my manliness. How can I let a defenceless young girl go out there alone like that? Same reason they all let her go out there alone, that's why. A perfectly reasonable fear of the half-naked love-lorn Kong; plus she's not really all that defenceless. Shit it, I'd better go and take a look. I can always stand inside the reception hall bit where he probably won't see me and all this lot will think I've gone outside. I leave the bar and come out into the hotel reception bit. I can hear

Diane warming up her vocal chords outside. I stick my head round the outside door. They're in an orange street light glare over by the cathedral gate. Twiglet's naked waist up, thank God, and shouting at Diane that she doesn't listen. She's stringing together a bugger load of pot-kettle arseholes and easily outmatching him for volume as they circle round each other by the parked cars. I step outside. There are a few people stopped and watching from the High Street and I think I'm safe enough to cross to the edge of Cathedral Square. Holy shit she's got a tongue on her. A man with a thinner skull or a brain bigger than one of the thicker dinosaurs would have long since picked up on the hints she's dropping that she's no longer keen, but Twiglet is ideologically and alcoholically convinced that endless repetition and being much bigger than everyone else will eventually win out as the more effective argument.

I edge closer keeping out of sight close to the memorial thing or whatever it is. All Twiglet's got is, 'But I love you and I want you back.' Whereas Diane's making up new swearwords like 'pinkydickest' and 'mongnut.' So Twiglet goes back to threatening suicide and Diane stops to breathe in for the first time in a couple of minutes.

'Go on then,' she says, 'Jump off the cathedral tower if you've got the balls.'

'I'll cut my heart out for you.'

'Cut your heart out?'

'Aye, cut my heart out.'

'That'll do then, cut your heart out, save your fat arse a climb.'

'I will.'

'Then stop only saying it and fucking well get it done. Either cut out your heart and put it in my hand, or fuck off.'

Twiglet pulls something from his back pocket. Oh no, that just glimmered like a blade. Diane's only a few feet from him, she sees it but she doesn't even step back an inch, she stays rooted to the spot with her hand still out waiting to receive his heart.

'Scissors?' she says, 'You're going to cut your heart out with a pair of scissors?'

'Aye, I am unless you'll go back out with me.'

Diane says nothing but keeps her hand out. Twiglet puts the scissors to his chest, the kitchen-sized handles on the things obvious now. The blades part and he cuts, and oh my no, really very no, that's really not nice at all. An eye shaped hole is left in his chest and the blood, black in the street light, wells up and streams down him. What he slaps into Diane's surprised hand isn't his heart exactly; but it is his nipple.

For a moment, Twiglet looks at Diane and Diane looks at what Twiglet's put in her hand and then the pain hits Twiglet and the disgust hits Diane. Twiglet lets go an anguished roar and bends double grasping at the blood pouring hole where his left nipple used to be. Diane, over the top of Twiglet's agony, shouts at him, 'What the hell'd you do that for?! Are you terminally wrong in the mind?!' A pain bent 'I love you.' is all the reply he manages before he drops to his knees. Diane transfers the severed nipple to between her thumb and fingers and looks at it and looks at Twiglet before her on the ground screaming in agony. She hunkers down in front of him, some might imagine to provide immediate first aid or emotional relief.

'Do you seriously believe,' she bellows in his face, waving his former nipple before his eyes, 'That handing me this is somehow making you more attractive to me? You moronic fucking dipshit, am I supposed to think you're sexy now, am I?'

She stands back up as Twiglet roars again, the blood pouring from his chest between his fingers and she says as much to herself as to him, 'You unbelievable twatbag.' She looks around and sees some of the people who've been standing watching.

'Can someone phone an ambulance for this lump of idiot please, he's messing up a perfectly good road with all his blood. And could I maybe get a towel or something over here too? He doesn't deserve it but then neither does the person who'd have to clean up his carcass if he bleeds to death in the street.'

There's movement among the onlookers as they immediately comply with Diane's bidding, at which point she notices me.

'Findo you bollocks, get over here.'

I comply too, but more slowly as even if he has dropped his scissors, my task involves approaching the groaning wounded bear-sized Twiglet.

'Shift your arse.'

I shift it a little. She steps over to me, grabs my wrist and presses the slice of human nastiness into my palm.

'Go and put that in some ice,' she says. 'They might want to sew it back on.'

I look at her in a manner entirely appropriate for someone who's just placed her ex-boyfriend's bloody severed nipple in my hand without so much as a by-your-leave.

'Don't be such a wimp,' she says, 'Now shift it.'

I don't look in my hand but I can feel it there like a wet ravioli.

Chapter 22

Secondary 4

After I hung up on Cousin Dan for the second time, I lay in bed awake most of the night, waiting for the police to arrive. They didn't come that night. They didn't come the next day either, as I walked around school feeling as nervous as the biggest lobster in the restaurant aquarium. Every door slammed or bag dropped, I imagined was a SWAT team coming to get me through the walls. In biology I was wondering if they were to shoot tear gas canisters into the classroom, would I be able to escape under the tables wearing the big glass plant experiment jar on my head. I was so out of sorts that the teacher to whom I was usually invisible, asked me with some concern if I was feeling okay.

'No Miss, not really. I'm waiting for the police to come and arrest me for a hate crime I accidentally committed while I was carrying out an unrelated act of terrorism.'

I didn't say that though. I said, 'I'm fine Miss.'

I had no appetite that night and told Mum it was because her fish fingers were off, yet the police didn't come that night or the next day either. They came the day after that.

Cousin Dan hadn't been in school but I didn't think anything of it because he was so close to leaving he'd mostly already left. When I got home my appetite was back and I was planning on eating half a packet of biscuits before dinner as an aperitif, but Mum wasn't in the kitchen heating anything up, she was sitting in the living room with a couple of plain clothes detectives. Everything that she so obviously wanted to say was all over her face but she was suppressing it. Suppressed anger, suppressed tension, suppressed shame, suppressed fear and suppressed disbelief. She was so suppressed that she'd made tea, put out some crisps in a bowl and was being an agreeable hostess. As soon as I was through the door and saw them I didn't have to be told who they were. My mind raced over all the scenarios I'd played in my head and how much they might know and what forensic evidence they might have gathered to lead them here to me. I needn't have bothered. I found out later that Cousin Dan had been boasting to one of his arsehole friends, the son of a police sergeant.

However, ignorant of that fact, a pit of pure black dread opened up within me and almost swallowed me whole. For an endless second, as the three faces looked at me and no one said anything, I found myself rooted to the spot, felt my skin empty of blood, and I saw that the life I'd had up to that point had actually been a good one, but that life had ended. I was caught, completely screwed, knackered and dead. Yet somewhere, somehow, down through it all, underneath the rigid terror, something deep in my gut told my lead-filled feet to force themselves from the floor, one at a time, and move myself into the room all casual-like and not shit-scared looking at all. And from somewhere, back aeons before humans evolved, back when everything that was anything lived in the sea and had no intention of ever going on the land because why would you and what even was land anyway; somewhere, right back in the very depths of my stomach, a brain far older than my brain, shouted up at my brain, and told it to tell me to bluff it.

'What's up?' I asked with what I hoped was my best innocent/casual tone of voice, but that came out higher than a pre-pubescent mouse.

'These are policemen, Findo' said Mum, not buying my innocent act, given she'd already been informed of my likely guilt, 'And we'd all like to hear what you have to say.'

'Say about what?' I asked like a newborn lamb.

'Thank you Missus Gask, if you don't mind, have a seat Findo, I'm DS Hairy Nose and this is DC Rugby Tackle.'

I can't remember their names, but there they were, eating crisps, taking up all the space in the living room and telling me what to do in my house, and what's more, I was doing it. I sat down.

'Just deny it,' Cousin Dan had always said, and with Mum sitting there looking as black as one of those clouds with a tornado inside

135

it, I certainly wasn't going to start admitting anything if I could possibly help it.

'Could you tell me Findo, were you were on Sunday evening? The twenty fourth.'

DS Hairy Nose's voice was all measured and controlling and while the two policemen were the biggest physical presence in the room, I was most aware of Mum's eyes boring lasers into me as she sat off to the side. No way was I going to look over there, and I couldn't look at the floor because that would look bad, so I looked back at DS Hairy Nose. Fat DS Hairy Nose. The question was still hanging in the air and I realised that if I told them anything at all, they'd start to drive wedges into it till I had to tell them something else, and then they'd split that apart too until my guilt was obvious because I'd be forced to admit it. I didn't know if they'd got to Cousin Dan or Maxwell yet and what if the stories didn't match, because of course they wouldn't. Cousin Dan would say the first thing that came into his head and expect them to believe it no matter how ridiculous, and Maxwell would be locked in his attic shouting down at them that he had a shotgun.

'Just deny it,' said Cousin Dan's voice.

The question still hung in the air. Where was I on Sunday night? I tried to think of all the old episodes of 'The Bill' I'd been forced to sit through and how the major criminals who ran the drugs gangs on the Jasmine Allen estate would cope under questioning. Mind you, they didn't usually have their Mums sitting watching them and they usually weren't fourteen.

'Just deny it,' said the voice.

'Well Findo?' said Hairy Nose.

'Findo.' Mum was being impatient. 'Tell the policemen where you were. You were with your Cousin Dan.'

'Please, Missus Gask,' said Hairy nose, shutting Mum up.

I looked over at Mum and she had a face on that wasn't expecting to take any shit. She wanted a complete confession there and then, no arguments, out with it Findo, right now. A ton of thoughts were flashing through my head, most of them too quick to catch.

What had Mum told them?

What had they told Mum?

She knows I did it.

They know I did it.

Cousin Dan wasn't at school, they must have him.

What's he told them?

If he's told them, why haven't they arrested me?

Have they arrested me?

What will Maxwell do?

What would Jesus do?

'Just deny it.'

I'll get expelled.

Do they still have borstals like in that film?

Can they even do anything to me? Aren't I too young?

'Just deny it.'

Do they have any proof?

'Findo!' snapped Mum.

And I knew what to do. I looked at Mum and saw that whatever punishment she could dream up, I could deal with easily. I looked at DS Hairy Nose and PC Rugby Tackle and I saw they had already positively identified me as the cross burning racist they were looking for. But I knew that's not what I was, and even if I accidentally had been, I wasn't any more. No, I wasn't a founder member of the Highland Chapter of the Ku Klux Klan, I was the star of my very own episode of 'The Bill'. I was a kingpin heroin dealer on the Jasmine Allen Estate. So I looked at them with the cold eyes of a cockney master criminal and decided that they could prove whatever they liked but they were getting no help whatsoever from me. I wasn't going to admit anything, I wasn't going to deny anything, I wasn't even going to say 'No Comment.' I located the insufferable smartarse part of my brain that can't help answering back and I switched it off. I turned my ego right down, sat on my desire to make up something plausible, and most of all, I bit down hard on my almost overwhelming fear. Then I looked around, sat back and waited to see what I would see.

Ten minutes and another cup of tea later, once they realised I was taking the mute act seriously, they decided to take me to Inverness to interview me down the station, and Mum couldn't decide whether to support me or go mental. I wasn't handcuffed or anything as I wasn't under arrest. Mum and the detectives agreed that I was going to voluntarily help them with their inquiries and I may be a bit more inclined to be a bit more voluntary once I'd seen the inside of a police station. Mum came along because there needed to be an adult there, and getting into the back of the police car she was badgering me, imploring, threatening and saying lots of things containing the words 'for your own good'. I stuck my face to the window and as we pulled off I noticed everything outside the car looked more normal than usual. Super-extra normal. The street had never looked more like itself, the boys in the park appeared specifically placed to demonstrate the normalness of kicking a ball about, and the primary school looked uncommonly like an educational establishment for young children. Avoch had never looked so Avochly and the fields had never appeared so intended for growing crops. At Munlochy bay the tide was in, and really high, which I liked.

I tuned out Mum's jabbering completely and the trees flashed past. By the time we were on the dual carriageway and shooting out over the bridge towards Inverness police HQ, she'd more or less given up. Then I noticed that somewhere underneath all the fear, at the very bottom of the dread black hole which had yawned open and eaten me the moment I saw the detectives sitting in there: underneath all that, a tiny maladjusted part of me was starting to enjoy itself.

The interrogation was easy. A lifetime of being made to watch crappy cop shows by Mum had prepared me better than I could have dreamed. I sat in placid silence through good cop/bad cop; angry cop/angrier cop; slowly shaking of the head cop/list of terrible consequences cop; understanding cop/no biscuits for you cop; and frustrated cop/why are we even bothering with this arsehole any more cop. They eventually gave me some dinner and it was surprisingly tasty: big sausages and chips with broccoli. They questioned me again, Mum consistently trying to convince me that confessing everything would somehow be to my benefit. I thought otherwise, I sat there like a log. They let me go.

They said they would come and arrest me soon. They whispered to me I was marked and they'd be watching. They told Mum they thought I was potentially dangerous, and someone would be available to drive us home but we'd have to wait a couple of hours. Mum phoned Gran. Gran wasn't happy. It was 11.30 pm. Mum wasn't happy. I wasn't best pleased either but I saw no point in mentioning it. While we waited I sent a text to Cousin Dan and Maxwell telling them, that if they hadn't already, to destroy their hard drives, wipe the website and burn everything else. The Darwinian Terrorist Organisation was shutting down and disappearing. Before I went to bed that night the innards of my computer would be living under the insulation in the loft. Gran pulled up in the drizzle wearing a coat over her pyjamas. Getting into the car I was expecting the worst from Gran, yet all the way home they talked about me like I wasn't there, so I stayed silent in the back and played along. They talked about how easy I had it and how I'd been given too much slack and never brought into line since Dad died, and Mum talked about the end of her tether, and Gran talked about how it was in her day and Mum couldn't understand why I'd do such things and Gran said it was because I thought I'd get away with it. Gran, as usual, was more or less spot on. She dropped us off and vanished up the street as Mum unlocked the front door. Then as she opened it, she stopped and said, 'Things are going to be very different around here from now on.' And feeling slightly put out, I petulantly retorted, 'But they didn't charge me' thinking that was somehow the most appropriate thing to say. It obviously wasn't though, certainly as far as Mum was concerned, as she promptly burst my lip with the house keys wrapped in her knuckles.

Chapter 23

Saturday 13th April, 11pm

What a superb and fantastic fun filled big night out I'm having. No friends; just me, my drink, the table, and a man's nipple in a pint of ice. The barmaid didn't seem bothered at all when I asked for the ice to put the severed tit-end in. Stuff like this probably happens to her all the time. She even gave me a little clear plastic bag to pop it in so it doesn't get wet. She knows her stuff that barmaid.

Turns out I'm not as squeamish as I thought I might be either, even if I am drinking noticeably faster than I was. Hardly minded at all peeling the sticky bloody teat off my hand and I'm sure the image of Twiglet slicing off the hairy little chunk of himself is one that won't stay in my mind for any length of time. This drink's nearly done, I'm going to need another.

I'd go outside to help only someone's got to look after the nipple. Diane's got it all under control anyway. She stemmed the blood flow, calmed him down and handled the crowd until the ambulance came, and then when Twiglet jumped up and took off like a tank down Union Street, she was the first one to go after him. Yup, as far as I can see there's nothing for me to do out there in the world, and someone's got to stay here and look after the nipple.

Chapter 24

Secondary 4

Mum said things were going to be different. She was one of those parents who really objected to being taken off to a police station to watch her son being questioned for suspected Ku Klux Klan activities. Middle class I think they call it. Even though we're not middle class. Mum says she's middle class and Gran insists we're upper working class, but the truth is the Gasks are villagers, no more, no less, and Highland villagers at that, and no amount of technology or painting the living room with a feature wall is ever going to change it. Just as we can spot a mile off the people who've only been around here for two or three generations, they can spot us equally as fast too, sitting on our walls with our community eyebrows. But Mum, being true to her imagined status as someone from a respectable family unknown to the police, set out how things were going to change: and change they did. She took my phone off me, my computer, she banned me from seeing Cousin Dan, banned me from going anywhere except school and she delivered and fetched me herself. Her commitment to the new regime was serious, as unlike her previous attempts this one lasted a whole two days. On the third day I fished out my phone from the pasta jar where she'd hidden it and got the bus into school because she couldn't afford to take any more time off work to drive me. I phoned Cousin Dan before Physics and found out he'd been questioned too. I didn't want to say too much in case the police were bugging us, so Cousin Dan said he'd come over to Fortrose and meet me at lunchtime.

He turned up in the cathedral car park in, even for him, some really crappy old car I hadn't seen before that stank of animals and fags.

'Well?'

'Well what?'

'Did you tell the police anything?'

'Course not. Did you tell the police anything?

'Course not.'

'You sure?'

'Course I'm sure, are you sure?'

'Course I am, I didn't say a word.'

'Neither did I.'

'Well that's alright then.'

'Well I suppose it is as long as you didn't.'

'Well I didn't.'

'Well that's alright then.'

'I suppose it is.'

'Did they charge you with anything?'

'No, you?'

'No.'

'Well that's alright then.'

'I suppose it is.'

We looked at each other closely. Cousin Dan told lots of lies all the time and it wasn't always easy to tell. I doubted he was telling me the exact truth though, and then the scarecrow shitehawk had the nerve to doubt me.

'Are you really sure you didn't tell them anything?' he said.

'I just said I didn't. I didn't say a word, seriously, not a single one. Nothing. Ask your Mum to ask my Mum if you don't believe me, she was there the whole time. Though I wouldn't actually ask your Mum to ask her 'cos she's really pissed off at you. And how come if they got you first, they knew to come looking for me? And how did they know to come looking for you?'

'I don't know,' he said. 'Forensics. Satellites maybe. But I didn't tell them anything. Ask your Mum to ask the social worker if you don't believe me.'

'What social worker?'

'Mum and Dad wouldn't come to the cop shop so I had a social worker in my interview. Doesn't matter anyhow. Even if I'd said something, which I didn't, they can't touch us because you're about five and I'm not sixteen for another two weeks yet. They can't do shit to you when you're under age. It's like shoplifting, you can

142

do it as much as you like and they're only ever going to give you a warning.'

'But it was on TV. Of course they're going to do something if it was on TV. It was on TV.'

'Nah,' said Cousin Dan, unconcerned. 'We can do what we like and they can't do anything about it. Anyhow, they can't prove anything and even if they could, so what? Have you spoken to Maxwell?'

'No. Just texted him to destroy his computer and all the stuff. You?'

'Aye. You didn't mention his name to the police did you?'

'No, I told you, I didn't say anything. You've destroyed your computer and all the shed stuff haven't you?'

'Aye, 'course.'

Cousin Dan pulled out his phone and dialled Maxwell. 'Alright boy, how's it going? … Aye, no bad … Aye, he's here with me now, says he's behaved himself … aye … aye … aye …' Cousin Dan handed me the phone 'Wants to talk to you.'

'Yo, Findo you fat arse biscuit, you won't believe it, I got something to show you.'

He was sounding unusually happy on the other end of the phone. I didn't like it.

'The police haven't spoken to you have they? Did you get my text? Did you destroy everything?'

'Police? Nope, no policingmen here, nothing to worry about police, but you need to come over, I've something to show you. It's as cool as …'

'What's he saying?' interrupts Cousin Dan.

'He wants us to go over. What was that?

' … snowball's totally rolling.'

'What?'

'Give me that,' and Cousin Dan grabs the phone back. 'Aye, it's me. What were you saying to the boy? Aye … aye … no … tell us now then if it's so good … 'spose we could … Aye … in a bit then.'

Cousin Dan pockets his phone then says 'We're going to Maxwell's.'

'What? Now? I can't. I've got Geography in half an hour.'

Cousin Dan looks at me like I'm the moron. 'Geography? Oxbow lakes and that?' he says. 'Christ on a mountain bike Findo, you really are a twat.'

'Why? What did Maxwell say?'

'Not much, wants us to come over though. Sounds good.'

Cousin Dan then silently sticks on his fake driving moustache, baseball cap and old man glasses. 'You coming or what, oxbow lakes?'

'I didn't really have to think about it too long. I'd no idea how, but it was already all around school I'd been arrested for TV racism, and no one cared that I'd only been questioned and released without charge. So usually at school, where I was only stared at or ignored, that morning people were muttering loudly behind me, bouncing marker pens off my head and one second year girl asked me if it was true I'd set fire to a black guy.

'Ok,' I said.

'That's more fucking like it. Fucking oxbow lakes.'

Once out of town I braced myself for Cousin Dan's light speed or death driving style but fortunately a vibrating wheel and an overheating engine kept him from tying to outrun the sound of the rattling bodywork.

'Where did you get this piece of shit?' I asked, noticing that while there was no stereo in the stereo slot, there was a box with half a dozen of them on the back seat.

'Off a guy in Alness.'

That meant he'd either swapped it for stolen stuff, stolen it, or was still in the act of stealing it.

'Why didn't you bring the white one?'

'White car's dead. Bounced it into a ditch when the police were after me.'

I was too surprised to say anything but, 'What?'

'Aye, there was a new pothole on a corner with adverse camber, so when I went over it, it bounced. Usually make that corner no problem at all.'

'The police were chasing you?'

'Aye,' he said, as calmly as if he was talking about going to the shop later. 'I saw them coming up to the farm so I took off past them before they could ask me anything.'

'And?'

'And what? I didn't know what they wanted me for, it could have been anything, so I wasn't hanging about to find out.'

'And they chased you?'

'Most of the way to Killen till I bounced it, and then they were all very policey about the whole thing.'

'I thought you said you didn't get charged with anything.'

'Aye I didn't, not for the Ku Klux Darwin stuff, only for the motoring offences. Calm yourself down Cousin, there's no problem here.

My idea of what a problem was and Cousin Dan's seemed to be different, and then he got pissed off with me because I was pissed off with him.

'It's not a problem,' he reiterated. 'I'll just get banned again. It's not as if I even have a licence anyhow.'

'And you don't think it looks a bit suspicious, you doing a high speed bugger off before they even get out of their car?'

'Aye, but it wouldn't have mattered if I'd got away, would it?'

I was really frustrated with him now.

'But they were at your house, looking for you, at your house. Where did you think you were getting away to?' Surely he had to understand that.

'Aye, but if I had got away, they wouldn't have known it was me would they?'

Cousin Dan was an exasperating shit-for-brains and now I wasn't even entirely sure if he didn't have a point. I let it drop. He took this as a victory and drove the rest of the twenty minutes to Maxwell's in smugness and silence, me wondering a little what Cousin Dan had really told the police. They hadn't charged me, and he said they

145

hadn't charged him, but who knew? Cousin Dan didn't seem to care either way. Maybe he was right, maybe they had nothing on us, but in that case, how did they know it was us they needed to come looking for?

'What happened to your face?' he asked. My lip was still swollen where Mum had knuckle-dusted me with her keys.

'Nothing.'

We pulled up at Maxwell's and he answered the door wearing some sort of Kung-fu pyjamas. 'Come in gentlemen, come in.' he said, all perky like there might be a girl inside who'd gone in voluntarily. We went through to the living room which was slowly being lost under chip wrappers and fanta cans. Cousin Dan cleared himself a space and sat down. I stood. Maxwell disappeared into the kitchen asking as he went, 'Anyone want a beer?'

'I'll have one,' said Cousin Dan.

'Not really but might as well,' I said.

'Not really but might as well,' came Maxwell's piss poor imitation of me.

'Your Uncle not about?' I asked.

'Offshore,' came the expected reply as he re-emerged from the kitchen and handed us a can each. He settled into the armchair, popped his own can and sat looking pleased with himself waiting for one of us to ask. I gave in first.

'So what's new?'

'Oh you know, this and that. I hear you had a visit from the law.'

'I did. And so did he. And he got chased.'

I looked at Cousin Dan who was sucking his beer a bit too nonchalantly, and then back at Maxwell. I wasn't telling Maxwell anything he didn't already know.'

'So what did you tell them?' he asked.

'Bugger all,' I said.

'He's telling the truth,' said Cousin Dan. 'Ask his Mum.'

Maxwell exchanged a look with Cousin Dan that I couldn't read, then Maxwell brightened again.

'I knew it,' he said, 'They're a bunch of cocks who wouldn't know a cock if it cocked them. Come and look at this.'

He got up and went through to the spare room we'd been using as the production hub for Darwinian operations. I followed and Cousin Dan dragged himself in behind us. I'd been expecting, hoping, to see the room cleared out and hoovered of all trace of Darwinist activities. Instead it was as packed and messy as ever and one of the walls was piled high with new boxes. My heart started sinking.

What's all that?' I asked.

'Stock,' said Maxwell. 'We've got a shitload of printing up to do. Have a look at this.'

He turned the screen of his laptop round towards us and pointed. It was a video on a website. I slowly realised what it was.

'Oh fuck, you didn't,' I said. But of course he had.

The video was titled 'The Highland Cross Burning' and was the grainy, low light footage of a balaclava'd Cousin Dan and a balaclava'd me digging a hole in a lawn with a pick and shovel and pissing ourselves laughing as we tried to do it quietly. Then dragging a cross mock Jesus fashion and doinking it in upright into the hole with a few big rocks to keep it upright. We'd pre-wrapped the thing in ancient potato sacks and doused them in pink diesel, so when the two balaclava'd figures in the video threw a flame at the base of their construction, the fire slipped quickly up the post. As the blaze reached out along the crosses' arms, the light reflected behind from the façade of a pretty Victorian Highland parish church. The balaclava'd figures in silhouette laughed and shouted things like 'Fuck 'em all' and 'Knock their cocks off' while at no point mentioning the strongly held Darwinist principles that were actually behind their action. Cut to a wider more artistic shot of a cross wreathed in flame and the church behind it flickering in a lovely ambient orange glow; then a shout somewhere off to the left of, 'What's going on there?' in, when you listened to it, an unmistakably African accent. One of the balaclavas exclaims 'Run!' and the camera's grabbed and there's darkness and footsteps and running, breathing, swearing and laughter before the camera cuts out.

'Take it down,' I say to Maxwell immediately, and I'm not kidding.

'Don't be stupid man, you need to see that,' he said as he stabbed at the screen with a greedy finger.

Cousin Dan and I leant in towards it to see what it was. It was the hit counter. Seven thousand four hundred and seventy six people had viewed the video. We were all going to prison.

'7476. It's gone up over a hundred since you phoned.' said Maxwell, beaming like the psycho who invented the basement.

I dug my nails into my palm before I replied in as calm a way as I could.

'Aye. And while on the one hand that's all very fantastic, on the other hand, you've got to take the video down now, and then delete the video and delete the website, and then delete everything off your hard drive and take the hard drive out of your machine and throw the tiny smashed up bits into the sea. Me and him have both had the police on us, and if they see that they're going to come back and do us all.'

Maxwell remained singularly unconcerned. 'Bollocks man. You've balaclavas on and you're under age so they can't do shite. 7479 hits and rising. That's our marketing snowball rolling there, that's what that is. Why do you think I've got all the blank t-shirts and T-towels in? We're getting enquiries, people want to buy stuff.'

'Em ...' said Cousin Dan.

At last he was going to speak. Come on you shitebag, back me up here and put this nob-end in his place.

'Em ...' he repeated, visibly choosing his words before finally saying to Maxwell. 'So do you think we can make more money out of being the Ku Klux Klan than we can out of being Darwinists, or should we maybe do it as a separate company?'

I exhaled the word, 'What?'

Maxwell said, 'I think we bung it all up on the same site and see what sells. Findo can do us a KKK design, call ourselves the Highland Klan or something, and see if anybody wants to buy big tartan hoods instead of the white ones they usually do. Look at that, 7490 hits now.'

148

My brain felt like someone had started a slow blender inside it and it was all getting swirled round and mashed up. I was staring at Maxwell and there were stars at the edges of my eyes trying to float across to the middle and I had to concentrate on them to make them stop. I had to make them stop.

'No!' I screamed, and got their attention at least. I stared at them and they stared back.

'Whoa. No need to go mental there Findo boy. If you don't like tartan hoods, we won't do tartan hoods.'

But there was clearly every need to go mental, so I told them as much.

'There's every need to go mental, every need. Because understand what I'm telling you. Understand! You, me and him, the three of us, us in this room. We are NOT in the Ku Klux Klan! Not now, never have been. Not in the Ku Klux Klan. Understand? We're Darwinian Terrorists. Darwinian Terrorists! Because of our principles, because we believe in it, because we're trying to topple religion, and because it's the right thing to do. And I am NOT; NOT joining the Highland chapter of the Ku Klux Klan just to sell some tartan fucking hoods.'

For a moment they were taken aback. For a moment I thought maybe the power of my argument had made them see sense. And Maxwell said, 'Then why did you stick a burning cross on a black guy's lawn?'

'IT WAS AN ACCIDENT!'

And then I did go properly mental. I dived to the computer to try and delete the video and when they stopped me I tried to grab the computer to smash it or take it into the woods or something. When they stopped me doing that I went after the screen printing frames so they couldn't make any more t-shirts and when they stopped me again we were in the garden and Cousin Dan was sitting on my legs and Maxwell was sitting on my chest. We stayed like that for a long time and eventually I agreed to be calm and they agreed not to be corporate racists. Cousin Dan drove me back to Fortrose so I could get the school bus home. I had nothing to say to him on the way back because there was nothing to say any more, and when I got out all he managed was, 'Twat.' And so ended my Darwinist dream for a brighter religion-free future. I could have gone back to school for my last class, but instead I went down the beach and sat on a bench. After a while I decided I shouldn't hang about with nutters any more, and I felt a bit better.

Chapter 25

Saturday 13th April, 11.40pm

Diane swings into the bar spots me where I am and stomps over. She's a bit out of breath.

'We caught him half way to Rosemarkie,' she says. 'I talked him down and he's agreed to go to hospital so I'm going to go with him. Ambulance is waiting outside, I just need this. S'been a lovely evening, see you later.'

She picks up the pint of nipple and is turning to go as I stop her.

'Wait. What, so I'll just meet you back at yours later then will I?' I ask, not too pleased at the thought of having to find my own way back to Avoch.

Diane looks puzzled. 'How do you mean?' she says.

'Well, how long do you think you'll be? I mean, I am staying at yours tonight. Aren't I?'

'First I've heard of it, I thought your Granny was coming for you.'

And now I remember I never actually asked her if I could stay. Still, it'll be ok.

'Sorry, you can't stay at mine,' she goes on, 'I'd have said if you'd asked but Dionne's having a sleepover thing tonight, the house is full of wee girls and you know how Mum thinks you look like a paedo even if she's pretty sure you're not.'

'Could I not just stay on the floor in your room?'

'Can you not phone your Granny?'

'She'll have taken a lot of drugs and gone to bed by now. She said earlier there was no chance of a lift off her.'

'Sorry Findo,' says Diane. 'Honestly can't help you tonight, you know what Mum's like. Any other night and you'd be welcome. I don't know how long I'm going to be stuck dealing with Twig anyhow, can't you just phone your Granny, I'm sure she'd come if she knows you're stuck.'

'She won't.'

'Aye she will, if she knows you're stuck. Anyhow sorry to bail but I've got to get this tit back to the other tit.' She raises the pint glass to me, says, 'Good night though, lovely times. I'll text you or whatever tomorrow'. And she turns and goes.

Shit, shit, buggering pissing shit. What the hell am I supposed to do now? There's no point phoning Gran, not a single point in the world. I wonder if Mum would discharge herself to come and get me? Can't see Gran reacting very well to that even if it is her fault I'm stuck, the pill popping old crone. I'll try Alex, he'll still be with those girls so even if I can't crash at his, maybe they'll give me a lift. I phone him. It goes to voice mail. I phone him again, it goes to voice mail again. I text him 'Emergency, need lift or crash pad, where are you?' I wait. No reply. I drink some beer and as I have no choice I'll have to phone Gran. I'm going to phone Gran. No choice. She'll be mad, properly mad, but she'll come and get me. Who am I kidding, she'll tell me to sleep under a hedge. There's no way she'll come out when she's already told me there's no way she'll come out. I ring her anyway. She doesn't pick up and it goes to voice mail. I hang up. I call her again. If I call enough times, I'll maybe make her think it's the hospital calling about Mum and then she's bound to pick up. Voice mail again. Once more. No reply. Once more. Voice mail. And again. Voice Mail. Shit, shit, shit. She's not been stingy with the self-medication tonight. So what now? No Gran, no Alex, no Diane. Or is it really no Alex? He didn't pick up because he doesn't want me disturbing him with his three girls, but maybe he just doesn't want me to know where he is so I can't disturb him. I bet he's been through in the public bar the whole time keeping his girls and his lifts and his places to stay to himself, the greedy ginger fingerer. Anyway, it's a straw, so I grab it.

I pull on my jacket, drain what remains of my latest banana beer and head for the door. I find my balance is a bit off and I knock someone's table a little but don't spill anything. 'Sorry.' I right myself and concentrate my aim at the door. Shit, shit, shit. I've not nearly enough money for a taxi and I'm facing a ten mile walk unless Alex and those girls are in the public bar. I step outside and I'm pisster than I thought I was. It's cold and clear and there's no way I can walk ten miles like this. I check my cash. No notes, less than a tenner in change. That's a cab to where? Half way, probably not even that. And it's beer money not cab money, hard saved beer money goddammit. Can I walk five miles? Can I bolloksy. I go out and round the corner and into the public bar, it's busy and noisy. I pause near the door to look around. I recognise a couple of faces who left school a year or three ago. They don't look as scary as they used to but still worth avoiding. I'm lounge bar material me, public bars are too full of people who sat exams where you get marks for getting your name right. I move further in and see a couple of guys from my year who I don't talk to and their ridiculously sexy fifth year girlfriends who would never talk to me. No Alex anywhere unless he's down behind those … no he's not. Shit. Maybe out the back smoking. S'cuse me, s'cuse me, s'cuse me, s'cuse me, don't move then you lanky … s'cuse me. I push out the back door into the cold light of the smokers' yard. A couple of faces look at me and a couple of faces don't, none of them Alex's or any of those girls from earlier. Turdbags. I go back inside and scanning the bar once more, propped up by a wall, I spot a face that's having trouble focusing past his pint. His hair's totally different from the way I remember and how long's it been since I've seen him? A year and a half. Two? Not since Uncle Robert's funeral when they let him out for the day. I hardly spoke to him then and I don't really want to speak to him now. Not that everything was my fault or anything. It wasn't. Totally wasn't. I wonder if he might be good for some taxi cash. Fuck it, no choice. I make my way over towards him. S'cuse me, s'cuse me, s'cuse me, no, why would you move you lanky … s'cuse me. And there he is, the total state of him. I can't believe his hair's even worse than it used to be.

'How's it going Cousin Dan?'

Chapter 26

Secondary 4

I told them to take the video off the internet and they didn't listen so of course the police saw it and of course they came back to get us. We were both charged with a racially motivated hate crime and Cousin Dan had all his police car chase stuff added on too. Because I was fourteen and Cousin Dan was a week and a bit short of sixteen when we did it, the papers and TV weren't allowed to name us but everyone around the place and at school knew who it was and so I couldn't have been less popular if I'd taken to wearing a Nazi uniform which had been skilfully woven out of fresh shit. Still, just because no one else would talk to me it didn't mean I was hanging out with Cousin Dan, as now that he'd left school I was perfectly happy not to be running in to him in the corridors any more and I wasn't making any efforts to run into him anywhere else. And as for that toilet stain Maxwell, I heard he was going around Cromarty telling anyone who'd listen that he was going to be the principal witness for the prosecution. No more Sundays at Cousin Dan's either as Mum decided I was now old enough to be locked in the house whenever she went out to church, and as the trial date approached, Mum and Auntie Roberta stopped talking too and even ended up getting us different lawyers, because in trying to decide between them which of us was the worst and most to blame, Mum had given Auntie Roberta a black eye. It was probably around this time Mum started hanging out more in the bookies and I had to learn to cook chips and pot noodle.

My lawyer was a short man from Conon Bridge with an out of proportion beer belly and an even bigger motorbike. He said I should consider pleading guilty. I said I didn't do it. He said he'd seen the video and it looked a lot like I did do it. I said that could have been anyone under those balaclavas and whoever they were, neither of them was me. He said I was a good lad and I had to keep on saying that. He said the prosecution case was really weak and they were only going ahead because of all the media exposure, so if I could keep up the bare faced lies no matter what, we could go for a not guilty and I'd probably get away with it.

The trial happened at the end of the summer holidays before I was due to go into fifth year. I was shitting it like I'd never shat it before. My lawyer had come off his motorbike a week earlier and detached both retinas so he couldn't come, so I got stuck with someone who'd been found wandering nearby but who had his own name badge. I'd mostly given up cigarettes as I wasn't being driven anywhere by Cousin Dan any more, but I took them up again with a vengeance outside the Sheriff Court. The defendants in the other cases were always obvious too, because although smoking is compulsory for the families of the accused while standing outside a court building, the defendants are always the ones who are sucking on their fags the hardest. On the last day of the trial I swear I smoked a king size cigarette to the filter in ten seconds.

Cousin Dan had pleaded not guilty too and it turned out that my blind lawyer had been right: they really didn't have that much on us except one grainy video shot at night of two people dressed in black and wearing balaclavas. Maxwell, the supposed star witness was never even called as the police had reckoned he was 'wholly unreliable'. So my name badge lawyer, probably because he hadn't read anything about the case, told me not to take the stand and to stay silent. Cousin Dan's lawyer gave him the same advice and although he didn't harm himself by having to answer any awkward questions, on the first day he was heard to say quite loudly that the Sheriff, 'looks like a cunt'. And then on the last day that he, 'still looks like a cunt'. Nevertheless, on the charges of being racist hate criminals there was insufficient evidence for a conviction and we both got off. I almost fell over and wet myself with relief.

That only left Cousin Dan's car chase charges and two counts of contempt for calling the Sheriff a cunt, and since the TV crews were outside waiting to see the Highland racist teens get their comeuppance for something, and since the Sheriff wanted to look like a hard nut, in response to all the mitigating circumstances that

Cousin Dan's lawyer laid out, the Sheriff basically said, 'Tough shit, it's been on the telly. Take him down'.

He was inside for a year.

Chapter 27

Saturday 13th April, 'bout midnight

'Steal me a tractor.'

My dear old Cousin Dan is completely pissed. He's slurring his words like a Glaswegian junkie who's just back from the dentist. In another half pint or so he's going to slide slowly down the wall that's currently keeping him upright and then he'll probably puke on his own knees. Right now he's simultaneously looking at me, through me, somewhere in the air between us and inside his own head, in an attempt to find either a thought or a way to focus his eyes.

'A tractor,' he says again, remembering I'm here. 'I know the one I want, I've checked it out. You go and get it. And I'll give you twenty for a taxi.'

He's not going to remember this conversation tomorrow, so I say.

'Ok. I'll get you one. Where is it? Where do you want it put? I'll need the cash up front.'

His eyes focus on me in clarity for a moment, then pointy drunk that he is, he stabs me in the chest with his finger then waves it in my face.

'Bollocks you will,' he says, almost spitefully, then he leans his head back against the wall, the anger in his face floats off and he becomes thoughtful. He speaks without looking at me. 'You should be helping me get a tractor you should, but where the fuck have you been? You owe me a tractor shite fingers. Get me one.'

'Couldn't you just lend me the cash for the taxi?'

'Nope.'

'So is that what you're doing now? Robbing other farms?'

His eyes come down from the ceiling to mostly meet mine. 'That'd be what you think,' he says, trying to touch his nose in the international sign of secrecy, but in a way that only a fifth rate master criminal who's too drunk to touch his own nose can effectively manage.

'Of course that'd be what I think. That'd be what you're saying?'

157

'Except you know balls,' is all he bothers to slur back at me.

'Miss being in prison do you?' And as soon as I've said it I regret it.

Cousin Dan comes to life and points his drunk finger. 'Young Offenders Institution,' he corrects me. 'Not the same thing at all. Not that you came to visit you shit piece.'

He has me there.

'Mum wouldn't let me,' I say, and I can hear how weak it sounds. It happens to be true but we both know it wouldn't have stopped me if I'd wanted to go and see him. I don't like feeling guilty. I usually ignore the feeling whenever I get it. How else would I have been able to give my dangerously ill Mum hardly a second thought all night. And even if I do sometimes feel a bit guilty about some things, I don't act on the guilt because then the guilt wins. Far better to ignore it till it goes away. Not for me any religious based guilt or the pseudo-religious eco-guilt or the eat-this-delicious-thing-now-feel-bad-later food guilt that all the girls at school seem to enjoy having so much.

'You know,' says Cousin Dan, possibly reading a possibly guilty look on my face. 'If you weren't such a wank-boy-mummy's-boy, boy, you could have been ...' He sticks his wonky pissed face right up to mine and focuses his rolling eyeballs and prods me again in the chest, saying in a lowered voice. ' ... Major Snowballs.'

I think he's on more than just drink but I bet he won't give me any. He eyes me for a second or two as if somehow the shite he's talking has significance, then he says, 'I'm going for a pish now.' He levers himself off the wall and sways towards the bog. He's never going to give me taxi money in that mood. I wonder how he's getting home. The farm's as far away from here as Gran's and he doesn't seem to be out with anyone. He must be taxiing back. Or maybe he's driving. Would I get into a car with him in that state? Am I drunk enough to do that? No, not quite I don't think. He must be taxiing it back anyway. I need to talk him into letting me share. Even if he won't drop me off anywhere near home I could always crash at the farm.

The bell goes for last orders. Cousin Dan's pint is down to the dregs. I've no choice, I'll have to invest most of the cash I have left in a couple of pints. Then, if my generosity doesn't persuade him to give me cash or a lift, he'll probably pass out anyway and I can rob him. I join the last minute throng at the bar.

If he wants one so much, maybe I should steal him a tractor. How hard could a tractor be to steal? A newer one might be tricky but an old one would be a piece of piss. But then it's not my fault he went to junior prison and it's not my fault Uncle Robert died while he was in there. Turns out lots of people die from falling over when they're trying to put their trousers on. Quite common apparently. And so it's not my fault their farm's gone to shit. Cousin Dan always hated the natural world and the seasons and all that stuff, so why would Auntie Roberta be surprised when he never lifted a finger to plough anything. I heard Mum tell Gran that Auntie Roberta hasn't been coping well at all, but what's that got to do with me? Nothing. That's what.

'Two pints of your finest cooking lager please.'

Maybe if Cousin Dan hadn't been such an arse to his Dad his whole life then he might have got left the farm, but he was so it wasn't. Now it's all held in trust for his tiny little brother Stan, so even if Cousin Dan did get off his arse to herd a cow or whatever, he'd be working for his four year-old brother. Suppose if I was him I'd be pretty pissed off too. Suppose if I hadn't started the Darwinian Terrorist Organisation maybe some things would have worked out a bit different maybe, but mostly they probably wouldn't, and how was I to know anyway.

I pay for the pints and find a spare corner. Maybe I will steal him a tractor if that's what he really wants.

Chapter 28

Secondary 4 to 5

Cousin Dan went off to Young Offenders, I got away with it and Mum lost her job. When she told me we were going to move in with Gran in Kilmuir, I was so against the idea all I screamed was, 'Nooooooooooooooo!' Just like in the films.

Mum had run up online poker and bingo debts and hadn't been going to work and hadn't been paying the rent. As if living in Avoch, the armpit of the world, wasn't bad enough; now we were moving to Kilmuir, the world's very darkest arse crack, to live in a tiny cottage with a smelly old angry woman. Miles and miles from anything, a single track nightmare to get out of and it's not even a village, you'd struggle to call it a bollocking hamlet. Nothing but beach, sea, forest, hills and scenery – totally fucking useless. Not even a shop, unless you count the hippy who sells crochet owls on sticks out of her spare room in the second last house along, and I don't. I thought I had it bad in Avoch, I really did. I didn't know anything. Welcome to Kilmuir, Findo Gask, your ancestral shit pile.

Mum tried to sell it to me as us going back to where we belonged, how once, everyone in the village was either a Gask or married to a Gask, and how it was right that there should be Gasks in Kilmuir. How great Kilmuir was, like when she was young how it was still quite common for people to pull sixty pound salmon out of the sea from the slightly illegal nets everyone put out and how once, someone brought a fish into the house which was bigger than she was. I told Mum that whales aren't fish and I think she took it a bit personally because she's so fat. In spite of the reality of having to get my bed shortened to fit in my new room; Gran's personal habits, like cutting off the rind of dead skin off her heels with scissors while she's watching TV; and there being nothing whatsoever for me to do until the day I leave home; Mum tried to interest me in history crap like the Armada story which I'd heard a million times before from Gran. About how the Gasks are descended from a sailor off the Spanish Armada ship that came ashore near Avoch because the

Captain's cheap map made him think he was rounding the top of Scotland instead of sailing into the mouth of the Moray firth, and how the sailors who didn't drown were robbed and stripped and sold or imprisoned, except for the original sailor Gask, who having been robbed and stripped, and having escaped from the cannibal Avochies by swimming the mouth of Munlochy bay as the tide went out, caught the eye of a young maiden who kept him safe in the woods until together they founded Kilmuir and populated the coast with salmon poachers. And I even got Mum's tame version of the Bonnie Prince Charlie's spoons story, which differed considerably from Gran's robbed-him-and-ran-away version. According to Mum, a brave kilted Gask, fighting at Bonnie Prince Charlie's side at Culloden, saved his life from the unwelcome advances of some redcoats with their bayonets out, and so to thank the brave Gask, Bonnie Prince Charlie quickly presented him with a set of his own personal silver spoons before buggering off into the heather dressed as a girl. Nice try Mum, but made up history to engender a sense of belonging didn't alter the fact my new bedroom was a former cupboard with a skylight.

So on the day of the historic returning of two thirds of Clan Gask back to Kilmuir, Gran looked at the van full of stuff we'd brought with us and told us it would all have to go in the shed. Gran had made her front room into a bedroom for herself, Mum got Gran's room and I got the cupboard, which Mum had always used as an example of how hard she'd had it when she was young, but which was now suddenly, 'perfectly good enough for me when I was your age'. And while she listened to my complaints to start with, after a few weeks, she talked less about how we'd be getting another place of our own soon, and more about how it would be nice to have some help moving some of her bedroom furniture in from the shed as soon as she could make some space.

'Your Auntie Roberta phoned your Mum,' said Gran one day, a few months later. 'She's going to the young Offenders to visit your Cousin Dan. Do you want to go with her and see him, do you?'

There was no suggestion that I should go in her voice. There was no anything, so I assumed it was up to me.

'Not really,' I said. And after that he wasn't mentioned in the house again for the whole time he was inside, except for the time around when Uncle Robert died and Cousin Dan got out for the day and sat in the crematorium with a guard in a car outside like he was in the Mafia or something. When my Dad had died I think that maybe I went a bit mad, except that I was too young to know that I was mad because I didn't know what mad was, so it was sort of hard to tell, although I did sort of nearly become a hell-fire preacher for a while when I was seven, so perhaps that was a bit mad. So I could guess how Cousin Dan was feeling, yet I couldn't think of anything to say to him. He was looking a bit too unstable in his eyes to approach, like he was all paranoid and thought everyone was pointing at him, which the more distant relatives all were. Afterwards, while we were waiting for people to bring cars round, I mumbled to him, 'So they let you out then.' to which he replied 'Compassionate'. I didn't mention how sorry I was about his Dad, or how well I knew and shared his pain, even though we both knew that my Dad had been far better than his. Instead I hoped that the words 'So they let you out then'. had somehow conveyed all my shared sense of grief for him and his Mum and his nearly two year old brother, and maybe the feeling too that I was sorry for all the stupid stuff that had sort of been my idea, but that he was in prison for. I hoped I'd communicated all this to him, but on reflection it's a little unlikely.

And I didn't go and visit him after they took him back, and when he got out I didn't go and see him either because I really didn't want to. And he didn't come and see me. At school my reputation was essentially that of an ugly loner racist nutter, (nice eyes though and good at science and that) and so if I was ever, ever, ever, even once, ever, going to get a girl to let me at her with my cock, I was going to have to re-invent myself as something a little less off putting. Something ...something ... maybe a mystery man, or a man of action. Basically I had no idea, but Mandy Duplin had a perfect neck and did ceramics, so at the start of sixth year I took ceramics and started hanging around the art room. And that's where Diane found me, and in an idle moment made me her pet.

Chapter 29

Saturday, no, Sunday 14th April, Kicking Out Time

Where's Cousin Dan got to? He must have passed out in the bogs but I can't go in looking in case he's just taking a big dump. I'll give him a couple more minutes.

Ok, the top third of my pint is gone and he's still not emerged, but as I need a piss now anyway I can safely go and see if he's asleep on the pan without it looking odd. Off I go. My balance isn't everything it could be and I re-adjust my trajectory to make the middle of the bog door. I bang a bit heavily through it, surprising someone who's in the act of writing something on the wall in big red letters with a big red marker pen. He simultaneously jumps and turns. It's one of the guys from my year. So far he's written 'Gavin enjoys a big salty coc'. The vandal gives me an embarrassed glance and without finishing his work he heads out the door straight past me.

'Hi Gavin,' I say.

'Hi …' says Gavin, deciding quickly at the last moment not to use one of my nicknames.

Gavin Hellier, who'd have thought it. But now I'm alone. Cousin Dan isn't in here, passed out, drowned in the bog or otherwise unconscious or dead. I piss and go back to the bar. The crowd has started to thin out and he's not here either. Maybe he smokes now or is hanging out with them. I stick my head out the door where a couple of women are puffing away like their court case is about to begin, but Cousin Dan isn't there. The shit-hamper must have left while I was buying him a drink. He's abandoned his own Cousin the cock-wank-scarecrow-bastard.

Maybe he's gone down to the Inn for last orders there. Should I try and catch up with him? I return to my pints and take them to an empty table.

I text Alex again, the revolting ginger runt.

'Stuck in Fortrose need a lift anywhere where the very hell are you?'

The minutes tick by and no reply. It's properly chucking out time now. My only chance is to catch Cousin Dan coming out of the Inn, if he's even there. I sink the remainder of my pint, put on my jacket, sip the top off the pint I bought Cousin Dan and slip the nearly full glass carefully into my big inside pocket. I stand up slowly and walk as steadily as I can to the door, while trying to affect the air of complete innocence that someone who isn't stealing anything can manage without trying. Once outside and a few paces clear of the stragglers round the door, I retrieve the pint and not a drop spilt.

There are figures down at the bottom of the High Street dispersing from the Inn, so I pick up my walking pace and quickly find that the pavement is too narrow to negotiate with any confidence.

'Findo my me,' I say out loud to myself. 'You are drunk I am.'

I abandon the too skinny pavement in favour of the middle of the street. When I get to the Inn there's no one about outside. I stash my pint up the alley and stick my head inside the pub door.

'Shut,' says the barman at me, but not before I see that there are only a few people left inside and none of them are Cousin Dan. I am, not to put too fine a point on it, fucked.

I retrieve my pint and walk back into the High Street. It's totally deserted now. Everyone who can go home, has. The town is absolutely dead. I stand in the middle of the street and sip my pint. A ten mile walk home at three miles an hour, no, be realistic, I'm pissed and have unnaturally short legs. Let's say two miles an hour. I'll be home by six am. Except of course I'll die first because I can't walk that far. So it's either die walking, or find a shed or an upturned boat or something and sleep there, except of course if I do that I'll die of the cold. So I either die walking or die sleeping. I step out of the way as a lone car coming up the hill has to slow because of some pissed young idiot standing in the middle of the street. If it'd been going the other way I could have hitched a lift.

I get a text. I fish my phone out. It's from Alex, the ginger erection. Is he coming to get me?

'I made a new friend. I'm beyond Dingwall.'

So I'm hitching back home. And what motorist wouldn't stop to pick up a big drunk teenager at past one in the morning, particularly if he's standing helpfully in the middle of the road to make himself easier to spot. However there are no cars anywhere so I start walking. I've half a pint left in the glass but I don't want it any more, as it's making my hand cold, so I lob it over a high stone wall and hear it bounce on soft grass or something on the other side. I wanted it to smash, I feel a bit annoyed at it.

A car is approaching, I stick my thumb out. I've never done this before and it's a weird feeling and it's not just that I'm drunk, it's like I'm admitting I'm a tramp or something. The car doesn't stop. It was going the wrong way anyway.

So who exactly is going to pick me up? Judging from the state of me and the time of night I know I wouldn't stop for me. My only chance of a lift is from some psycho who'll want to stab me with a knife after he's stabbed me with his cock. So I'm to either die walking, die of the cold sleeping, or die getting knifed and cocked. A couple more cars pass, and if anything they speed up. Looks like I've chosen to die walking.

Twenty minutes and I'm only just past the edge of town. What's that, half a mile? Not even. Then again I did stop for a pee, and now I'm having a little rest while I look at all the lovely stars. There are a lot of them. I can feel my hippy tendency trying to kick in and make me say, 'Wow'. A car's coming. It's in the wrong direction for hitching but as I'm lying on my back in the middle of the road I should really get out of its way. I topple up to my feet and step out of the headlights as the car has to slow to pass. I start walking again. I think, yes, the car's stopped behind me. Best not to turn round in case it's full of no-necked Cromarty boys. I hear a car door open. Keep walking, the Croms are coming to get me.

'Findo?'

It's a woman's voice. I turn around. Some woman I don't recognise and can't see has got out of the passenger side and is staring into the darkness towards me.

'It is Findo, isn't it?'

'Yes.' I say, because it is me.

'We thought it was you. Are you stuck?'

'Em, yes.'

'Well come on, in you get, we can't leave you out here all night.'

I'm too surprised to blink. I think I might be saved. There may still be Croms lurking on the back seat waiting to pounce, but I totter over towards the idling car deciding to act as sober as possible while I figure out what's happening. I can see the woman better now. She's smiling, fortyish or something, neat short hair and I have no idea who she is.

'Jump in the back,' she says.

I squeeze into the little car. The driver is a lot younger but I can't see her face so no clue as to who she is either. The woman gets into the passenger seat and turns round to me and says.'

'Alison said she passed you a bit earlier. I've been at a friend's in Avoch and she's come to collect me. How are you Findo?'

The car's moving off, it's warm in here, I don't want to die and the price of not dying seems to be polite conversation, so fine, I'll do that; but I have no idea who you are woman and who the hell is Alison? Alison who? There are a few Alisons knocking about and I think I'm pretty sure I don't know any of them. Who the shit are you people?

'I'm very well,' I say, 'And you?' I smile at her to try to cover how slurred that sounded, and I'm hoping she'll answer with her full name and how she knows me.

'Oh, we're fine thank you. So how did you come to be walking the streets at this hour?' she asks in a smiling way.

'Oh, I was supposed to be staying a friend's but, um, she had to go and look after a sick friend.'

'No room at the inn, eh? You weren't going to walk all the way to Kilmuir, surely? Are you still living over there?'

'Em, yes, and yes.' I hope the first yes made me sound adventurous, and how do you know where I live? She's looking out the front as she talks now and in the street light I try to look more closely at her face, maybe it is a bit familiar. The driver must be her daughter but I can't see enough of her to place her, and she's not saying a word to help me out.

'Goodness Findo, you must be fit to walk all that way,' says the woman. 'And but well, it's a little late to drive you all the way out there now, so we'll find a warm corner for you tonight and sort you out in the morning. That sound alright?'

'Em, yes. Thanks.'

There's a noise. I think Alison snorted, but the woman doesn't notice. We're back up into Fortrose now. They're friends of Mum's maybe? Or of Gran's? Maybe Mum knew them when we lived in Avoch. Neighbours or something?

'How's your Mum?'

Bingo, friend of Mum's. Except Mum doesn't have any friends, does she?

'I heard she was poorly,' she adds.

Holy shit, this woman knows everything.

'Em, yeah. It's, well they don't really know yet. She's in Raigmore. Stable though,' I say, hoping that she is.

'You must be worried.'

She seems genuinely concerned. Should I be more worried? She's turned around to look at me and I look back and I nod. She smiles at me. She's nice this woman. I don't think she's blaming me at all for being out on the piss while Mums on a drip. I think she understands. Now if she'd just tell me who the bloody hell she is, everything will be just dandy.

Alison the snorter drives us down past the school and into the old council houses off Dean's Road, where she parks up. I don't know anyone who lives up here.

'Here we are then,' says my new friend, and we all get out. I take a look at Alison. I do know her face, from school, I think, maybe. She must have left when I was maybe in second or third year or something but she's so plain and un-anything, I don't think I ever even knew her name. And now I think that maybe Alison's Mum is a little bit pissed. She's giggling and wandering up the path to one of the houses like she's a rubbish tightrope walker. Alison doesn't seem impressed and overtakes her to the door. The woman turns to check I'm still following and I almost have a flash of recognition. I think she maybe used to be fatter and have long hair maybe.

Inside the front door the hallway smells of coffee and a bit like cat piss too. No clues to who anyone is. No family photos, just a picture of a desert with the photographer's name printed really big below it. The picture's not even that good you wanker, why'd you need your name so big? I hang up my coat as instructed and follow the woman through to the living room. It's small and has lots of Scandinavian catalogue stuff and she gets her decorating advice off one of those shitty do-up-your-house-like-we-tell-you-to programmes. And in the middle of it, by the window, sits a clue. It's a tall, skinny, baldy clue, and he's looking as surprised to see me as I'm horrified to see him.

'Vincent,' says the now fully identified woman to the tall skinny clue. 'You remember young Findo, don't you?' Vincent clearly remembers, so Mrs Egger continues. 'He got a bit stranded so we've brought him back for the night. Sit down Findo, I'll make us some coffee.'

Mrs Egger disappears into the adjoining kitchen, Alison's already vanished and I take the seat as far away as possible from Vincent Egger, which isn't very far away at all. I suddenly feel quite sober(ish). Since when did the Eggers live in Fortrose? The Eggers live in Munlochy, and in a much nicer house than this. Vincent's eyeing me like he can't decide whether to throw me out before or after beating me over the head with a coffee table. If it wasn't for the baby asleep on his lap I think his evangelical holiness would be up and showing me the door with his foot.

'How are you Findo?' he says, trying on his usual lovely guy act but all simmering underneath.

'Fine,' I say, and I attempt a little smile that maybe comes out a bit sneery.

He doesn't say anything else. He just looks at me. Alison comes into the room and before she can do anything, Mrs Egger sticks her cheerful head round the other door and says to her, 'Take André off your father and put him up in his cot will you love.'

'I'll do it in a minute,' says Vincent.

'No need. Alison will do it.'

Alison moves to pick up the baby but Vincent gives her a tetchy, 'I said I'll do it'. And she retreats and sits on the other end of the sofa I'm on. Standing in the doorway, Mrs Egger gives him a look of 'Suit yourself, I was only trying to be helpful you uppity overly-Christian-arse-wank.' I recognise Alison now too. She's the older of the two sisters and as dull and nothing-to-say as she ever was, though I don't remember her having such nice tits. She asks Vincent if the baby has woken and Vincent says, 'No'. It occurs to me I don't know whose baby it is. Is it Mrs Egger's' and Vincent's, or have Alison or the other one been indulging in the kind of pre-marital activity that would make Jesus cry? Or maybe the daughters are all married and Jesus is happy on his cloud because wedlock babies get to go to heaven.

Vincent's staring at me. Was I staring at Alison? Why's he not saying anything? I've nothing to say to him either, but isn't he even going to try and smarm on the charm? Nope, he's trying to put the frighteners on me. I'm sitting in his living room, not invited by him and not sober, and he's not happy about it. He knows I'm in his power and he's biding his time. He's going to kill me in the night. Should I say something to him? The silence is really uncomfortable now. Alison's sitting there like a toad and Vincent's giving me evil mongoose eyes. Well bugger it then, I'm not going to say anything either: I can do awkward silence as well as the next fucked-up family.

Mrs Egger re-appears in the door and thank God starts a conversation with me. She asks about school and exams and what my plans are when I leave, and whether I want tea or coffee. I make up some answers and she wishes there'd been such a thing as a gap-year when she'd left school. She disappears into the kitchen again and Vincent asks Alison, 'Did you change the car stereo back?'

Alison says, 'Yes'.

Is it just me, or does Alison not like him either? Mrs Egger comes back in with three mugs. I get one, Alison gets one and she keeps one for herself. Vincent mustn't be thirsty. Mrs Egger sits in the armchair opposite me and gives the room a general smile. She says to Alison what a good sleeper André is and then she smiles at me and asks me what bands I like. I name a couple, and weirdly she's heard of them and knows a little bit about them too. As we talk, Vincent gets up and leaves the room carrying the baby. As soon as he's gone the atmosphere seems to lighten and even Alison has a thing or two to say, although it's all dull and poorly informed. She's so dull I start to wonder if I might stand a chance with her. She's way older than me, four, five years? But she's got ok tits and she must be pretty desperate, and she's also currently well inside the standards set by how much I've had to drink. I test the water.

'What are you up to these days?' I ask her, only slurring my words a tiny bit.

She says, 'Not much. I'm going to bed now.'

Wow. That's either the most successful chat up line in history and an invitation to join her, despite her mother sitting right there; or a total disaster, but never mind because she's so dull. She gets up, takes her cup into the kitchen, comes back out, says 'Goodnight' to her Mum and leaves without so much as a come-hither-me-Findo look. So I'll assume no luck there then.

'She's had a long day,' says Mrs Egger, covering her daughter's rudeness and slouching back into her chair. 'She was up early and I was at my friend's tonight a lot later than planned.' And then she adds in an almost conspiratorial whisper, 'Two bottles later to be precise, so she's not too happy she had to stay up to drive me back'. She smiles, trusting me with the confidence, and it feels like when she used to sneak me extra biscuits to see me through the tedium of Vincent's bible group. She's about to say something else when Vincent's re-appearance in the doorway cuts her short. There's something weird going on here as he's got a coat on. Does Vincent work nights or something?

'André didn't wake when I put him down,' he says. Then, 'Can I have a word?' His tone turning into a cross between being annoyed, and pretending not to be annoyed.

'Don't mind Findo,' says Mrs Egger, smiling at him.

Vincent obviously does mind Findo though, so instead of whatever he was going to say, he says 'I'll phone in the morning'.

'I expect you will,' replies Mrs Egger, unconcerned.

Holy mother of shit. I think Mrs Egger just gave Vincent a verbal middle finger; and the most self-righteous prig-hole since Noah battered off his drowning neighbours with an oar, hasn't even answered with a Jesus will burn you for that quip. In fact, now he's buggering off out the door at I don't even know what o'clock in the morning. And Vincent's away. What the hell's going on?

'Would you like a nightcap Findo?' says Mrs Egger.

I saw a black and white film once, so I know a nightcap's booze.

'Em, yes please.'

Two minutes later and everything's clear. I have a glass of brandy in one of those big glasses that's supposed to be all sophisticated, and it's doing the trick, as I'm even starting to feel a bit sophisticated. Mrs Egger has just used the words 'Since the divorce', like she assumed I already knew about it or something. She maybe found out about Vincent kissing and boob touching that other woman, or maybe she just realised what a monumental dickwad the skinny wanksock is. So this is Mrs Egger's house, Vincent was only here to baby-sit, though I still have no idea whose baby it is. Mrs Egger's sitting talking to me like I'm a human being, so I'm trying to concentrate the effects of all the booze away, and pretend I am one. A sophisticated one.

'You don't like Vincent very much, do you?' she says, taking me totally off guard.

'Eh …' I say, and wonder if I should be diplomatic since I have a big brandy glass in my hand. Meanwhile Mrs Egger takes my inability to decide what to say as politeness and adds,

'Well I can't say he hasn't given you cause'.

I think it's kind of her to say, so I tell her as much and that seems to please her. Mrs Egger must have been there when Vincent grabbed me over the pews and dragged me out of the church that time for being young and having opinions. She must have even known how he was sitting behind me on purpose, waiting to get me if I said something loud and Darwiny, which of course I did. She might not know how he slapped me one outside, but then I expect Vincent probably told her. He was probably quite boasty about it.

'I scared the shit out of an eleven year-old, you should have seen it. God would have loved it, it was as holy as sex within marriage,' he probably said.

I wonder if Mrs Egger knows it was me who vandalised their car back then with the Darwin-fish? She maybe must do, after me going to court and Cousin Dan going to prison for all the other stuff we did too. But she's so friendly I feel like I could tell her all about it, as I think she'd be cool. But then again, you never can tell with old people, so I more wisely decide to bite my stupid homeless tongue and keep my trap shut. Brandy out of big glasses must make you more honest, I'll have to watch that.

Now Vincent's gone I can feel myself going back to feeling drunker again. Mrs Egger just told me a really cheesy joke and I genuinely nearly pissed myself. Really, my bladder about gave way. I'm now in the bathroom having a sit-down pee, as I can't trust my accuracy and there's a fitted carpet that looks like a stainer. That's how well brought up I am Mrs Egger, I'd rather pee like a girl than pee on your floor.

I weave my way back down to the living room and Mrs Egger (who says I've to call her Marie; no chance) has pulled out the sofa bed for me and thrown on it a tiny pink duvet with ponies that looks like it won't reach to my knees. Still I'm not complaining, I could be dead in a ditch but instead I've been fed brandy and seen Vincent twatting Egger cast out into the street. Despite being someone's Mum, and maybe a Granny too, Mrs Egger is quite a good laugh. She says, 'Nighty night' to me and I briefly remember my manners and thank her for saving my life. She laughs, and hangs about for a minute to tell me where to find biscuits if I'm hungry, or a glass of water if I'm thirsty, or do I think I'll need a bucket if I start to feel unwell; so she's spotted I'm a bit pissed then. I say that I'm not a puker and that puts her mind at rest and makes her smile, and although I am a puker really, it won't be till tomorrow afternoon.

Mrs Egger goes off upstairs and I can finally be me again. How the hell did I end up here? Egger central. I feel like a burglar who hasn't the nerve to touch anything. There are some photos on the wall beside the sofa. Alison Egger and the other daughter, whatever her name is. They have faces on them like they've been living in a German cellar. I look around and feel like I want to steal something but I know I shouldn't and it's all crap, so I'll not. I'll go to bed. I should maybe go for another pee but I don't want to be wandering upstairs in the dark in case they think I'm up to something. Could I pee out the window without anyone hearing? I test the window handle. Smooth, silent UPVC, and grass in the garden beyond. I listen. Silence. It's worth a try and it goes well, till the end when some goes on the windowsill. Curtain takes care of that.

I sit on the sofa bed and take my clothes off, except my t-shirt and boxers, and a sock it turns out I can't be arsed reaching down to my other foot for. I get into the sofa bed and realise I'll have to get up again to turn the light out. I get up, turn the light out and only crack my shin a little against the bed frame as I find my back. It smells weird in this place, like goodness or something. There's a bit of street light orangeing in around the curtains and I'm knackered and pissed so I'll pass out easily now.

Except it seems my brain won't shut up. It must be the weird room. The sofa bed's not uncomfy or anything, though my naked foot keeps touching the cold frame and now I wish I'd kept my other sock on. I move diagonally to sort out my cold foot but no matter how I try and position myself my brain keeps going. I'll visit Mum tomorrow, of course I will. I've probably enough change left for a bus all the way into town, and if I don't, I'll make Diane come and give me money. She owes me. Her and every other bugger, buggering off and not so much as a text to see if I was dead in a ditch or under a hedge getting eaten by foxes. I don't expect anyone to give a shit but it would be nice if my friends at least pretended to. All too busy pulling or helping the nipple impaired.

There's a noise from upstairs, someone moving about or

something. It stops. Cousin Dan will be in proper grown up prison soon if he's nicking tractors and stuff for a living. Most of that stuff has trackers on it. A bit of farming would probably be an easier option, even if it is his little brother's farm, but there's no point trying to tell Cousin Dan that. Knob-end wanker wouldn't even give me taxi money.

I think it's Mrs Egger walking about up there. I wonder if Jesus will let Vincent into heaven now that Mrs Egger's divorced him. I wouldn't if I was Jesus.

'Sorry Vincent, too many self-righteous babyfisters in here already. The holy ghost keeps letting them in every time it's his turn on the door. No Vincent, I'm not going to send you to hell, there's no such place you ignorant fanny-wad, you can piss off and spend all of eternity in Alness.' Hell's got nothing on Alness, it's like the worst Baltimore ghetto but with hanging baskets.

The noise from upstairs is on the stairs. The noise is coming down the stairs. Maybe Alison's fallen for my charms after all. The door handle to this room turns and I freeze. The door opens with a scrape on the carpet.

'Findo.'

It's only Mrs Egger.

'Uh huh,' I reply, pretending I've just woken from having just fallen asleep. And I look over with one eye open in the orangey light. Bloody hell Mrs Egger, that's a very small nightie for such a very old woman.

Chapter 30

Sunday 14th April, 7.24 am

A short peaceful moment of nothingness, and then from somewhere daylight creeps into my conscious and it's painful. I'm in a bed. It's not mine. The pain is dull but wide. The duvet I'm under is pink. Oh yes, back it comes. The pubs, the booze, no way to get home, the Eggers, that's where I am. And there was brandy, the noise on the stairs, the door opening, and it all floods back into my head like a tsunami coming down a hill. Reader, she wanked me off.

She said she thought I had lovely eyes. She said she'd always liked my eyes. She'd come into the room and closed the door and sat on the edge of the bed, really close, and I had to move my elbow so it didn't get trapped under her bum. She said the thing about my eyes and I didn't say anything because of the combination of the terror of the old woman in the nightie sitting on the bed, mixed with the sprinkle of curiosity that this was how a porno film might start. In the orangey light she locked me into eye contact and undid the front of her nightie, which undid at the front. And there they were. I couldn't break eye contact with her because I thought it might be rude, and I didn't know if I was allowed, but all the same, in the orangey haze in front of me were tits. Actual women's tits. A very old woman's tits, but I sensed that they were substantial and plump and not pointing at her knees or anything and the nipples were still attached, which was a very positive thing, and they were mostly pointing at me.

While I still kept my eyes politely pinned on hers for all I was worth, she reached under the pink pony duvet and found my hand, and took it, and placed it flat just below her neck and drew it downwards. Annnnnnd I was feeling a tit with my hand. I broke eye contact and looked where I had to. I didn't care that she might be a granny, well I did a little bit, but I threw that thought into a mental box marked 'not now' and dropped it somewhere down the back

175

of my brain. I now knew what an actual tit felt like. Softer than I expected and baloony and squeezy and I wished that there was more light, or maybe I didn't. My hand had now guided itself round the tit, and up and down the tit, and round the tit again, and I found that I didn't have the confidence to move off the tit and on to the other one, or indeed anywhere else, just in case this was the only tit I was allowed to touch. So I stuck with what I knew, and moved my hand round the tit, and up and down the tit, and round the tit again.

While I was engaged in up, down, round, up, down, round, I'd also gained the confidence to do it all in the opposite direction too, and was seriously considering moving on to the other tit soon; when Mrs Egger's hand glid under the duvet. Now I was really hoping she wasn't someone's granny. Someone's mum sticking her hand inside your pants and touching your cock could almost be considered cool, except of course that it isn't. Someone's granny … No, out thought, out. A hand was touching my cock, a woman's hand, owner doesn't matter, owner doesn't matter. The hand had found a cock that was already delighted to have seen its tits, and I experienced what I'd imagined a thousand times, even though it was nothing like I'd imagined. At some time I'd imagined Mandy Duplin and I'd imagined most of the girls in my year, some in the year above, most in the year below and even despite my own moral objections, one or two in the year below that. But mostly I'd imagined Mandy Duplin. Mandy Duplin. She's not someone's mum and certainly not someone's granny. Out thought, out. I was having to learn that reality is always different and this reality was very different indeed. I was getting a wank now, no doubt about that and when I glanced up at the face of the person wanking me, she said I had, 'lovely eyes' again. Nice of you to say so Mrs Egger, now you just keep wanking and I'll continue with my clearly very expert tit rubbing. This went on for a minute or so, and a minute or so later was when it first occurred to me there might be a bit of a problem on the horizon.

As new and as interesting and intense as it was having Mrs Egger chugging away at me, I started to realise that I was so very pissed, there was a real possibility I was too drunk to come. My years of fear that when I finally got round to it, I'd end up emptying my bin bags before my flies were even undone, were proving totally unfounded. Instead the very opposite was threatening to happen: although my cock was as hard as a winter Mars bar, something in my brain was telling me that regardless of the amount or quality of the manipulation, my bin bags were fast asleep and were intending to stay that way. There was only one course of action, only one way out. Time to fuck Mrs Egger. A few seconds to think about it and my tit hand left its tit and moved down the corrugations of her stomach, but before I even reached the top of her pants her free hand grabbed my tit hand and replaced it on the tit.

'Fine where it is', she said, not unkindly, but in a tone that also said, 'You're getting nowhere near my fanny'. Perhaps it was best. What would a granny's fanny be like? Out thought, out. Concentrate on the hand and look at the tits. For reasons known only to herself, this semi-naked woman had taken a semi-fancy to my body, and it would be very rude indeed if I couldn't even do her the courtesy of spunking into her hand. So in order not to appear rude, it was going to be best if I concentrated on all the new physical sensations, and maybe cast up a few images of every good looking girl I could think of in an effort to go over the top. This may very well be the only bin day I was likely to experience in my life and it would be criminal to waste it. I just had to concentrate.

And, it, was; endless. Mrs Egger plugged away and I slowly became aware that she too might be aware that my balls weren't quite as plugged into my knob as they might be. She changed tempo, and pressure, and as far as was possible, direction. Afraid to risk speaking to her in case she just stopped, I found myself communicating with her in very quiet sub-human grunts. More, less, definitely not, let's stick with that for a bit. All the while imagining it was Mandy Duplin naked on top of me instead of someone's granny's hand. Please, not that thought again, that thought isn't helping, get out thought, get out. Think Mandy Duplin in her pants, think Mandy Duplin out of her pants, now look at the old lady's tits and imagine they're Mandy Duplin's. Mmmm, Mandy Duplin's getting on a bit though. Out thought, out. And on and on it went, and all the time Mrs Egger was looking at my eyes, 'such lovely eyes'. Probably the only bit of me she could stand to look at.

Her arm got tired, she swapped arms. That arm got tired, she went back to the first one. I sensed she was reaching the end of her will to go on, but neither of us wanted to admit failure. I knew why I wanted to go on and it was probably pride keeping her going too. I'd mentally run through every sexy girl at school, doing every sexy thing I could think of to me, and I'd used up all the sexy stuff I could think of from the telly, and all the porn I could recall that had fixed itself into my impressionable young mind, and yet still my balls were unconscious. But if I was going to come, I was going to have to do it soon or probably never get to do it again with another person in the room. So I concentrated like never before and flicked though a dozen images testing for effect, and an image popped up and I felt a tweak in my undercarriage as it nudged me just a touch towards the brink. So I concentrated on the image, and expanded on it, and animated it, and the image inhabited the room with me and it blended into the arm movements below, and finally, finally, finally? Yes, yes, finally, there we nnnnnnaaaaarrggghhh!

And thank the very fuck for that. My brain re-surfaced, and as it did it was with far more relief than pleasure, and as my brain swam and the image I'd created melted away, Mrs Egger wiped her hand on my leg, the dirty cow, and with a smile in her voice said, 'I think we'll both sleep well after that'. For a moment I thought she was going to climb in with me, but she leaned over, gave me a peck on the lips and left the room pulling her nightie closed as she went.

I lay in a triple haze of booze, tiredness and the weird, unsettling, empty-balled glow of whatever the hell it was that just happened. I was about to start worrying about what might happen in the morning, when it occurred to me I was a man now and I fell asleep.

Chapter 31

Sunday 14th April, 7.25am

Awake. Awake and remembering. The sunlight is piercing through the Egger's crappy thin curtains and I have to get out of here as fast as possible. My head hurts to move. Mum warned me about the dangers of drink, but if she'd said that getting wanked off by a possible granny was one of them I might have taken more notice. I look into the daylight over the edge of the bed. My trousers are there on the floor. I reach to them and find my watch in the pocket. 7.55am and is that movement upstairs already? I should scarper before anyone comes down. I can't look Mrs Egger in the eye, no way. But maybe I can close my eyes for just a couple of minutes more first, my head just isn't right, a couple more minutes should fix it. There are muffled voices coming down through the ceiling now, what am I going to say if they come down? I could try and play it cool. Nope, no way, time to go. I drag myself to the edge of the bed and sit up. My brain feels like it's about to murder me while puking up inside itself. I have to take a moment to let the room go still. I ease my feet to the floor and the metal bed frame freezes the backs of my legs. I wonder why I'm wearing one sock. I can just about bend down far enough to reach my trousers before the waves of head pain get too much, and I start to try to drag them on over my feet. Shit, someone's coming down the stairs, do I get back into bed and play dead or try and get my trousers on a lot faster than I am doing. I try to do both and pivot myself back under the duvet with the trousers still well below my knees. Whoever it is has reached the door and I'm lying in the bed with my feet sticking out the bottom of the tiny duvet and my trousers round my ankles. To the casual observer I could hardly look more like I'm having a wank.

'Findo?' says a voice on the other side of the door. I think it's Alison.

'Mmm,' I say, trying to sound like she's woken me.

'Mum says, can you make yourself decent and then we'll come through and make breakfast in ten minutes.'

I manage a, 'Yes, ok.' And she goes back upstairs. Too late to run.

I put my clothes on. I need a pee but I'd have to go upstairs to where all the Eggers are and I don't want to do that. For lack of anything else to do I tidy up the sofa bed and fold it away, then sit and wait. If I was Alex, the ginger shag maniac, I'd be out the window and half way up the road with a neighbour's daughter by now. I briefly, seriously consider running, but some kind of social conditioning's kicked in and I find I'm staying put as there's a rumble at the top of the stairs and the herd starts to come down. Mrs Egger's dressed in a tracksuit like she's some kind of jogger or something and her ancient head is sticking out the top of it and it wishes me good morning like nothing's going on and what would I like for breakfast? I try to get out of eating so I can just go right now, but she's all polite and insistent just exactly like anyone's mum would be if there hadn't been a marathon festival of cock pulling last night. Maybe she thinks I can't remember. She goes through to the kitchen. I sit in the living room willing time to pass more quickly.

Alison comes in with the baby, doesn't quite manage a smile or a grunt and goes straight through to the kitchen, then the other daughter, who must have been in bed when we showed up last night, comes in and looks at me like I'm a shit on the carpet, which is fair enough. She's about nineteen or twenty and is dressed to depress. She's a skinny long-faced version of her bible-toting dad and I can't remember her name. I wonder if she overheard what happened last night. Or maybe her mum told her, maybe that's what kind of family this is. Are good Christians that honest? I bloody hope not. I'm in a nightmare of cosmic proportions. It's like one of those films where everything is so ridiculously normal that you just know something appalling's going to happen: only in this case, the appalling thing's already happened, but everyone who knows about the appalling thing's being extra super normal, so the people who don't know about the appalling thing don't find out. And my head, which is trying its best to burst out through the back of my eyes, can't cope with either the appallingness or the super normalness and I don't know whether to run screaming out the door or have a cup of tea. They're all in the kitchen now so I go upstairs for a piss, feeling somehow that I should have asked someone for permission first. I lock the bog door behind me. My brain is a pain jelly and my cock looks like it didn't pay its Mafia debts. I try and pee on the edge of the bowl so as not to make any splashing noise. I flush and wash my hands and I wet my face like they do in the films but it doesn't cure my hangover. I linger because I don't want to go back down there. I clean my teeth with some toothpaste on my finger, then wash my hands again, then splash more water on my face. I'm still violently hung over. I look at myself in the mirror mostly obscured by things in pink containers. I have to go back downstairs now and have breakfast with a woman who's probably a granny and whose tits I interfered with, while her children who might have heard everything sit looking at me. I have to wonder if it was worth it.

We're sitting packed around a tiny kitchen table eating poached eggs on toast and drinking glasses of ethically squeezed juice. At least three people in the room hate me. Alison Egger hates me, the younger daughter whose name turns out to be Miriam Egger hates me; and me, I hate me. Mrs Egger is chatting away politely to everyone as if all the air in the tiny kitchen isn't filled with Findo-hate. The baby is sitting silently in a high chair next to me. I'm not sure if the baby hates me. I manage no eye contact answers of a syllable or less whenever Mrs Egger directs one of her cucumber cool, run of the mill, everyday enquiries towards me, in a manner that suggests there's no way she's the kind of lady who'd even know what sperm was, let alone the type who'd clean it off her hand by wiping it on my leg. I've been given cereal too and it's gone mushy and I can't eat it. Alison Egger feeds the baby with something out of a tiny jar while Mrs Egger forces more toast on me. If I eat it, maybe she'll let me leave. I think the baby is Alison's, I think Mrs Egger is a granny. I could ask but do I really want to know, plus I think it might be rude and I'm being rude enough already saying nothing and squirming to get away. But if I say things, then I might get forced into a conversation and I'll be here even longer. Miriam Egger's looking at me like 'Who the hell are you and what are you doing here and why are you having breakfast with us?' It's because I drank a lot Miriam, it's because I drank a whole hell of a heap too lot. I glance at Alison Egger with the baby and she looks like its mum.

I've eaten the toast as quickly as I can and Mrs Egger mistakes it for hunger and offers more. I refuse and she puts another slice on my plate anyway. I wonder if I detect some kind of meaning in the extra slice giving, but I don't know what it is if there is any and I don't want to know. I just want to leave. She offers me a lift home.

'No thanks, it's all right.'

'It's no trouble Findo, I wouldn't want to think of you stuck.'

I need to get out of this. 'No thanks really, it's ok.' I can't be alone in a car with a wank-granny, surely she knows that. Is she toying with me? Does she want more? I look at her. I have no idea. Maybe she's really just offering me a lift.

'I'm going to stop off at a friend's in Avoch,' I say, 'So I'll just take the bus.' That sounded almost plausible.

She looks like she's going to insist on taking me to Avoch, and then she lets me off the hook. 'If you're sure then.'

'Yes. Thanks.'

I eat the last of my toast and then suppose out loud that I ought to be going, and I'm positive I don't want anything else to eat, and I'm sure that I have enough money for the bus, and I'm positive I've got everything, and I'll certainly pass on all their best wishes to my mum. And I'm away from the table and through the living room, passing the sofa bed, out into the hall and grabbing my coat. So close to freedom I find I can start to join in with the weird super normalness. I thank Mrs Egger for letting me stay, as she sees me all the way to the door. She says, 'A pleasure Findo, and don't forget us now you know where we are'. And out on the front step she tries to give me a look to communicate something extra, like 'Our little secret', or possibly, 'I hope it meant as much to you as it did to ...' But I don't care as I'm out. And as I step down the path there's a

182

miracle. Mrs Egger turns back into the house and as the door closes I hear her say to a lurking daughter, 'Take your little brother upstairs and get him dressed for me will you'.

Inside my head I'm skipping to the gate. I'm out of that house and I'm free, and far more importantly I wasn't wanked off by someone's granny, because the baby is Mrs Eggers. Not a granny, not a granny, not a granny: just someone's really, really, really old mum. And maybe possibly a bit of a paedophile too, but at least I'm not a pervert.

It's a sunny morning, which will warm up soon, and I stroll towards the bus stop. If there was even a single person about I'd probably smile at them. I reckon I've lost about thirty percent of my virginity, which is exactly thirty percent more than I ever thought possible at this time yesterday. I count the change in my pocket and find I have precisely enough to cover the bus fare to Kessock. What a fantastic day.

Chapter 32

Sunday 14th April, 9.10am

The crappy Sunday bus service won't be here for an hour. I phone Gran. She doesn't want to come and get me and she says she's too busy to even come and pick me up from the bus stop in Kessock, so I'll have to walk back along the beach, selfish old cow. How can she be too busy to come and pick me up? It's Sunday and she's old. I take a seat at the bus stop. Fortrose is a buzzing metropolis, my only problem is which of the multitude of leisure options open to me I'll choose to while away the time. There's a solitary scabby man coming down the other side of the street walking a tiny dog that his wife picked, so that's all the sights of Fortrose taken care of and I didn't even need to move: you can't top that in your Londons or New Yorks. I suppose I could go down to the harbour and sit there for a bit, or I could go round to the cathedral and sit there; or if I really wanted to live fast and die young I could do both. But then again I've got a long walk at the other end of the bus, every heartbeat is a small grenade going off in my head and my cock feels sunburn raw from having mostly been worn away. I'll just sit here quietly unless I have to nip into the cathedral grounds for a puke.

I'm not going to stop off in Avoch like I told Mrs Egger. I text Diane to find out what happened to her and text Alex to remind him that he eats his own ginger penis-cheese with a spoon. I'm not going to mention my experience last night because they'd laugh and tell others.

The more you want to leave a town the slower time gets. Diane doesn't bother texting me back and Alex texts to inform me that it's well known I cock rabbits, and that the rabbits are dissatisfied with my girth. So I remind him that he's a convicted dolphin fingerer, and he points out in return, that I happily knock my own front teeth out to give better oral satisfaction to the History Department. And on it goes. Forty minutes later it's warm enough to start me sweating. The bus finally throbs down the High Street and the text conversation with Alex is starting to descend towards filth. It's nearly empty on the bus and I sit near the back so if the diesel smell and engine vibration make me throw up then there's a chance I might get away with it. Fortrose, sea, Avoch, fields, Munlochy, trees, Kessock. I get off and phone Gran again to see if she's changed her mind about coming to pick me up, then I start out back along the shore to Kilmuir. No money for a can of anything at the Spar and it looks like the annual day of summer's happening early. By the time I'm out of Kessock and under the bridge my foggy brain is already heat swollen and my feet don't want to go on, but whereas I'd usually need to have a few sit downs, hangover or not, I find I decide to plough on. It must be because I'm thirty percent more of a man than I was yesterday and I notice I might be walking with my chin a little higher than usual, and that despite the sore feet and rubbing pain from my grated cock, I may even have developed a bit of a swagger.

The sea is flat and shimmering all the way across and the tide is full in and very high, so that means if I want to get past the rocks at the end of the road without drowning, I'll need to go up the hill past the newt pond house and then down through the woods and back out on the beach at the boat house ruin, which is a pain in the arse as it's longer and steep, then branchy and thorny and fency, and I'm already sweating out the top of my t-shirt and down the backs of my legs.

As I finally come scratched and half dead out of the woods, over the wire and back to the sun-beaten shore, having been forced to quench my thirst from the little burn that runs into the newt pond, I find the tide is so high that it's up over the grassy turf at the top of the pebbles. I'm forced to pick my way between the sea right up at my feet, the hidden rusty pools of rotting crap in the grass, and all the spiky stuff poking through from the wild side of the fence. Why the fuck won't some fucker build a fucking road along here?! By the time I've negotiated my way to within fainting distance of Kilmuir I feel like the lone survivor of a desert plane crash, whose left foot is somehow soaked to the ankle and whose trainers are never going

185

to be the same colour as each other again. Finally back on tarmac and twenty metres to the house, I'm going to collapse and sleep and drink lemonade, and do nothing else for the rest of the day.

'Ah there you are, we're going to visit your Mum after lunch and I need any of your clothes you want washing before we go. You look the worse for wear boy, I hope it was worth it, I'll get you a cup of tea shall I?'

I haven't even shut the front door behind me before Gran is up and off to the kitchen. It smells like she's been baking for one of her old people things. Warm cakeyness hangs in the air. I could maybe bring myself to eat some cake. I dump my jacket and lever off my trainers and sit at the foot of the stairs to get off my wet sock. I decide I can't be bothered with stairs and I sore-foot it over to lie on the couch where I may have to stay forever. Walking's not for me, it's not my thing. I'm more built for sedentaryness, for staying put and for lying about. For dozing too, and for longer naps, maybe drifting into outright sleeping. Then for waking up, but not for going anywhere, just for looking about and then closing my eyes again. These people who do the West Highland Way and stuff and think hills are for climbing should be herded off the top end of the country at spear point. I'm against hills. They're stupid, they stop people building roads where roads could go and they get in the way of the view. Gran comes back through with my cup of tea and some paracetamol.

'How was your night out?'

'Diane's ex-boyfriend cut his nipple off with a pair of scissors.'

'Why'd he do that?'

'You'd have to ask him.'

'Hmm. Probably bottle fed. Are you suffering?'

'Yes.'

'Where did you go?'

'Avoch and Fortrose.'

'Who were you with?'

'Diane and Alex mostly.'

'Where did you stay?'

' … Diane's.'

'And is she your ...'

'No.'

'Want a fairy cake? They're just out of the oven.'

'I want four fairy cakes.'

After my fairy cakes I shut my eyes for a moment. I dream of the little bridge over the burn before Munlochy, and the school bus has broken down on this side but I can't go across the bridge for some reason, so I climb into the field to try to cross the burn and Mandy Duplin's there and she's not unhappy to see me, and we're about to have some very bendy sex when Gran's voice from the kitchen reminds me where I am. I turn my back to the kitchen door to hide my erection and let it recede and I notice I've been dribbling on my arm.

'Well?' says Gran from the kitchen as if she's already asked me something.

'What?'

'Do you want something proper to eat before we go and see your Mum or not?'

Could I eat? I think I could. My hangover doesn't feel nearly so bad now as it did and I notice I've been asleep for two hours.

'Yes, I could eat,' I say, and close my eyes again.

'Well you can go up and have a shower first, you smell like a pub floor.'

I make it up the stairs and shower and change, and eat the cheese on toast with brown sauce that Gran gives me and half a packet of biscuits she doesn't. After she's hurried me along to get ready to go, I sit and watch TV for two minutes which turns into twenty as she attends to lots of last minute pointless nonsense with the urgency of a glacier. 'Is that off? Your Mum'll want these. Now where did I put them? I'll put this there while I look for that other thing. Did I turn that off? Here it is, I'll need a bigger bag. I'll leave those there, now where's my light tan bag? I'll take these out of it and I'll need some extra ones of those, and I'll just rearrange this while I remember. Ok now, put that thing off now I said Findo and come on, we'll be late for visiting at this rate.'

Chapter 33

Sunday 14th April, 2.20pm

A couple of hours later I storm out of the hospital and over into the big car park positively boiling with disbelief. Total ridiculous arse load of wankers. Not possible, not possible, not possible. Not even a tiny bit possible. Totally impossible. Absolute bollocks, no fucking way, stupid doctor arsehole bastards. I kick someone's car that's in my way and nearly burst my toe as the pain explodes up into my head and back, but it hardly wipes out my incoherent disbelief for a second while my other leg gives way and the tarmac takes chunks out of my hand as I hit the ground. I stumble back to my feet because fuck the pain and fuck it, and the only other thought in my head is shouting, 'Not True'. I look around to see if anyone saw me fall but no one did and fuck them even if they had.

I find Gran's car and I stand beside the locked piece of shit with my jaw clenched and my mind seething and wanting to take it all out on something. Everything around me's looking just as it did before I went in there, and that angers me even more. Cars, car park, trees, town. Bollocks to the lot of it.

I yell, 'Fucking Cuntshits' at the sky, and some woman crossing the car park a dozen cars over scurries a bit faster towards the hospital entrance. She's wasting her time, the bitch, they don't know a fucking thing in there, not even the fucking basics. 'Fucking idiots don't know fucking shit!' Now she's really picking up her pace.

Not possible, not true, fuck them and fuck standing in this car park bollocks. I need to be somewhere else smashing the fuck out of something. I need to take that doctor apart. It occurs to me that a psychologist might refer to my current state as one of 'denial' but what the imaginary psychologist has failed to recognise is that sometimes a person is in denial because the thing they deny simply isn't fucking true. And because what isn't physically possible can't be physically true, my denial is perfectly justified and my anger is perfectly reasonable; so imaginary psychologist: go and fuck yourself.

I fume and stand and consider kicking something else, but there's nothing but tiny gravel and cars, and my toe's already in agony from the car I've already kicked. I lean against the car but I don't feel like leaning so I pace and then stand. Eventually Gran creaks up towards me.

'It's not possible, it's totally fucking impossible and I know what I'm talking about. It's bollocks.' I shout at her as she approaches, rummaging slowly in one of her bags for the keys. When she finally gets the car unlocked she looks at me from the other side of the car roof and says, 'We'll talk when you calm down'.

And I can see it in her face. She believes it. She actually believes it. A total impossibility, a thing which absolutely could not happen, but because the idiot mouth it came out of had a doctor attached, Gran has accepted the bullshit as gospel. Stupid old bitch. I don't know whether to shout, smash, argue or walk calmly back into the hospital and go on a spree. Am I in shock? Maybe I am. No, I'm not in shock, I'm two or three bus stops past shock, I'm in something else entirely: as if Isaac Newton sat under the apple tree and watched all the apples float gently away on a breeze.

I stand here feeling the breeze on my face. Gran starts the car and winds down the window to say something to me.

'It's not possible,' I say to her first.

'We'll talk later,' she says.

I get in the car.

189

Chapter 34

Monday 15th April, 7.10am

Monday. I'm awake before the alarm clock goes off. That never happens. It feels like the world has tilted on its axis and I'm the only person who knows. Everything looks the same and everyone will go about doing their stuff as if everything is the same, but it isn't, and all those lucky complacent bastards haven't a clue. 'Carry on as normal,' Gran said. What's normal now Gran? Tell me that. What's normal? What would normal behaviour be? How can I act normally when normal's gone forever? Normal has pissed off and left … what? And Gran seriously expects me to go to school today?

They'd put Mum in a plastic tent thing. They'd said she was getting better but they'd put her in a plastic tent thing. They said it wasn't anything we should worry about, just a precaution, and then they told us why they'd put her in the tent.

On Saturday night, after sixteen years, four months, eleven days and about three and a half hours; an actual woman voluntarily interfered with my penis. A momentous event in every young life, never to be forgotten. And so what if I can't tell anyone about it ever because she has kids who are older than me, it was momentous nonetheless, it was one of those rites of passage things and it opened up the possibility that if one woman on the planet was willing to do it, there may be others out there somewhere who'd consider letting me go further. But now, only two mornings later, a middle-aged woman with her tits out cracking me off for over an hour, is by about a million miles the smaller of the two events from this weekend that I have to keep to myself. I seriously can't believe Gran expects me to go to school but she's shouting up at me like it's any other day. Any normal day. Shut up, shut up, shut up.

'OK!'

I get up and it's not like any other day. It's not and it never will be again.

Teeth, shower, dressed, three slices of toast and a mug of milky tea. Gran's acting far too everyday for it to be anything other than an act. She doesn't mention what happened in the hospital yesterday and neither do I. It looks like I'm going to school then. I grab a couple of chocolate bars and snatch up my coat and bag as Mrs Hughes sounds her car horn outside.

I get in the back of Mrs Hughes' car. Mrs Hughes says good morning and so do I, and Charlotte Hughes doesn't. Normal day. Out of Kilmuir and up the endless hill, at least Mrs Hughes isn't chatty. When it's the McLeod-McLeans' week Mrs McLeod-McLean never shuts up. We pick up the two small McLeod-McLeans at Drynie and they squeeze in beside me and talk to each other all the way down to Kessock in their stupid Muppet voices. We pile out at the top Kessock bus stop where about twenty people are already waiting, and not one of them do I have anything to say anything to. Normal day. For the first four years the people at this bus stop ignored me, for the last two I've been ignoring them. The school bus comes and because I'm sixth year and bigger than everyone else, no one is sitting on my seat, bottom deck back seat right corner. I look out the window to try and avoid Palsy telling me about whatever he's seen, or heard, or played, or ate, or bought, or compared, or considered since Friday. I turn as far away from him as I can manage and wonder what I'll say if he asks me how my weekend was. He's probably picked up on my mood though as he isn't saying anything. I look out the window and watch it go by. The firth, the hills, the fields, the forests. All just stuff for tourists and hippies, no use at all if you have to live in it and look at the stupid shit every day. I find I'm getting very angry at the scenery, useless same ten mile bus journey bunch of shit that it is. Scenery bollocks. Shit fields and village arseholes and all those don't know fuck about fuck hospital bastards. Palsy had better not talk any of his usual bus shite at me right now as I'll bite his face off.

Chapter 35

The first nurse had looked shifty.

'I'll check for you,' she said, and she flicked through some papers on a clipboard behind the desk. She looked at one and ducked into the little office behind her. Gran and I could see her through the Venetian blinds having a quiet word with another nurse. It had been a simple enough question, 'Where was Mum?' We'd shown up to see her, but her bed on the ward had some woman with purple cheeks and clouded up eyes in it. No one had told us anything and Gran was thinking Mum had died and been wheeled out in the night, but she was pretending to me that that wasn't what she was thinking. It was the other nurse, older, more senior, who came out to talk to us.

Chapter 36

Monday 15th April, 8.45 am

Fortrose Academy, Academy Street, Fortrose – Trying to teach Avochies how to speak English since 1791. For some reason the school bus doesn't like going down Academy Street in the morning so they dump you on the High Street and you walk down. It's the only bit of walking I've never minded, even on my first day in first year when I was shitting it. It's very narrow at the top end and all the walls are high and the buildings old. People with cardigans and green jackets live in them. It's always felt like a serene kind of street to me, even when the contents of the Kessock bus spews down it, trying to give each other dead legs and nicking each others stuff to shouts of, 'Give us back ma phone ya tight fuck, that's tight as fuck'.

This morning I'm walking down Academy Street in a whole new state. Not serene at all. Very far from serene. I read somewhere that some guy, after a whack on the head or brain cancer or something, had started to believe that his wife and kids weren't really his wife and kids, but had all been secretly substituted with identical looking impostors. He admitted that there was no reason he could think of why anyone would go to all the trouble of stealing his family and replacing them with doppelgangers, but as far as he was concerned that didn't mean they hadn't done it, because the people currently claiming to be wife and children were definitely not the real thing. This morning I feel like someone's replaced me with an impostor. I've been stolen and another me has been put in my place. And as I also used to be the previous me, I can be absolutely positive that the me I'm now experiencing as me, definitely isn't me. And while I'm not on any drugs whatsoever at this moment in time, the new me will be considering some serious drug taking as a future lifestyle option. In the meantime, the jaws of the school yawn open before me and like a good robot I go in. I head for the common room not making the slightest adjustment in my course to get out of anyone's way, and I plough straight on as I knock some people a bit on the arm, or into a wall. I'm ignoring the complaints of a third year I nearly bounced off his feet when I see Alex swaggering down the corridor like a tiny ginger John Wayne. He nods, stops and is going to speak to me. I can see I'll have to try some normal conversation. I wonder if I can do it.

'Alright Findo, how's it going?'

'No bad, yourself?'

'Aye, no bad.'

My turn to talk. I was annoyed at him for some reason wasn't I? Why was I annoyed at him again? Oh yes.

'Where did you piss off to on Saturday then?'

'Aye, I meant to tell you but the girls were keen to get going and I couldn't see you.'

Couldn't see me? I'm six foot three. What he means is that I turned my back and they all ran out of the pub pissing themselves laughing. Usually when he does it I pretend not to mind. Today I find I'm considering a head butt.

'Aye, sorry anyway,' he says, perhaps sensing my internal twitch. 'Ended up at a kind of free-love scented candle party up in the hills somewhere out past Dingwall. Little cottage, middle of nowhere, lots of people who said 'creative' a lot and think that bits of shiny stone connect them to something. Drank some punch and saw Jesus waving at me from up in a tree. Eventually stayed in a caravan up the back, and I know you don't like to pry so I won't tell you what we all got up to.'

Usually I'd rise to it at this point and call him all the jammy syphilitic bastards under the sun. Today, and without any feeling at all because I genuinely don't give a shit, I say,

'I'm very happy you had a lovely time.'

This throws him. He looks at me with all his ginger wiles for a moment, and possibly senses I've been replaced by an impostor, but is unwilling to admit it to himself as in the normal run of things it's pretty unlikely. Even so, he expresses his misgivings as eloquently as he can.

'Fuck's the matter with you?'

'Nothing.'

'You're not really properly pissed off I pissed off on Saturday are you? I didn't know you were going to need a lift. Anyhow, is it true the Twigger cut his own nip off to impress Diane?'

'It is.'

'Did you see him do it?'

'I did.'

'Was it horrible?'

'I suppose.'

'And did he really use scissors?'

'Yeah.'

'And?'

'And what?'

'Jesus, you're a mine of information aren't you.'

The bell goes and the corridor turns into a torrent of first years. Alex and I ignore the bell and only after the corridor clears do we start to amble towards our registration classes.

'So how did you get home on Saturday?' Alex asks.

And this is my chance, it's the conversational opening where in a normal world I'd jump in and coyly brag 'As it happens, I didn't go home on Saturday night'. And after all the times the wee ginger stiffy has forced his own tales of cockmanship on me, here I am, at very last with a story of my own. Yes, I could say; actually Alex, a sexual thing happened to me on Saturday. No, not a girl Alex, a woman. Yes Alex, a woman. An older woman, yes, well obviously a bit older, that's how a woman would be defined. Quite a bit older I suppose. Ok a lot older. If you must know I thought she might be a granny but luckily she was only a mum. No, no actual sex, no. No, not that either. With her hand. Well I was so pissed it took about an hour and I only just managed to come before the old girl's arm gave out. Perhaps some stories are better left untold. I let the chance pass.

'I got a lift home with my cousin,' I say instead.

Walking down the corridor towards us is Lyndsey Jack, beautiful and perfect Mandy Duplin's evil little bitch of a best friend, who so kindly pointed out to me getting off the bus on Saturday that I've no chance with Mandy, ever, ever, ever. I find as she approaches that I want to give her a little smile, so I catch her eye and the smile that comes out of me must appear to her to be full of genuine warmth. This clearly confuses the hell out of her, and as she passes she pretends badly that she hasn't even seen me. I think I'm going to smile at Lyndsey Jack often now. Partly because she clearly doesn't like it, and partly because it was a conjured-up image of Lyndsey in her gym shorts and jiggling about with her fat little tits, that finally sent me over the top on Saturday night and spared Mrs Egger a more serious repetitive strain injury. So thank you Lyndsey Jack you heartless little bitch, I owe you one.

Chapter 37

Sunday 14th April, 1.55pm

The second, more senior nurse, had taken the edge off Gran's rising panic. It was all to do with the beds. She'd been moved to a different ward, that was all, and she was surprised we hadn't been told, as in fact her condition had improved. So up we went in the lift to the new ward and asked for Mum there.

And yes she was there, but no she wasn't in the general ward. And yes her condition had improved slightly, but it had also been decided to put her into a private room for the time being. Gran made sure it didn't mean we'd have to pay, and if we wouldn't mind waiting for a moment the doctor would like a word.

'Which room is it?' Gran asked but the nurse had already gone to find the doctor. Gran sat to wait and I wandered along the corridor looking into the rooms. The layout was the same as the other floor with half a dozen private rooms between the lifts and the main wards. On some the blinds were closed, on some they were half closed so I peeked in. Mum's room was the second one along, she looked asleep. When the doctor appeared from one of the wards and came down the corridor to Gran, I already had a question waiting for her.

'Why's Mum's bed inside a big plastic tent?'

Chapter 38

Monday 15th April, 9.35am

I'm not paying any attention in this class. Chromosomes, phenotypes, punctuated equilibrium; arse biscuits. I no longer believe in any of it. Look at that ridiculous man wearing a lab coat even though he's not a scientist, and banging on about DNA as if he knows anything about it. If he really knew anything he wouldn't be teaching it, he'd be gene splicing bits of pig into things to mess about with the flavour of potatoes, or growing hormones on apple trees to counter the spread of radical Islam. But no, he's sweating in his lab coat and spouting out all the entry level easy crap that challenges neither him nor us. I wonder how hard the science got before he gave up trying to learn it and decided to teach. I suppose the trouble is, the closer you look at anything scientific and the more you get into it, the harder and more complicated it gets, until you reach a point where you either can't understand it any more, everything you thought you knew turns out to be bollocks, or you can no longer prove what you believe to be true. At which point you take a few steps back, pick a place where you sort of had the gist of it, and go and obtain the appropriate teaching qualification.

He's asked me a question.

'Well, Mr Gask?'

Well this is going to be pointless. He knows I wasn't paying attention and I know I wasn't paying attention. He's looking at me and I'm looking at him and I don't know what the question was let alone the answer. Usually I'd say something to prove what a smartarse I am. Today I'm not in that kind of mood. I'm just going to keep looking at him in silence till he goes away.

'Mr Gask?' he says again, a bit more impatiently.

I'm saying nothing Mr Sweaty Lab Coat Man, not a sound. You'll die of old age waiting first. Less than ten seconds and he cracks.

'Well as Mr Gask seems to have lost his voice, does anyone else know?'

Anne Finlay sticks up her hand, of course she'll know whatever the hell it is, the Finlays don't even have a TV. I've had enough of this class, I'm not paying any more attention.

Chapter 39

Sunday 14th April, 2.00pm

The doctor had given me a patronising little smile so I asked her again.

'Why's my Mum inside a big plastic tent?'

'It's a precaution really,' she said, addressing her reply to Gran. 'We're sure she's past any infectious stage, so it's simply to be on the safest of safe sides.'

Gran seemed happy with the explanation but I wasn't.

'So if she's not infectious, why's she in that tent?'

Gran butted in, 'The Doctor just said Findo, it's to be on the safest side,' and she smiled at the doctor like she wanted to offer her a cup of tea and talk about how proud her parents must be to have a doctor in the family.

'So can we go in and see her now doctor?' asked Gran.

And the doctor hesitated a moment too long before replying.

'I believe she's sleeping at the moment.'

'I can wake her,' I said, and the doctor interrupted my walking off.

'It's probably best if you don't disturb her right at the moment, she's had a sedative and will be a bit out of it for a little while yet.'

And finally Gran was curious too.

'Why's she had a sedative doctor?'

Chapter 40

Monday 15th April, 11am

The interval bell goes. I phone Diane because I'm under standing orders to, and she comes over from her absurdly advanced maths class. She wants to nip up the road to the shops and she's in an unusually good mood. The morning's warm and only a couple of little fluffies throw quick passing shadows over the tennis courts and bowling green as we go by. I'm going to have to ask.

'You haven't got back with Twiglet have you?'

She whacks me on the arm.

'Are you some kind of a spakking idiot? Get back with him? He cut off his own moob top in the street and ran away from the ambulance because he's frightened of stretchers. It was eleven yesterday morning before I got home and he's already phoned my mum to tell her to tell me that he thinks they stitched it back on upside down. He says the hairs are growing the wrong way. So no, no, despite the seductive charm of the evening I didn't get back with him. So how come you didn't phone me yesterday and how come your face is still sad my sad boy?'

Now if there was anyone in the world I could even possibly begin to tell about what happened at the hospital yesterday, then it would be Diane. As despite her bulldozer personality, her superficial lack of empathy and her great big enormous mouth; she can be trusted with the stuff that matters. Plus of course she's the only real friend I've got, so who else would I tell anyway. Alex? Ha! And yet there's no way I can tell Diane this one, no way in the world, not ever. Not on my deathbed, or on her deathbed; or even if our death beds happened to be bunk beds. She simply wouldn't be physically able to keep it to herself. She'd have to tell someone, even if she didn't want to, she'd have no choice; she'd blab. The life destroying implications to me of speaking the knowledge would fall by the wayside, as like it or not, we live in the kind of world where some pieces of gossip are simply far too juicy not to share. And now she's looking at me and she knows something's up, but what to tell her and how to frame it?

'Been worried about my Mum.' I say.

She whacks me on the arm again only this time it's out of kindness. 'She'll be fine Findo. Promise.'

At the top of Castle Street we turn into the High Street and head to the chippie. Sweets and Fanta for me, ice lolly for Diane. I step outside first and into the path of a small herd of dumpy fourth years squeezing for the door. The High Street's at its narrowest here and the pavement's one person wide, so I step out on to the road and become aware of an approaching roar. An old Massey Ferguson's rumbling straight down towards me and I wedge myself back on to the pavement so it can thunder past my face. My brain takes a moment to register before informing me what I've seen. I don't quite believe it, so I turn to take a better look at the figure inside the departing Massey's cab, exactly as the figure in the cab turns round to see if I've spotted him. Hello there Cousin Dan. He's fully regaled in his impenetrable driving disguise of fake moustache, dark glasses and baseball cap, and as he rolls away down the High Street in what must be a stolen tractor, I can see he's wearing a Darwin-fish t-shirt, but it's a Darwin-fish t-shirt that's wrong.

Two or three years ago I screen printed tons of Darwin-fish t-shirts in Maxwell's spare room. We wrapped them up and posted them off and then all things Darwin-fish went tits up after we burned a cross in an accidental black man's garden and Cousin Dan got locked up. But we never made any t-shirts like the one Cousin Dan's got on, as he vanishes out the bottom of the High Street. The design's different and we never made any in those colours. Cousin Dan's Darwin-fish t-shirt is new.

'Diane.'

'Mmph?'

She's just emerged from the chippie with a mouth full of lolly.

'I need to borrow your scooter.'

'No way. Why? And I mean no way though, but why?'

'I just need to borrow it.'

'Well in that case, no way. Why?'

'I can't say exactly. I just saw my cousin. I've got a bad feeling about something and I need to go and check it out.'

'That's a very interesting story which tells me nothing whatsoever, so no way.'

'Diane, stop pissing about. Really, I need to borrow it.'

'Now I don't think you know the difference between "want" and "need" young man. You don't "need" my beautiful scooter, you "want" it. But I'm not letting you have it because you're being all mysterious and evasive on me, plus I think you're far too agitated to drive it with the love and care it deserves. And then there's the question of licences and insurance, which we've never really bothered about before, but which I believe the authorities will take a great deal of interest in if you crash it.'

'JUST LEND US YOUR FUCKING SCOOTER!'

Chapter 41

'The sedative was to help her sleep, she became a bit agitated and given that she's still quite weak, we felt it was best to let her get as much good rest as possible.'

'What was she agitated about, doctor?' said Gran.

'Why don't we take a wee seat,' the doctor said, and she led Gran to a little waiting area cut into the side of the corridor. I followed and stayed standing.

'Your daughter's case has developed some unusual elements,' said the doctor to Gran once she'd sat her down. 'You see her illness presented like any other case of flu, serious, but nothing out of the ordinary. Then from the blood work we did, one or two things showed up that made us think that perhaps there may be something else going on.'

'What things?' I said.

The doctor looked at me like I was a rude young man, and then because she was too polite a doctor to tell the rude young man he was being rude, she decided to give the rude young man a one word answer.

'Proteins,' she said.

'What?' said Gran.

'Proteins. Unusual Proteins. Proteins which really had no business being where they were.'

'Where were they doctor?' asked Gran

'Well, they were in her body,' said the doctor.

'Oh, I see. And where should they have been?'

'Em, well, not in her body.'

'Oh, I see,' said Gran, nodding her head sagely, and displaying the kind of rigorous and integrated understanding that a barnacle has of the oil rig it's attached to. The doctor tried again.

'Yes, so what I'm saying is, that the proteins we found led us to believe that your daughter's illness may have a genetic element to it.'

And then, as if she couldn't help herself, the doctor glanced up at me, and accidentally gave away a look that said she was sitting on the kind of news that took specialist training to break. I remembered when we'd been in here a few days before, they'd taken samples of our blood too, mine and Gran's.

Chapter 42

Monday 15th April, 11.20am

'Oh great queen of beauty Diane, perfection in all things, who makes Helen of Troy look like a bus driver's arse, very pretty please with sugar on, will you lend your magnificent royal scooter to … what was it?'

'An unworthy, festering foul-mouthed wank-job who will be very, very careful with it or find that he has to eat his own bollocks on dry bread.'

'Yes that.'

'Say it then.'

From my position on bended knee in the middle of the High Street I can't help thinking that queen of beauty Diane's enjoying herself far too much.

'Say it' she insists.

'An unworthy foul-mouthed wank-job who will be very careful with it.'

'Ok, close enough.'

I stand up and she throws me the scooter key on its pink fluffy key fob. An old woman who's stopped on the other side of the street because she probably thought she was witnessing a proposal, goes on her way looking deeply unimpressed with the state of the world these days.

I hurry back down towards the school, Diane striding along beside me. The five minutes of begging she made me do means that morning interval will be well over by the time we get back so it's going to make it even more conspicuous when I depart on her scooter from the bike shed.

'If Mr Fraser asks, tell him I'm in Chemistry doing project stuff and if I'm not back by the end of lunch tell Alex to tell Evil Bob that I'm in Art, doing project stuff.

'And where are you going to be?' asks Diane.

'I told you, I need to chase down my thieving cousin.'

She's smiling at me in an odd way and I'm suddenly very suspicious. I stop walking.

'You didn't even bring your scooter in today did you.'

The pleasure evident in her face tells me I'm right.

'Nope, it's at home. Do you still want to borrow it?'

I turn on my heel and walk back up towards the High Street, and the bus stop, shouting over my shoulder as I go, 'I've half a mind to crash the bloody thing now.'

And she shouts up the street after me, 'Well if you do, you'd better say you stole it, then at least the bike's insured even if you're not.'

I hurry up towards the bus stop on the off chance there's one due now. There isn't. I've half an hour to wait. I could almost go back to school and let Cousin Dan do whatever the hell he likes with someone else's tractor. At least, I could if it wasn't for that t-shirt he was wearing.

Why would Cousin Dan make a new Darwin-fish t-shirt? It's not as if he understood or particularly gave a shit about the anti-religious principles behind my Darwinist Terrorist Organisation, he just liked doing the vandalism and getting in the papers. So why would he go to the trouble of making a new t-shirt when he was far happier spending his time lobbing stones at stained glass windows, or trying to do a shit through a church letterbox. I pull out my phone and look up our old Darwinian Terrorist website, it hasn't been there since the police got involved and it isn't there now. Is that tractor he stole the same one he wanted me to steal for him on Saturday night, or is stealing tractors just what he does now? Why's he made a new t-shirt? I search for Darwin-fish t-shirts, but if he is selling them his page isn't ranked. He'd better not be starting up the DTO again without me. It was my thing, my idea, and nothing to do with him till I asked him to join, so he can't be going off making new t-shirts. And if he's making cash then I'm entitled to a cut. Intellectual property rights and that, the thieving git. Maybe he needs a tractor for Darwinian Terrorist purposes. Ploughing for Darwin maybe? Though why would he need to steal a tractor anyway, he lives on a farm, they already own at least two. Most likely he's nicking farm equipment for cash, which is fine because it means he can afford to give me money for nicking my idea for t-shirts.

At last the bus, at bloody last. The short hop along the shore to Avoch and I'm almost breaking out into a run up to Diane's, but as it's right up the hill I settle for a fast walk. I hope Diane's mum isn't about. The house looks quiet and there's no car, so I slip down the side and round the back to where the scooter sits by the kitchen door. There's no movement or sound from in the house so I retrieve the helmet from inside the seat, strap it on, start the engine, and buzz out the front gate on a powder blue scooter wearing a pink helmet. If I could see myself, even I'd think I was gay.

It's a twenty minute buzz to Cousin Dan's farm. On the long straight bit between Avoch and Munlochy I stick my head down and try and coax out a bit more aerodynamic speed, till a lorry overtakes me and nearly blows me into the ditch. Head back up and with a little adrenaline boost, I feel the wind in my face and looking around it's a beautiful day. If every single aspect of my life and my being wasn't totally screwed up, I could really enjoy a day like today: escaping school, just me and the open road, and no one around to notice the colour of this helmet. I'm not sure I even care much whether Cousin Dan's gone back to the farm or taken his tractor elsewhere. Maybe I don't even really care what he's up to. Maybe I'm more wanting to take my mind off the other thing that's on my mind. Maybe I want to be me again, even though I'm not; or maybe, now I'm not me, I can do whatever the hell I want. Though what am I even going to say to Cousin Dan if he is there?

'Hi Cousin Dan, I know you sort of went to prison and you might blame me a bit for that, but if you're selling t-shirts for a thing that was my idea, can I have some of the money?'

Or what about,

'I'm glad you're stealing farm stuff it's a nice career for you, and if you go back to prison, this time it'll be totally your own fault, but the Darwin terrorist fish logo is mine, and you can't do anything with it without my permission'.

Or I could go with the more simple approach of,

'What are you up to you dodgy fucker and where'd you get that t-shirt?'

I buzz past the top of Munlochy and past the Cloutie well, the load of old bollocks magic fairy well where the ignorant locals used to, and still do, tie rags to the branches round the spring to make their wishes come true. A few years ago they added a car park to attract the tourists to join in, because it's all so magical, and now it looks like an Oxfam shop threw up in the woods. I buzz on through the forestry towards Tore, turn off before the village and head up the hill, quickly coming within sight of Cousin Dan's farm, or rather, my four year old Cousin Stan's farm, since dead Uncle Robert left Cousin Dan nothing. I haven't been back here since his funeral, and as I come out from behind the hedge to where I can see the place properly I slow down to take a look. The whole farm looks totally, unfarmed. Cousin Dan always swore he wouldn't be a farmer and unless he's getting European funding to keep nothing, plant nothing and cut nothing, to encourage butterflies or weasels or fuck-knows-what, then it looks like he's being as good as his word. The soil hasn't been turned for at least a year, the fields have all gone to weeds and there's no stock that I can see at all. I turn on to the long straight drive, open up the throttle and arrive in the yard as noisily as possible, doing a half decent skid to a halt in the dust on the concrete by the house. I expect to see Auntie Roberta sticking her head out the kitchen window, or Cousin Dan walking out of the big barn eating a bacon roll. A bit of me even expects to see Uncle Robert passing in between the sheds looking grim, but there's no one. I get off the scooter, hitch it on to its stand, dump the helmet inside the seat, and for the first time in my life I feel like I should knock on the kitchen door even though I know it's always open. I knock and wait. No one comes. I knock again, louder. There are a couple of crappy old cars parked in one corner of the big shed but no stolen tractor. I decide to go into the house anyway for a pee and a drink, and on trying the door I find it's locked.

I walk over to the first of the old sheds and have my pee against the corrugated iron. Then as I'm wiggling I hear a noise of metal on metal. I know instantly where it's coming from. I zip up and walk round in the direction of the old shed at the back which Cousin Dan kept his scrap and crap in. As I come round the back corner of the old cattle stalls I can see to the end of the buildings, and sticking out the big door of Cousin Dan's shed, the front half of a stolen Massey Ferguson. I hear something beside me but not in time to consider either the arrival or the impact of the punch which pops my jaw out of its socket and sends me straight to the ground in a second of pure unconsciousness as I drop. My eyes open, my arms are pinned behind me and I'm dragged back to my feet and force-marched towards Cousin Dan's shed. Twisting my face round I see the owner of the fist, that sociopathic, up-himself turd of a video uploading shit-for-brains, Maxwell.

Chapter 43

Sunday 14th April, 2.05pm

Gran looked at the doctor with all the authority of total ignorance, and said 'Well if it's genetics she's got doctor, it'll be from her father, we never had any genetics on our side of the family'.

'Em, well, yes …' said the doctor.

'So,' I asked, 'is that why they took our blood? To see if we've got what Mum's got?'

'Pardon?' said the doctor.

'On Friday, they took our blood. Mine and Gran's.'

'I'm sorry, who did?'

'The hospital. Here.'

'They said it would help and they needed to check something,' added Gran.

'Em …' said the doctor, flicking through her clipboard. 'I don't think that would have happened. They … if you'll excuse me for a moment I'll check up on that for you. One minute.'

The doctor scuttled off and when she didn't come back after two minutes Gran said. 'Let's look in on your Mum.'

In the little room, lying still in her bed inside the wrinkly clear plastic tent, Mum looked a bit too much like an overweight alien autopsy, so I rolled up the side of the plastic nearest us and tied it at the top near where a big tube was sucking air away and where there were ribbons attached to tie it to. Gran had taken a seat beside her and I gave Mum a prod to wake her. When she opened her eyes she looked like she'd woken up from one dream straight into another. She didn't look like she was all there, she took a couple of long blinks as we said hello and she tried to work out what was real. Then Gran said her name to her and she turned her head a bit and sort of focused on us. She was doped up past her eyes but she didn't look too happy about it. Looking confused, she reached for Gran's hand.

'Mum,' she said, 'Have they told you what I've got?'

'Yes,' said Gran. 'We've just spoken to the doctor just there, she said it's genetic but you're going to get better soon.'

'No Mum, it's not,' said Mum, looking glassy and anxious. 'That's not what they told me.'

Mum's brain went far away again like she was trying to catch a thought, or maybe had Alzheimer's and couldn't remember what a fridge was. Then she seemed to come back and saw Gran, and focused on her again.

'They said I have an animal disease,' she whispered.

'No sweetheart,' said Gran 'We were speaking to the doctor just there now. She said they've given you a sedative so it sounds like you've been having junkie's dreams and imagined it, you know, like Lucy up the hill used to have, before, well, you know.'

'No Mum,' she said, sounding sure despite her drugged up state. 'I've got an animal disease. They said I've got distemper. They said people don't get it, but I've got it. It's not something people get Mum, it's not something people can get. And they put me in this plastic bag and gave me something very strong. It was lovely, but I didn't want it. I didn't.'

Gran didn't know what to believe or what to say and she looked at me, but I was no help so she turned back to Mum and said, 'No sweetheart, I don't think so. Distemper's something dogs get and we were just there talking to the doctor, and she said it's genetic what you have, so I don't think it's distemper or she would have told us, and you're not a dog now are you sweetheart'.

'They said distemper. That's what they said,' replied Mum and she closed her eyes. Gran and I raised our eyebrows at each other but the silence wasn't broken till the doctor came into the room.

Chapter 44

Monday 14th April, 12.45pm

'Give me a hand, grab him,' insists Maxwell's voice behind me and who's a hell of a lot stronger than he looks. I'm struggling to twist away from him but he has my arms locked and the rest of me off balance as he bundles me into Cousin Dan's shed. I hear someone else behind me and see the bird's nest hair and smell the diesel and mud as Cousin Dan joins in and grabs my legs with his nail bitten hands.

I say, 'What the fuck!' and 'Fuck off!' a lot, but my jaw screams with pain when I move it and this pair of insane dick-wads are paying no attention to me but are talking to each other.

'What'd you bring him in here for?' asks Cousin Dan.

'I didn't know where you were.'

'I was round the other side.'

'Well he came round this side.'

Then the manky bastard Maxwell twists my right arm from thumb to shoulder and I have no choice and topple face first to the concrete floor, breaking my fall only a bit with my left hand. My jaw is singing with pain and as I realise they're not trying to pin me down, I turn over to see what I can see and to swear at them both at lot more.

I've been dumped in a big space at the back of Cousin Dan's shed that's stinking of diesel and old manure dust. The tractor's parked half in half out of the door and is hitched to a big trailer which is taking up most of the space inside the shed, leaving only two narrow passages down the side to get out of here. Blocking the way down one side is Cousin Dan, doing his best to look like a hard man, but coming off more like an angry scarecrow. And now looming directly over me is Maxwell, who's taken to wearing a tweed suit like he's got a few thousand acres for grouse tucked away up in the hills and who's picked up a three foot length of scaffolding pipe in his gloved hands.

'I think you broke my jaw you fucking piece of shite,' I mumble through clenched teeth to Maxwell before tentatively checking whether my mandible is still attached to the rest of my head.

'What the fuck you doing here?' spits Maxwell.

'Yeah Findo,' echoes Cousin Dan. 'What the fuck?'

'What do you mean "What the fuck?" What the fuck did he hit me for, and what the fuck did you jump me for, and what the fuck's he waving that scaff bar about in my face like he's some kind of henchman and not just a dick.'

'Because he wants to know what the fuck you're doing here.' spits Maxwell, referring to himself in the third person, which is never a good sign from a general sanity point of view.

'So fucking tell us,' he says, raising the scaff bar in a gesture designed to threaten my head with being completely stowed in. I see his eyes are shining a bit towards the psycho end of the spectrum and deciding he probably thinks he's serious, I feel appropriately threatened. I look in appeal to Cousin Dan in the hope of some sense of protective family bond or cousin-ship or something, but even a glance at the angry scarecrow tells me I'm well off his Christmas card list.

'I really think you broke my jaw you fucker,' I mumble again to Maxwell, angling for a bit of sympathy. It doesn't work. He says, 'Last chance before I do your ribs. What are you doing here?'

'Why do you fucking care so much?'

'None of yours, but I do care very much. So?' and he raises the scaff bar to the top of his swing.

'Ok fuckwit, ok. Because, well, because …' And my mouth blurts out the excuse, 'Because I thought he wanted me to steal him a tractor.'

'What?' says Cousin Dan.

Maxwell pauses and holds his weapon over me in a slightly less imminent way and looks over to Cousin Dan.

'What's he saying?' Maxwell asks him with a hint of suspicion in his voice.

'My Cousin Dan asked me to steal him a tractor,' I say again,

214

sensing I might have found the thin end of a wedge and giving it a little tap.

'Bollocks, he's talking shite,' says Cousin Dan, advancing a couple of steps.

'What have you been saying?' says Maxwell, turning towards Cousin Dan.

'I've said fuck all,' replies Cousin Dan adamantly. 'I haven't even seen him in years. Apart from like I said when I drove past him in Fortrose earlier, but I didn't stop and I didn't talk to the fucker.'

Looks like Cousin Dan was too pissed to even remember meeting me in the pub on Saturday. I move into a sitting position but don't try and stand up.

'Then what's he doing here and why's he talking about you talking about tractors?' asks Maxwell, increasingly peeved.

They both turn slowly back towards me, and although I think the immediate threat of violence has passed for the moment, they're both super edgy and I'm in a lot pain and a state of confusion. Why is Cousin Dan still hanging about with Maxwell when it was Maxwell posting the accidental Ku Klux Klan video that got Cousin Dan sent away for a year?

'Why are you saying I've been speaking to you when I've not?' Cousin Dan asks me.

'Why are you hanging out with Maxwell when it's his fault you got locked up?' I ask right back.

'None of yours you dick. Now why are you saying what you're saying?'

'Because you asked me to steal you a tractor.'

'Fuck you and shitsticks I did,' he says, stepping towards me and filling the dusty air with his spittle. Then a speck of doubt touches him from somewhere and he says, 'When?'

I wait till he thinks I haven't got an answer, and then I say, 'In the Crown on Saturday night'.

Cousin Dan's speck of doubt condenses over his face into a cloud, which Maxwell pierces with disbelief.

'I don't fucking believe it Dan, what have you said?'

And then to me, 'What has he said? And who have you told?'

And then to Cousin Dan, 'And who else have you told, and what have you fucking told them you pissed up … FUCK!?'

Maxwell's anger reaches a peak and he batters the scaff bar on the back of the big tractor trailer with enough force to dent the sheet metal an inch and reverberate a couple of pigeons out of the ceiling. Maxwell then turns and focuses my way, strides back up to me, sticks the end of the scaff bar in my face, and looking one hundred percent serious says, 'What did he tell you in the pub?'

'He asked me to steal a tractor for him.'

'What else?'

'That's it.'

'What else?'

'That's it.'

'Who else was he talking to?'

'No one I saw.'

'Who else?'

'No one.'

'And what the fuck are you doing here?'

Now that's a trickier one, think fast Findo.

'I didn't believe he was serious when he asked me in the pub but when I saw him driving down Fortrose High Street earlier, I saw that he was, and figured if he really was nicking tractors for a living now, then maybe I could help and maybe make a bit of cash out of it.'

A near total lie, but reasonably plausible. Maxwell seems to be buying it and he moves the roughly sawn end of the scaff bar off my cheek.

'Yeah,' he says, 'Well we've got all the tractors we need for the moment and we're not hiring, so you've wasted your time.'

'Well I'll be on my way then, lovely to see you both.' I start to try and stand up and Maxwell shoves me in the chest with the scaff bar hard enough to make his point. I sit down again.

'You picked a bad day to visit,' says Cousin Dan from over Maxwell's shoulder.

'Aye,' says Maxwell. 'Because you picked a bad weekend to get chatty in the pub. Get something to tie him up.'

'Tie me up? What the fuck? Seriously now you dickwads, what exactly the very fuck is going on here?'

'Should we keep him here or stick him somewhere else?' asks Cousin Dan, as he walks to one of the long junk strewn benches that line the sides of the shed and starts picking among the piles of stuff.

'Might as well keep him here. Don't want him to go all escaping on us.'

'So you don't want a hand with your little tractor thing then?' I venture.

'No Findo,' says Cousin Dan, extracting a reel of baling twine from the depths of his junk pile. 'We don't want any help and particularly not from you, you gutless arsewipe.'

Cousin Dan approaches unfurling the twine while Maxwell stands over me.

'You tie me up, and that's kidnapping and false imprisonment. I could have you back inside.'

Cousin Dan and Maxwell share a glance and both burst out laughing, genuinely amused.

'Could you now,' says Cousin Dan, smiling at me. 'Well wouldn't that be a truly terrible thing. I'm sure I wouldn't like that at all. Hands behind your back or we'll brain you.'

Gutless my arse. Do this pair of shits seriously think they're some kind of agricultural gangsters. I put my hands behind my back to avoid a hefty tap with the scaff bar, but with a resolve to visit retribution on these wankers at the first opportunity. As Cousin Dan starts to wrap the twine round my wrists I push hard against the binding as he wraps so he thinks it's tighter than it is, while I'm really creating a gap between my wrists. I'm hoping it'll give me enough slack when he's finished to squeeze a hand out. The twine is sharp and cutting and he wraps me up tighter than I hoped, but not as tight as he thinks.

'Where'd you get that t-shirt?' I ask him as he finishes and stands up.

He doesn't answer. They sit me on an upturned plastic crate and tie my ankles together, very tight. Deciding that's not enough, the pair of turds hop me to the wall, put a loop of much thicker nylon rope between my feet and hands and hitch the end of it through an old ring bolt in the wall. False imprisonment, no fucking question. They give me the plastic crate to sit on and move everything metal, sharp and escapesman-like well out of my reach. Cousin Dan reaches into my pocket and takes out my phone, then they give each other self-satisfied smiles and Cousin Dan pats me on the head and tells me to be a good hostage.

'Where'd you get the t-shirt?' I ask again.

'I think he needs something else,' says Cousin Dan, looking down the other side of the shed under the bench. The fucker. He's shaking fifty years of dust out of an ancient hessian potato sack and checking it for holes. He walks back to me and pulls it over my head. I choke in a murk of dried dirt filling my hair, nose, mouth and eyes. I try to flip the bag off by shaking my head, choking even more as I do, I drop to the floor and shake and scrape it off inch by inch by dragging my head along the floor. As I free my head from the mouth of the bag and try to open my gritted up eyes, I see Cousin Dan and Maxwell standing by the trailer chuckling at me. Pricks.

I rotate myself back up to a sitting position with my elbow.

'Where'd you get the t-shirt?' I ask him again.

'What's it to you?' says Cousin Dan, impatiently.

'It looks new.'

'So?'

'So, the Darwinian Terrorist Organisation was my idea, so how come you're still making t-shirts for it?'

'You quit. What do you care?'

'I didn't quit. I ended it. It was my thing, which I ended. My thing.'

'Not so much,' says Maxwell. 'You quit, we kept going.'

'What? How do you mean? Kept what going? He was in the young offenders and it was losing money. There wasn't anything to keep going.'

Maxwell looks at Cousin Dan and an agreement passes between them.

'Aye, we just sort of told you it was losing cash so you'd keep working for nothing,' Cousin Dan says.

'Aye, you were a good little slave while it lasted.' adds Maxwell. 'But then you turned into a girly-wimp-I'm-all-afraid-of-the-police pain in the arse. And as it happens, the business did really well when he was inside. We had an internet marketing snowball going off the back of Scotland's most notorious Ku Klux Klan member here. We shifted a ton of tea towels because of it. Turns out racists love a tea towel.'

'They do.' echoes Cousin Dan. 'Pity it also turns out the Ku Klux Klan is a trademark of the Ku Klux Klan. They got all lawyery on us when they found out that we were making a few quid off them.'

'Aye, it's a pity they didn't want to franchise,' says Maxwell.

'Aye, a pity,' says Cousin Dan 'The racists really do love a tea towel.'

'So now we're exclusively Darwinist again,' says Maxwell.

'Hence the new t-shirt,' adds Cousin Dan. 'Satisfied?'

I'm seething in a way I've never seethed before. This pair of jumped up shit-for-brains have taken something which I thought up and believed in; something that had a point to it, an ideology, a higher purpose, and which was about far more than painting people's cars and trying to sell them a t-shirt: it was about turning religion on its head, about direct action against ignorance. And then these fuckers come along and they've got me to work for them for nothing, for nearly a year, while they creamed off the profits and never even gave a crap about why we were doing it. And me, me who was once considered a prodigy, I've been beaten up, tied up, conned, humiliated and basically totally done over by a couple of well known total nutter fuck-wits. I am really, really, really annoyed.

'He doesn't look very pleased,' Maxwell is saying to Cousin Dan.

'Nah, he doesn't,' says Cousin Dan.

'Stick the bag back over his head.'

Chapter 45

Sunday 14th April, 1.36pm

Everyone's heard of bird flu, the Asian poultry virus which always seems to be trying to wipe out the world, by making the evolutionary leap into humans from some South Korean chicken with a bit of a cough. Everyone's heard of swine flu, another keen-to-kill-us-all virus, which is constantly working on ways to wipe out humanity because it's become bored with its day job of giving a Mexican pig a sore throat. And everyone knows that the media enjoy keeping us all a bit scared with the thought that a single infected animal is going to pass on a disease which will erase us all from the planet. But to be fair, every now and then, the bird flus and the swine flus do alright for themselves; like after the first world war when returning soldiers, sick of all the pointless death and destruction, brought home something they caught from a goose and wiped out more people than the war had. Of course it doesn't have to be the birds or the pigs that wipe out humanity, theoretically any nasty animal virus could make the jump, and with no natural immunity, the people of the world may all die in the streets wondering why they'd spent so much time worrying about an Asian chicken, when what's killing them started out as an itchy condition passed between consenting squirrels. You just never know.

And there was my Mum in hospital, being kept drugged up in a plastic tent claiming she's suffering from distemper, a serious canine disease that dogs get shot for at the first whiff of it, and there was the doctor, who'd five minutes before tried to tell us the problem was genetic. Gran was starting to smell a medical conspiracy and I was starting to sense the end of the world.

'So which is it doctor?' asked Gran. 'She says she has a dog's disease but you said to us just now it was genetic.'

The doctor finished rolling the side of the plastic tent back down and noticed we were both standing between her and the door.

'Well you see,' said the doctor, cornered at last. 'It appears that your daughter does indeed appear to have contracted a distemper virus, and naturally when we discovered this, it did raise some concerns of the possibility of cross-species infection and ...' and then rather than saying ' ... a resulting pandemic and the death of everyone on the planet.' She toned it down to '... problems with isolation.'

'However,' she said more brightly. 'Considerable resources have been brought to bear on your daughter's case, and from what we now know we can tell you that, well, firstly, the phocine distemper virus strain that your daughter has, isn't a dog's disease as you suggested. And secondly, we don't now believe that there are likely to be any problems with human to human transmission, as in this particular case, the virus doesn't appear to have mutated from its original form. So the reason for infection lies elsewhere.'

'I see,' said Gran. 'So what does that all mean doctor?'

And the doctor explained what it all meant and I went bloody mental, refused to believe a word of it, stormed out of the hospital into the car park and in an uncontrolled rage kicked a car knackering my toe as I went.

Chapter 46

Monday 15th April, around 1.15pm

The dust inside the bag has dissipated a bit now because I think I've breathed it all in. If I lean forward and stay still, it creates a bit of a gap between the bag and my mouth and I can inhale without disturbing too much more of the ancient dirt in here. I can mostly keep my eyes open now too, and as I've grown used to it, quite a lot of light is getting through the hessian but the weave is too tight to let me see any of what's happening outside the bag. This time Cousin Dan tied the bag at my neck so trying to shake and scrape it off just meant I nearly choked. I'm concentrating now on trying to get my hands free, squeezing and twisting and pulling at the centimetre of space I managed to create when Cousin Dan tied them. I can hear the two toss-pots at the tractor or on the trailer or moving things about outside, and they're sometimes talking in low voices or in cryptic references, aware that I'm listening, and not wanting me to know whatever it is.

'I'm going to tell your mum on you Cousin,' I say loudly, because besides the pain and the choking and the near blindness with my eyes full of dirt, I'm getting bored and want to provoke a reaction.

'Bollocks,' comes Cousin Dan's derisory reply from far closer than I'd thought. I didn't hear him approach but he must be only a few feet from me.

'The old cow moved to Wales or Cumbria or somewhere,' he says.

'When'd she do that?'

'When I made it obvious even to her that I wasn't going to do any farm work, by continuing to not do any farm work. The bitch sold all the machinery and pissed off.'

'So what are you still doing here?'

'She couldn't sell the farm, could she. It's in trust for baby brother Stan and she's not one of the trustees. Old dead Dad stuffed us both, the shit-fingers. She can't sell it, I won't run it, and no fucking tenant's going to touch it because I'm unevictable.'

A scraping sound and Maxwell's impatient voice comes from the shed entrance. 'A hand with this.'

Cousin Dan walks off saying to Maxwell as he goes, 'What are we going to do about him in the movie version?'

'We'll get some fat ugly mentalist with a disabled face to play him. It'll be an improvement.'

'No, I meant tying him up and that, it makes us look a bit dodgy.'

'What are you two idiots talking about?' I ask the world in the direction of their voices.

'Shut up,' says Maxwell to me, then says to Cousin Dan, 'We'll cut him out. He's nothing to do with anything any road so if we don't mention him, he never existed.'

'Are you two imagining a world where someone's going to make a film of you?' I ask.

'Shut up,' says Maxwell again.

'Aye Cousin Findo, you don't know shite about fuck,' adds Cousin Dan, eloquently.

'What's the film going to be about? Two farm boys against the world, on the run in their love-shack Massey? No? How to look good in a boiler suit? No, clearly not. How to be an alcoholic fuck-up by the time you're nineteen?'

'Fuck you Findo, if you're so fucking smart how come you're tied up on the floor with a bag on your head.'

'Because you jumped me and there are two of you fuckwits, though I realise that's quite a high number for you to try and comprehend.'

'You're really pissing me off now little cousin,' says Cousin Dan, proper anger in his voice. I tense up, half-expecting a kick.

'Don't mind the bag boy,' says Maxwell to Cousin Dan. 'He's been written out of history and he doesn't even know it.'

'Aye,' Cousin Dan agrees. 'You're written out bag head.'

'Just as well,' I say. 'I don't want to be in your pornography anyway.'

'He's really pissing me off,' says Cousin Dan to Maxwell.

I think I might have a bit of a kicking coming, but it's nice to know I can still push Cousin Dan's buttons.

'Let's tell him then, that'll shut him up,' says Maxwell.

223

'What? After what you were saying earlier, now you want to … ?'

The conversation between Cousin Dan and Maxwell is raising my interest the more it drops in volume. I stay as still as I can to try and hear.

'Yeah, but it doesn't matter now does it? At the weekend it did but where's he going between now and … ?'

'But once we're … what if he … ?'

'Why would he? And we can make sure he doesn't.'

'And if he did anyhow?'

'Then we only tell him … and not …'

'I s'pose. Would shut his smart face right up.'

'Yeah?'

'Yeah.'

'Findo,' says Maxwell to me in a nearly friendly but mostly smug voice, and I can hear footsteps coming towards me.' You know that bit in all the James Bond films where the villains reveal the master plan to James Bond, who's tied up with a tattie sack over his head?'

'He's not James Bond,' says Cousin Dan, his voice coming from very close to me now. 'No way he gets to be James Bond.'

'Aye, I know that, he's more of a dick with a tattie sack over his head, but anyhow … Findo, you know that bit?'

'Yes.'

'Well I'm in a position to let you know exactly why they do that.'

'Everyone knows why they do that,' says Cousin Dan to Maxwell. 'It's for the plot. It's so that when James Bond escapes, he knows exactly what he has to do, and by when he's to do it, to stop the evil plan from happening.'

'Aye,' says Maxwell, slightly frustrated. 'In the films it's for plot, but in reality it's not. In reality, it's because they've gone to a hell of a lot of effort doing the thing they're doing, and they take a lot of professional satisfaction in it because it's lovely and shiny and it's totally going to work. And they don't see why they shouldn't get a little acknowledgement of that fact before they, you know, destroy the world with a laser, or steal a fleet of submarines; or set off their lovely tractor bomb.'

There is a long pause and an eerie silence as they wait for that last bit to sink in through the tattie bag and properly into my head. And it sinks in, and it sinks in, and I can feel them waiting for my reaction.

'Are you two going to destroy the world with a laser?' I ask.

Another pause, this time not as long or so eerie.

'Take that thing off his head,' says Maxwell.

I feel Cousin Dan's fat hands grabbing at the cord holding the bag on as he tries to unpick his own knot. A few moments later he de-bags me in a flurry of light and dust. I try to blow away the thick cloud surrounding my head without breathing any more in and I blink away the extra caking in my eyes, desperate to be able to rub them.

When my vision returns, Cousin Dan is back to standing henchman-like a few feet away, and Maxwell is at the trailer unhooking the green tarpaulin that covers it down one side, at the back edge facing me, then up the other long edge out of sight. He reappears and flicks the back end of the tarpaulin up over itself and drags it towards the tractor end, revealing the trailer's contents.

It's a big double-wheeled trailer with an open top and metal sides a couple of feet high around the trailer bed. The sides have been built up with an improvised home-welded metal framework to a height of about eight feet, and held within that is a neatly laid brick-like construction made of fifty kilo bags of fertiliser. Hundreds and hundreds of them. If it really is a bomb, it's a very, very, very, very big one.

Maxwell has scampered up the side to the top of the pile and stands on it looking down at me with an expression of insufferable arseholeyness.

'What you can see before you,' he begins, 'Is a classic example of the genre. A tractor-based fertiliser and diesel explosive device with the very latest control features, and weighing in at … Dan?'

'Very heavy indeed,' says Cousin Dan.

'Very heavy indeed,' repeats Maxwell.

'What are you going to blow up?' I ask.

Maxwell taps his nose and Cousin Dan changes the subject.

'It's a very impressive bomb though, isn't it Cousin Findo. I mean, even to look at, it's got a lot of really bigness about it, and that's what you want in a bomb; really bigness.'

'And is it big enough for what you're going to blow up?'

'Well, honestly,' says Cousin Dan, walking over to the trailer and touching one of the fertiliser bags, 'We're not exactly sure. It's got all the farm's fertiliser in it from this year and last year and a whole bunch of other fertiliser we bought, but the website we got the instructions off was a wee bit Arabic in places, you know, and working out the blast radius got far too much like doing maths. We think it's either probably big enough, or it's way, way, way too big: which in practical terms only means we've got to stand a bit further back on the off chance.'

'And what? You're really going to set off a bomb? To what? Sell some t-shirts?'

'Don't be so bloody ridiculous,' says Maxwell, climbing down from the trailer. 'You think merchandising's only about t-shirts? There's going to be far more than t-shirts to this, and we'll be selling far more than 'some'. There's going to be a massive product range by the time we're done. Massive.'

'But you'll both be in jail won't you?' I quite reasonably point out to the idiots.

'Wrong,' they chime together, and more than just delighted with the synchronicity of their answer, they stand there smirking like their special school bus just stopped at an ice cream van.

'What?' I say, trying to work out their faces. 'You don't seriously think you're not going to get caught do you?'

'We want to get caught,' says Maxwell.

'But only I'm going to prison,' says Cousin Dan, in a matter-of-fact and couldn't give a toss kind of way.

I look at them, and think it over, and say, 'Eh?'

Maxwell replies first. 'As far as the law's going to be concerned, he planned it himself, and built it himself and set it off himself.'

Cousin Dan notices my confused look and says, 'It's not as if we're going to kill anyone, and we'll be making it clear that's not part of it, so I'll only get about six years maybe eight, out in three, four max. But before I get caught, I'll be on the run. I'll send videos and communicate with the police and papers and make manifesto statements and stuff, all through him.'

'So I become his PR face and the official unofficial spokesman for the Darwinist Bomber,' adds Maxwell.

'But all the fame and the blame comes to me,' says Cousin Dan.

'Then after, what, a week and a half, two weeks, depending on how the coverage goes, I talk him into coming out of the woods, or wherever he's hiding …'

'And I shout some pre-arranged marketing slogans at the cameras before the police Taser me.'

'And all the while we're selling the stories, and building his profile, and making him into a fight-against-the system hero that people can identify with. Then once he's inside I run the business on the outside till he's out.'

'And I sit on my arse getting more famous than any bitch with a fake tan and health impairing tit-job ever dreamed of.'

'Then when he gets out, it's all appearances and reality shows, and selling stories, selling stories, selling stories.'

'And lots of shagging.'

'And selling those stories.'

'And even more shagging.'

'And selling those stories too.'

'You're looking at the world's first celebrity terrorist,' says Cousin Dan.

I can hardly even repeat the words for disbelief.

'Celebrity terrorist? Celebrity terrorist?!'

'Aye,' says Maxwell adamantly 'Celebrity terrorist. Why can't there be a celebrity terrorist? Seriously. Why not? Think about it, see. There's a celebrity every other fucking thing, and we've got the animal friendly Darwin bit going for us, and people like animals, all David Attenborough and that; so it's not as if we're angry Muslims or angry Irish all beardy and shouty about whatever the hell they all want that no one gives a shite about anyhow. We're for the animals and nature and that, so yeah, celebrity terrorist, why the hell not? No fucking reason why not in the world, that's why not, so we're doing it first before someone else does.'

'Exactly,' says Cousin Dan. 'And don't look at me like that. Everyone's got a right to be famous, it's an absolute human-fucking-right. I've got a right to be famous if I want, and I can do whatever I want to get famous; everyone knows that, that's how it works, or haven't you been paying any attention to anything you book-reading spaz? I've got a right to be famous and I'm exercising my right, simple as that, and don't even pretend if you hadn't thought of it you wouldn't be doing it too.'

Unfuckingbelievable, and yet they seem to be taking seriously every word that's coming out of their mouths. I look at my Cousin Dan, soon to be celebrity terrorist, with his dusty scarecrow hair on top of his hope-I-don't-ever-meet-that-in-an-alley face, combined with his timeless farmhand dress sense. Then Maxwell. A brain full only of his own fantasy and a glint in his eye that would invade Poland as soon as look at it. It occurs to me that as I now know Maxwell's been involved since day one, when I get out of here I'll be making a point of mentioning to the police that Cousin Dan really shouldn't be going to prison alone. Though best not to mention it at this point as I might find myself strapped to the top of their little doomsday device. And as I'm thinking it, Cousin Dan, the bollocks, reads my mind.

'And just because we're tying you up for a few hours,' he says, 'Don't get the idea that you're going to be telling anyone anything about anything at any time, ever. Because that, you would find, would really totally piss us off.'

'Indeed Findo,' adds Maxwell, doing a reasonable impersonation of a calm sociopath. 'If you even attempt to fuck up our plans for the future, in any way, we'll be coming to fuck up yours whether you have any or not.'

'And anyhow,' says Cousin Dan, 'You owe me, so don't be a dick.'

And he says to Maxwell, 'Shall we show him the banner?'

'If you like, but quick, we're on the clock here remember.'

'You'll like this wee Cousin,' he says, and he disappears briefly then emerges from behind the trailer dragging a huge rolled up something. 'What do you think?' he asks, as with Maxwell they unfurl a huge canvas banner about five feet high and a dozen feet long. A massive Darwin-fish.

'Well?' he asks, genuinely interested in my reaction.

'Very pretty,' I say, and I notice a symbol in the bottom corner of the banner, next to the Darwin-fish's amphibian feet. The unprincipled thieving bastard motherfisters.

'You trademarked it,' I say, as calmly as I can.

'Yeah, we got to protect ourselves,' says Cousin Dan. 'Can't have people messing with the brand.'

'C'mon,' says Maxwell, tapping his watch. 'Let's get this rolled up.'

As their attention leaves me, I writhe, tense and contract my hands to try and will the swelling blood out by some deep and unused vein as I attempt to work the bindings over the heel of my right hand. Cousin Dan drags the rolled up banner away and I pause in my Houdini attempt as I notice Maxwell quietly considering me from the corner of the trailer.

'What?' I say to him.

He says nothing. I'm not going to give him the satisfaction of thinking I give a shit why he's being a silent moody twatter, so I say nothing more to him. A couple of minutes later, Cousin Dan comes back.

'About ready to go?' he asks Maxwell.

'Aye, only one thing.'

'Aye?'

'Aye. We'll have to bang him on the head.'

'What?' says Cousin Dan.

'What?' says me, but with far more conviction.

'You've seen all the films,' says Maxwell, mostly to Cousin Dan. 'When someone gets tied up in the films, so someone else can go off and do whatever it is they have to do, the tied up person always escapes, and messes it up for the people who were trying to get on with what they were trying to get on with.'

'Aye. So?'

'So we'll have to bang him on the head.'

'Kill him you mean?' asks Cousin Dan.

'Not kill him, no. Bang him on the head, enough to knock him out for the afternoon.'

As it's my head they're threatening, I intervene. 'Just fucking hold on there one minute,' my intervention begins. 'This isn't a film you know; you do know this isn't a film don't you? There's no need at all to bang me on the head, I'm tied up perfectly sufficiently to last the afternoon. No banging on the head required.'

'I dunno Cousin Findo,' says Cousin Dan. 'He's got a point. They always escape in the films. James Bond and that.'

'Yeah, maybe, but again, and I want to stress this point: This is not a film, this is real life. I am not James Bond and if you bang me on the head you're more likely to kill me than anything else. There's absolutely no way you can judge how or where to hit someone so it'll knock them out for a few hours. You'll crack my skull Cousin. I'll die, and you're going to be looking at a hell of a lot more time than the three or four years you think you're going to get for blowing up whatever it is you're going to blow up. And while we're on the subject, I think you're totally underestimating the time you're going to get for letting off a bomb half the size of a house, even if it doesn't kill anyone. Everyone knows the courts hate people who set off enormous bombs all over the fucking place, that's why most people tend not to do it.

I stare at them hard to see if I'm getting through.

'If we hit him with the flat part of a thick plank of wood, that probably wouldn't crack his skull,' says Maxwell.

'And if we use a softwood, pine or something. Not oak or teak or anything like that,' suggests Cousin Dan.

'You know,' I say, hearing a high note of scaredness, maybe even desperation, creeping into my voice. 'I don't think Charles Darwin

230

would approve of all this. I don't think he would. And you two can still walk away from it if you want. Just decide that instead of blowing things up, you're going to not blow things up instead. You could go and rob a sub-post office on a motorbike like everyone else your age.'

'Aye, we could do that,' says Cousin Dan, 'But as we've been to all the trouble of building our great big bomb there, as right-minded individuals, how could we not want to watch it go off?' And Cousin Dan disappears, looking for a suitable plank of wood.

I'm left looking at Maxwell and Maxwell's looking at me. No point trying to talk him out of anything, and I'm not begging, not to that hollow arrogant piece of Culbokie crap. I keep looking at him and he keeps looking at me.

'You're going to screw my Cousin Dan over too, aren't you.' It's as much a statement as it is a question.

Maxwell doesn't answer and his blank expression doesn't change. I now seem to be involved in a staring out competition with the turdbag. Well that's just fine with me you parochial lunatic, let's see how blinky or not blinky you are. And while I'm staring into your disgraceful excuse for a face, let me send the message from my eyes to your brain, you can try to bang me on the head if you like you filthy fuckstick, but it won't be before I head-butt you in the nuts and bite off your kneecaps. I can feel his desire to blink building up, I can hear Cousin Dan returning but we're too locked in eye battle to look his way and Maxwell's weakening and my eyelids are made of stone. Maxwell takes a step towards me, an intimidation tactic though it's not going to work dickwick. With a second step he kicks up the layer of old dirt from the floor and into my face, I have to blink it away. The miserable fuckbasket couldn't even do an honest staring out.

Cousin Dan's returned with a short length of heavy looking plank. Surreptitiously I'm still trying to work my hands free, a hair's breadth at a time. It's not going to be fast enough. Stall them.

'So what church are you going to blow up?'

'None of your business,' says Cousin Dan.

'So it is a church then.'

Maxwell gives Cousin Dan a withering look.

'What?' says Cousin Dan, 'I didn't tell him which one.'

'Give me that.' Maxwell takes the plank from Cousin Dan. 'I'll have to hit him a little harder now, to make doubly sure he's out all afternoon.'

'Till about five o'clock should do it,' says Cousin Dan.

'I was thinking around six, six-thirty' says Maxwell, looking at me with some diagnosable form of happiness.

The stupidity of their conversation barely even registers as I try to wriggle my hands free without them noticing any movement, and I'm getting close. I can feel significant progress and I'm almost nearly there as Maxwell approaches me holding the plank in both hands and raises it. My heart is beating out of my ears as the adrenaline surges. Fight or flight time as Maxwell stands over me and I give my bonds a huge final yank to free myself and ... nothing. Hands won't budge, I'm still tied up like a kipper. Change of plan. I scrabble to get my head into the corner between the wall and the floor where it's going to be trickier to hit and I fend him off with my tied up feet.

'Shit, grab him.'

As Cousin Dan drops on my legs I kick and squirm and kick again.

'Stay still you dick,' snarls Cousin Dan as he tries to pin me. I don't even waste my breath on a 'fuck you' but kick and squirm even harder, and as an arm tries to grab at my neck I twist round and bite it to the bone.

'Arrrgh! Motherfucker!' It was Cousin Dan's arm. He jumps back, the pressure off me for a moment so I stop writhing and grab a breath.

'Motherfucking shit bastard OW! Shit ... look at that. That's deep. Shit Cousin, you really fucking bit me.'

'You're trying to knock me out with a plank,' I say, twisting to where I can see him and Maxwell, now both standing a few feet back.

'Yeah, but even so,' he says peevishly. Cousin Dan is applying pressure to the wound just above his wrist and checks that his fingers are still working. I can't see any blood but I hope there's lots.

They regroup. Maxwell suggests a plan. 'Untie him from the wall, drag him out here, I'll sit on him and you can bang him on the head.' Maxwell offers Cousin Dan the plank but Cousin Dan has reservations.

'Why can't I sit on him?'

'Why?'

'He is my Cousin.'

'So?'

'So it shouldn't really be me that hits him with the plank.'

'Do you want to be famous or not?'

'Aye, course.'

'Well then take this plank and bang your cousin on the fucking head with it.'

Cousin Dan accepts Maxwell's winning argument and takes the plank. Here they come again. Maxwell unhooks the rope securing me to the wall and grabs my thrashing legs. They drag me into the centre of the open floor space and Maxwell suddenly drops on me with all his weight. I almost expire from lack of breath. Cousin Dan's got the plank and Maxwell presses my head to the floor pushing down ridiculously hard on my neck and temple. The agonising pressure of the sharp grains of dirt on the floor digging into the side of my head between my cheekbone and ear makes it impossible to move my head without scraping all the skin off the side of my face. Cousin Dan has stepped behind me, above me. I can feel him there lining my head up like a golf ball. The thought occurs that being about to die's at least mostly taken my mind of what happened yesterday.

'How much swing do you think I should give it?' asks Cousin Dan. 'About here? A bit more maybe? Here?'

I make another attempt to move but Maxwell has me pinned.

'Will you just bang him on the head,' he says.

I sense a swoop approaching and almost instantly, everything fills with light from the back of my skull to the front, and just as quickly from the front to the back, the light's replaced by nothing. Far more nothing than I ever thought there was.

Chapter 47

Don't know when. Might be dead.

I don't seem to have any physical form and I'm staring into complete blackness. I think time exists but I don't know how much because I really can't feel it. It might be going fast, it might not. I can see nothing but complete blackness in front of me, and other complete blackness to the sides which I can't focus on so well. It's easier to look at the complete blackness straight ahead, so I do that. I did have a physical form, didn't I? I look around and I don't have one now. I wonder where the hell it's got to. And how can I be looking at anything when I no longer seem to have eyes to be looking out of? What happened to me? I was at Cousin Dan's farm wasn't I? I wonder if I'm still there somehow? I remember I stormed out of somewhere, a corridor, a building. A hospital wasn't it, and then I went to Cousin Dan's. No, something else happened in between.

Phocine distemper virus. What's that? Where did that come from? I think it's something someone's got. Who's got it? Me? No, Mum. That's it, Mum's got it, but it's okay, because the rest of the world isn't going to catch it off her, particularly because I didn't. Who said that? A doctor? Gran? One of them I think. And they said it's not a dog's disease.

I was home upstairs. My toe was hurting, I'd kicked something had I? Someone called me down, must have been Gran. It was Gran, she wouldn't sit down till I did. She gave me a whisky. A big one. A single malt she said. Old. Absolutely disgusting. I had a tongue at the time and was capable of tasting things. I remember I downed it in one so I'd only have to taste it once. I thought she was going to talk about Mum for some reason, about something the doctor had said? She started talking about herself and granddad.

'He died before you were born, your granddad,' she said. I already knew that. Why was she telling me things I knew? She was in her seat, had she whisky too? Filthy Scottish filth. Why hadn't she given me a rum and coke? There was no one else in the house. Only Gran and me. Where was Mum? Gran was talking.

'He wasn't my first choice of husband, Findo. He was a good man though, mostly, but he didn't have much to say, and he didn't like to go out or meet people or do things. He was very self conscious about himself, your granddad, but he had the most gentle eyes. So big and gentle looking they were. Not my first choice of husband though. There had been, well, I'd been engaged to another man, before. And you're old enough to know what I mean when I say the other one broke off our engagement, not that we were ever officially engaged you understand, and I was left in what they used to call 'a situation'. And the other one wasn't quiet about it, and your granddad Gask, I suppose you'd say he took me on when no one else would. For which I was told I was supposed to be grateful. Don't give me a face, things were different then. Very different, and unless you were there you haven't a clue.

Gran's voice went all flat and measured. 'Anyway, the baby I had only lived four months. A cot death. He was called Alec, he would have been your Uncle and he'd have been fifty four now.' I had no idea. Gran didn't wait for me to say anything back to her, she just went on. 'And then for a long time after that, for one reason and another, years, it looked like your granddad and I wouldn't be blessed with any children.'

'Until Mum came along,' I added, trying to be helpful.

'Eventually, yes,' said Gran. 'But I was pregnant again before I had your mother and that baby didn't live to be born. He was a boy too but we didn't name him. Your granddad wouldn't hear of it. You see that baby had genetics, Findo. Genetics from the mermaid.'

'What?' I said, and looked at her like she'd lost it, because clearly she'd lost it. 'The mermaid? The one from the story? The story mermaid, the one that's a story? That mermaid?' Now wait; is this a dream I'm having now, or did it feel like a dream when Gran was trying to tell me the family mermaid story was real. The mermaid story I'd stopped believing in before I'd given up on Santa. The stupid old mermaid story I'd heard trotted out so many times I don't even have to think of it to remember how it goes, it's already here in my head.

Was it great granddad? No, it was great great granddad Gask who supposedly, when he was out fishing one day, caught a mermaid in his nets, and having somehow learned English, she asked him to peel off her scaly skin, which he did, and she turned into a beautiful woman, who of course he married. They lived happily together for years but eventually she started to long for her old life under the sea, as all mermaids seem to do eventually, and so she begged great great granddad Gask to give her back her scaly skin, with the promise that if he did, he and his family would never lack for fish again. However, great great granddad Gask had mislaid the scaly skin and it wasn't till many years later that one of their children found it and took it to great great granddad Gask to ask him what it was. He then gave his wife her scaly skin back, she put it on, and returned to the sea, disappearing forever. But true to her word, ever after, the Gasks became the luckiest of fishermen; not that I've ever caught a fish myself.

Now is this a dream, or did my actual grandmother actually try to tell me that the story was actually true? I remember she launched into telling me it for probably the millionth time, starting where she always did, with the inshore fishermen up and down the coast and what a tough life they had in those days. If I was listening it was because I was spooked out by two dead baby uncles I never knew I had.

'Your grandfather's grandfather,' she began. 'Which makes him your great great grandfather, made his living as an inshore fisherman up and down the coast. Now one day, when he was out fishing for herring, which is what they always fished for in those days, and it was a very hard life let me tell you, well one day he was out fishing, and he caught a mermaid in his nets and he took her back to shore.'

She'd forgotten about the peeling off of the scaly skin and I was about to point it out when she started including details I hadn't heard before, and then seemed to move into an entirely different version: so without pointing anything out, I shut up.

'Now for a long time, he didn't tell anyone about the mermaid, because in those days people were extremely superstitious and he wasn't sure how they'd react, so he kept her hidden in his boat shed which was along the beach a bit and over the rocks. But eventually, people started to notice that he was spending less and less time out in his boat, and bringing back fewer and fewer fish, so they asked him what he was up to and he admitted that he'd caught a mermaid, that they'd fallen in love, and that as far as he was concerned, they were as married as anyone else. Now of course the villagers were all very keen to see the mermaid, because not all of them had seen one before, so your great great granddad led them along the beach and over the rocks to his boat shed, and he'd opened the door slowly, and the creature that the villagers saw lying inside a wooden pen, was not so much a mermaid as it was a large grey seal. Now of course the villagers were extremely angry when they saw this, and even more so when they found out that the seal was pregnant, and they would have killed the seal at once and probably your great great granddad too, except that he fought them all off like a maniac possessed, with a broken old oar and a bucket of seal shit.

So all beaten up and dirty they walked back to the village, and what could they do? You see Kilmuir was far more isolated in those days than it is now, but even so, if it ever got out that a Kilmuir man was shagging a grey seal, well then: the whole village would be a laughing stock forever; the people wouldn't be able to hold their heads up anywhere, and no one would buy anything off them for fear of where it'd been. So everyone had a meeting in old Paterson's front room, which was also the pub, and eventually it was decided the best thing to do, was to let your great great granddad keep doing what he wanted, as long as he kept it in the boat shed. And in case the minister up the hill or anyone from outside the village should ever ask any questions, the villagers decided to simply call the seal a mermaid: as so many fishermen up and down the coast at that time were married to mermaids, they figured the chances of passing off just one seal amongst them were good.

Chapter 48

Intruding into the blackness, intruding into my dream, I feel something like pain. Wherever the hell my mind's been I realise I'm waking up from it. Yet I think the nightmare I was just in is possibly more than a nightmare: I think the nightmare may actually be my life. I think the nightmare is what I'm waking up into. In the dream, my great great grandfather is flailing around on a shit covered flagstone floor, with his bare arse out and his cock up a grey seal, which isn't nearly as keen on the idea as my great great granddad is. In the nightmare, the seal is my great great grandmother. In the reality I'm waking up into, I know from every mirror I've ever looked in, that what I see staring back at me every day, makes this as obviously and blatantly true as it is physically and biologically impossible. I'm waking up now and my head's turning into pain.

I open my eyes. A floor. Cousin Dan's shed floor. It's daytime. There's a lot more light in here than there was. It's because the tractor and trailer are gone. I'm still tied up. I move my head from the floor to look around and I'm engulfed in a huge throb of pain that reaches round my eye sockets and makes the light stop coming in. When it subsides I try to move again. Another huge throb but not quite so bad. The shitmonger's actually banged me on the head. I can feel they re-attached me to the wall too. I test the twine round my wrists. They haven't tightened it but it's no looser either. Another huge throb and I cough up a lungful of shitty dust which doesn't help my headache at all. Eventually the coughing and the pain drop to a level where I notice the arm I'm lying on has gone completely numb. I roll onto my stomach and wait to see if the blood is going to flow back into it or if I've lost the use of it for good. Slowly, thankfully, I feel the hot prickly blood creep down towards my elbow and into my forearm, the heat stopping at the bonds round my wrist. I've really nothing else to do but try to escape. I remember I thought I was nearly free before they knocked me out, so I start trying to twist and work my hands out of the twine. I think I can feel where a couple of strands are still tight to my wrist, so slowly, and bloody painfully, I stretch and pull and twist and lever, and bit by millimetre I work all the strands over the heel of my right hand. I pull and scrape the bunched up blood-inflated skin by the base of my thumbs and in front of my knuckles under the bonds. I slowly work all the wrappings of the twine to near my knuckles, then squeezing one hand up like an octopus through a keyhole, I'm over one knuckle, then another, and I'm out. I roll on my back, sit up and look at the state of my hands and wrists as the agony of the blood flow restarts into them. Purple, blue and lacerated. I feel my head where they planked it. No blood, but a lump that would qualify as a Munro. Feet still tied, I swivel to my knees, hop to my feet and unhook the rope securing me to the metal cow ring in the wall. I take small jumps over to the nearest bench where an old pair of pliers gets my legs and feet free.

And I've escaped. Just like in the films, and just like Maxwell was afraid I would, I've escaped their evil clutches. And now what? Home for some TCP and hot chocolate? Back to school? No. I think not. Now to thwart the pair of bastards. What time is it? Am I too late to do any thwarting? It's quarter past two, I was only unconscious for about an hour, they may not have even got to where ever they're bombing yet. God my head hurts. I need to find out where they've gone. A map with an X on it would be ideal. I look around the benches for clues but it's just piles of ancient farm crap and bits of cars and bomb making stuff. No sign of my phone either. I know it's a church they're after but there are churches all over the place. I need to think like Sherlock Holmes … nope, no idea how to do that. Okay, I need to think like Cousin Dan and Maxwell. They said they're not going to kill anyone, so it'll probably be somewhere isolated. No help there, it's the Highlands of fricking Scotland, there are more isolated churches than people, and Cousin Dan knows them all because at one time or another we covered the lot with spray paint. What other clues do I have? None. Not exactly James Bond. Might as well find a phone and maybe call the police. I have another look round the shed just to be sure Cousin Dan didn't leave my phone, but knowing him he'll have sold it already. A truly horrible thought occurs to me; worse than any bomb and nearly as bad as my great great granddad humping a large aquatic mammal. What if they've damaged Diane's scooter? I hurry as fast as my throbbing head will let me, out of the shed into the sunlight, back round all the outbuildings, trying not to imagine her face if they decided to go over it with the tractor. Back round the corner to where I left it and … it's still there, and it looks intact. And coming closer I can see they haven't bothered touching it. I feel in my pocket and I've even still got the key. Thank God for that at least, that really would have knackered my day.

I look around the empty yard. Where would I have gone if I was them? It occurs to me instantly. If I was them, I'd want to bomb the evangelical church on the hill above Fortrose, the church where Cousin Dan and I did our first Darwinist mass car spraying, the one I got chucked out of when I was eleven because they thought I was demoniacally possessed rather than a mouthy wee shit. That's the one I'd want to blow up if I was them: it's isolated, it's incredibly photogenic, with all the landscape and the sea in the background, and it's got a lovely tall spire. Then again I'm not them am I. That's just the church I'd most like to blow up if I was me, and I'm not even that any more. It's only one of a dozen or more possibles I can think of, and they might not even have gone for one of them. But, but, but, it's my best guess, and I've always been quite a good guesser. Now what would James Bond do? I suppose I could go and take a look. And then if I happen to be wrong, I'm near enough to school to give Diane her scooter back, catch the second period of chemistry and get the school bus home to find out which one they did on the news. But maybe I should just phone the police and let them thwart them, because Maxwell and Cousin Dan have an enormous bomb and a fanatical commitment to getting on the telly, whereas I have no weapons of any kind and a tremendous headache.

The farmhouse kitchen door is thoroughly locked and solid so I go round to the front and put a big rock through the living room window. I knock the smaller bits of remaining glass out with a smaller rock and clamber in. The room's been stripped. No furniture, TV, paintings, anything. Only the carpet, flat and dull where people walked, bright and fluffy where the sofas and cabinets used to be. Into the hall, stripped, the kitchen, stripped, even all the appliances gone. A few dirty forks left in the sink, some council tax demands addressed to Auntie Roberta and the evidence that Cousin Dan's been living on Mr Kipling's cakes and Pot Noodle. I head upstairs. Nothing left here either. A push on Cousin Dan's bedroom door, half expecting a booby trap or something, and it's more or less as it always was; distinctively smelling and piled high with his junk, with a sort of hollow in the middle of his litter strewn bed where he makes his nest. I go through the piles of crap on his desk. No laptop but there must be a map with an X on it here somewhere. A lot of car magazines, instructions on how to build a glider, auction catalogues, pornographic dominoes, a geology textbook from the nineteen fifties, pens, key fobs, post-it notes from farm suppliers and a manual for enriched air scuba diving; but no map, no X, no clues, no nothing. At least there's a phone, and it's got a dial tone.

So do I call the police or what? Maxwell and Cousin Dan were pretty specific that they'd rather I didn't and they're both clearly psycho enough to do something horrible to me. But then again, I've already been kidnapped, tortured and half murdered by them already today, so fuck what they want. But then again, what if they implicate me? I'm at a bomb making factory when I should be in school. My fingerprints are all over the place and I am their known associate from all that other business, which is essentially the same as this business. What if I send the police to the church I think it is, and it's the wrong one, and they think I did it on purpose when the bomb goes off somewhere else? I could just nip back to school and pretend I was never here, except my fingerprints and DNA are all over the place and they're bound to check for that kind of stuff whenever great big bombs are involved. And what if they find my DNA and it's like they said Mum's was at the hospital, with all unusual unexpected bits in it, and even though it can't be, what if it is, and my unusual DNA gets on the telly and all over the internet and everything. Think clearly Findo. So then; if I don't phone the police, everyone in the world might find out what my great great grandfather thought of traditional marriage to human beings, but then again, it's not genetically possible is it. What Gran said is absolute impossible shite, because you can't cross a great great granddad with a grey seal and get anything out the other end, you just can't. So what if Mum has porcine distemper, commonly known as seal flu, so what? It doesn't mean anything, and I don't have it so that proves it. And so what if my arms and legs are a little bit short and the rest of me is perhaps a little bit tube shaped? So what if my nose and mouth protrude slightly and I've got great big gorgeous beautiful brown eyes? Doesn't mean a fucking thing.

I dial 999.

As I speak to the woman on the other end of the phone I'm aware I'm possibly trying to overstress my complete innocence, and it all comes out in a bit of a random order. I start to wonder if I'd believe me, so I tell her again, trying to sort it out into some kind of sense. An everyday visit to my cousin, held hostage, a bomb. 'No they're not Muslims, a church, no really not Muslims. I think maybe they're after that one church in particular but I don't really know, definitely not Muslims, no. They're Darwinists. No, Darwinists, well they say they are anyway but they don't really believe in it like they should. They want to get in magazines and sell merchandise and have a reality series. No I don't think either of them has ever been to Pakistan. Well I couldn't say for sure but I don't think so. No, it's not strapped to either of them, it's in a tractor trailer. A couple of tons maybe. They said they're not going to hurt anybody, just blow up a church. No, not as a Jihad, more as a marketing exercise. It's part of their business plan. Yes, I do realise how that sounds. No I'm not. No. No. I imagine they're very severe. Because I'm telling you it's not a hoax. Because if it was, I'd have come up with something a bit more plausible. No, I've no idea what, but that's really not the point. But I've already told you that. But you have to send someone now, no I don't know where exactly, it's a guess, and it may be too late now anyway. Of course I know I'm shouting. As I've already told you, it's Findo Gask. No it's not a Middle eastern name.'

I hang up with instructions to sit and wait for the police to arrive. They don't seem interested in Maxwell or Cousin Dan, but they're very interested in me and want to ask a few questions in person to make a bit more sense of whatever it is I'm trying to tell them. Why didn't I just say they were Muslims? Then the SWAT teams would have been popping out behind a gravestone in every churchyard in the Highlands. As it is, when the police do arrive here it'll probably be a bobby from the nineteen fifties on a bike, looking for biscuits with his tea. Angry, kidnapped, half-murdered and now disbelieved too, I stand in the middle of Cousin Dan's bedroom and feel an almost overwhelming urge to smash the place up. Only what would be the point, he'd hardly notice. I could smash up the wild birds' eggs collection he keeps in a suitcase in the cupboard, that would piss him off, and then I remember what else he always kept in there too. I kick all the crap blocking the cupboard door out of the way, and behind the birds' eggs suitcase, there it is, just as it always was. I reach in and pick it up, feeling it cold and smooth in my hands. I'm not a genetic freak show, beaten up, abused and close to going mental any more: I'm James Bond. No: I'm Jason Bourne. Either way, I'm their very angry nemesis.

I power the scooter down the farm track and take the corner on to the road at full-tilt. Me, the sun, the wind and no helmet, because Jason Bourne doesn't need a helmet so fuck helmets. With Cousin Dan's crossbow strapped across my back, I'm off to right wrongs, to re-align a world that's become tilted off its axis, and to sort the fuckers out … assuming I'm going to the right church that is, the celebrity terrorist and his sociopathic PR machine really could be anywhere.

I buzz back through the top of Munlochy and on towards Avoch. Car drivers stare at me as they flash past, one pointing to his head and mouthing the word 'helmet'. Another beeps as he overtakes me. Their hostility is meaningless, their concern for road safety is nothing.

Or maybe it's the crossbow they don't like. Whatever, it doesn't matter because they don't exist. Throttle wide open through Avoch and one old bint with her wind-proof hairdo opens her mouth as if to object, but I'm past her and gone before her thought becomes a word. Out of Avoch, along the sea wall (tide's half out), into Fortrose and using the full width of the road to take the corners, up through the back of town. I skid to a halt where the town finishes and the road goes single track as it turns into the trees to go up the crazy steep wooded hillside to the church on top. Cones, red and white barriers, road closed. The scooter engine hums idly, I look at the barricade and I'm not convinced. There are too many cones all too neatly placed to block off such a minor, almost non-road. And more tellingly, the sign in front of the cones is stencil spray painted and declares 'Rode Closed'. I throttle forward, kick the sign over and barge between cones on to the steep single track a few hundred yards up through the trees. The scooter doesn't like the gradient and struggles as the town, now to my right, quickly drops away, becomes rooftops and gets lost below in the canopy which envelops the hillside. As I continue to rise, through the branches above I see the top of the spire appear: so if they are there, they haven't done anything yet. The road gets really steep for the last few yards before the lip of the hill and as I creep towards the top and the edge of the trees the roof line of the church comes into view. I stop the scooter, turn off the engine and listen. The wind is in the tops of the trees above and behind me but I can't hear anything else. I don't know what I was listening for exactly anyway but I'm sure that's what Jason Bourne would have done. I get off the scooter and walk, half crouching, to the lip of the hill, and as more of the church is revealed by the road I see something out of place, something flat and white near the front of the church. As more of it comes into view I recognise the top of a tractor cab. Motherfucking bingo! They're here.

I run, actually run, back down to the scooter. I unstrap the crossbow from my back and load it with the only bolt I could find in Cousin Dan's room. Back on the scooter, engine on, I balance

245

the crossbow from my lap to the handlebars, open the throttle wide and only manage an unfit snail's pace up the steepest bit of the hill, then as it suddenly flattens out, I power speed out of the trees and free wheel down the approach to the church. The tractor and trailer are there but no sign of Cousin Dan or Maxwell yet. I skid to a halt where the churchyard wall starts, turn off the engine and put the crossbow to my shoulder to survey the scene through its expensive telescopic sights.

In trying to get the bomb as close as possible to the church at the base of the spire, they've tried to reverse it into the churchyard and cocked it up. Looks like the gate wasn't nearly wide enough, so they've gone straight through anyway, taking out the wall on one side with them and parting the trailer from one of its axles. They've then forced the knackered trailer as far up the path as it would go, up-rooting headstones as they went, before it dug itself in at the base of a particularly impressive memorial standing a few yards short of the main door. The tractor's been detached from the trailer and abandoned at a rakish angle back in the road. Something flaps above. Suspended from a loop of rope that's been slung over the roof behind the spire is the huge Darwin-fish banner Cousin Dan showed me earlier. The huge amphibian Darwin-fish flaps gently in front of the spire of God's house, and even though the buggers who put it there stole the idea from me and then trademarked it and are going to get a crossbowing for their troubles: it does look kind of magnificent. I really think every church should have one.

Still neither of them have appeared. I put the scooter on its stand and start to walk closer, trigger finger alert, eye to the cross hairs. No one in the road, no one behind the church wall, can't see any movement behind the tractor. Ten yards short of it I stop and listen. No sounds of anyone lurking nearby, no twigs snapping, no gravel crunching on the far side of the church. I put a foot on the low churchyard wall and as I stand up on it, I'm aiming over the top of the bomb trailer. The tarpaulin's still in place and no one's skulking on top of it ready to pounce. I drop off the wall into the churchyard, not exactly as cat-like as I might have wished. I get back up, pick up

246

the crossbow and skirt round the trailer, no one behind. Then to the church door, no sounds within and locked. I go to the corner of the church and look round, nothing round there but the view. I'm completely alone with a great big bomb. I'm completely alone with a great big bomb which may well be on a timer. I stop looking at the world through the crossbow sight and retrace my steps with a growingly-anxious pace. As I regain the wall I hear a muffled something, maybe a shout. Despite my finer instincts I stop and look about. I hear it again. Looking into the big field which slopes up and away on the opposite side of the road, I see a distant figure breaking the skyline. It shouts again and waves at me. I can tell from the hair that it's Cousin Dan but I can't tell if he's beckoning me over, or urgently desiring me to fuck off. Either way he doesn't want me anywhere near the bomb and I'm in complete agreement with him. I drop off the wall, cross the road, clamber up the bank and climb over the barbed wire fence not very stylishly. Crossbow at the ready I half jog, half walk up the slope, passing a camcorder on a tripod pointed at the church and seeing another figure at the top of the slope moving about near where Cousin Dan is standing waiting.

'Wanker!' is how he greets me at fifty yards.

'Wanker yourself!' is my well thought out response.

'Piss off Findo, just piss off will you, we haven't time for your shit!' Cousin Dan is angry-loud and Maxwell has joined him looking angry-quiet. They're standing in a small hollow where they seem to have set up their command post. There's another camcorder on a tripod pointing down at the church, and on the ground, a couple of rucksacks, a walkie talkie and a bottle of Irn Bru. I approach slowly, keeping them both covered with the crossbow and I stop within talking distance. I notice that Maxwell is surreptitiously keeping Cousin Dan between himself and the crossbow bolt.

'Told you he'd escape,' says Maxwell. 'Bloody told you. Exactly like the films. You should have hit him a lot, lot harder.'

'I will in a minute if he doesn't piss off,' says Cousin Dan.

'No you won't,' I say. 'You'll go down there, turn off your bomb and piss off yourselves.'

'How the hell did you know where we were?' asks Maxwell.

'Because I'm Jason Bourne,' I reply, realising it sounds a bit mad but meaning it anyway.

'He must have found the map,' says Cousin Dan.

'You'd better turn your bomb off, the police are on the way.'

Cousin Dan looks at me closely.

'Bollocks they are,' he says. 'You beat the police here on a scooter? Don't think so. He hasn't phoned anybody. Now we really don't have time for this shite my cousin. You can only get one shot off that thing before we rush you and kill you in a messy way, and you're a crap shot anyhow, and even if you hit one of us we're still going to set the bomb off. So, either shoot now and take the last kicking of your life, or just piss off like I keep telling you to. Or, if you promise to behave, you can go and stand back over there a bit and watch. But decide now will you, we're in a hurry.'

Cousin Dan stands his ground and raises his eyebrows at me as if to say, 'Well, what are you going to do?' And I notice Maxwell has now edged almost entirely behind Cousin Dan. I wonder if I could get them both with my one bolt before remembering Cousin Dan's not wrong, I am actually quite a bad shot so I'd better not try to get too fancy. Of course Jason Bourne would have shot the pair of them by now and broken their necks to make sure, so I raise the crossbow to my shoulder for better aim and focus on my Cousin. He's nearest. I'll shoot him and run off. But Cousin Dan's not even looking at me.

'Shitlumps,' says Cousin Dan quietly to Maxwell, as he taps him with the back of his hand and indicates something down by the church behind me. Maxwell looks too, and I get the distinct feeling they're trying to do the 'look behind you' thing so they can batter me as soon as I do, yet I'm feeling a powerful urge to look anyway. Then I hear the sound of a motor and I can't resist a quick glance. Someone's pulled up at the church, and it's not a police car. I look quickly back to Cousin Dan and Maxwell and they haven't moved. They're fixated on the new arrival and glancing back down I see a figure getting out of the car.

'Shit on a shitting brick. Cousin Findo, can you hold off shooting us for a minute till we deal with this other guy?'

And since it seems reasonable, I say, 'Aye, ok.'

'In that case look, he's getting his phone out, get down there now.'

Maxwell takes off at a tubby sprint straight past me in a flash of tweed and on down the field. He starts shouting and waving his arms at the figure who's standing and looking at the semi-desecrated churchyard.

'Get over here and keep your head down,' says Cousin Dan, so I join him in the hollow, but at the far end and still keeping him covered, as we watch Maxwell reach the bottom of the field where he's successfully attracted the attention of the newly arrived guy.

'What's he going to do?' I ask, as Maxwell climbs over the fence, drops out of sight behind the bank and re-emerges as he crosses the road.

'No idea,' says Cousin Dan, picking a pair of binoculars out of a rucksack and flipping off the lens covers.

'Well, what's he doing?'

'Hang on ... he's talking to the guy. He's waving his arms about a lot and pointing up the road. Looks like he's making up some bullshit story. I think the guy's buying it. I know his face from somewhere too.'

'Who is it?'

'Dunno, but I totally know his face from somewhere, here ...' Cousin Dan shuffles over and offers me the binoculars. Finger still on the trigger and pointing right at him I stretch out my left arm and take the binoculars, and in the instant of letting go the binoculars, Cousin Dan plucks the bolt from the top of the crossbow. My bowstring is drawing on fresh air. I'm disarmed. I'm not Jason Bourne any more.

'You're a dick,' says Cousin Dan, snapping the bolt and tossing the bits aside.

'Piss off,' I reply, and I discard the crossbow pretending I never cared and turn to put the binoculars to my eyes to disguise the enormous sulk I'm about to drop into. Beyond furious at myself,

I peer vaguely in the direction of the church while trying to work out if there's any way I can seamlessly repair a snapped crossbow bolt, without any tools or glue, before Cousin Dan can stop me. While my mind is concerned with that, I locate some movement behind the bomb trailer and adjust the focus. I can see the top of the back of Maxwell's head and then to one side of that, a pair of arms appear which look to be trying to pull the Darwin-fish banner down off the church by the same rope used to hoist it. Maxwell's head disappears completely behind the bomb, and quite abruptly so do the arms.

'I don't think the guy's buying Maxwell's story any more.'

'What's happening?'

'Can't really see, they're behind the bomb.'

'Recognise the guy?'

'Haven't got a look yet.'

And though I haven't seen whoever it is, the feeling starts to take root that I might know exactly the kind of person who'd be visiting this particular evangelical church on a Monday afternoon, to tidy up sweet wrappers or polish the baby Jesus. As the fight rolls out from behind the trailer, I'm not too surprised to see it's a furiously slapping Vincent Egger who's trying to avoid being pinned down by the not nearly as tall, but far stockier, Maxwell.

In a way, the unfolding scrap in front of the church, looking so tiny with the huge landscape behind it, has something weirdly biblical about it. Not good against evil or anything like that, it's more the ancientness of the battle being fought down there, as Vincent Egger, scuffling like a girl, avoids being put in an arm-lock by pulling Maxwell's hair out by the roots. It's the never ending primordial animosity between one self-righteous arsehole and another. Vincent twists out of Maxwell's grip and the skinny old pretend pacifist hits Maxwell in the eye so hard his head nearly whips backwards off the top of his neck. I suddenly find I'm really, really, hoping that Mrs Egger hasn't told Vincent she wanked me off.

'What's happening?' says Cousin Dan as he tries to snatch the binoculars back off me.

'Hang on a minute,' and I keep my grip and re-focus on the action.

'Fuck sake Findo,' says Cousin Dan in my ear, as Maxwell regains his balance and rushes at Vincent, rugby tackling him and trying to punch him in the balls, while Vincent, grounded, sets about Maxwell's head with his elbow.

'It's pretty even,' I tell Cousin Dan. 'Maxwell's got weight and youth on his side but Vincent's like a terrier and he bites too.'

'Vincent?'

'Yeah, Vincent Egger, remember? The Christian twat who slapped me about, whose car we did the first time we did here.'

'Oh, shit yes!' exclaims Cousin Dan. 'That guy. I knew I knew him. Not as well as your mum obviously. Hey, check this.'

I look from the binoculars to Cousin Dan and he's holding a little remote control. He's hovering his thumb theatrically over a button. The button is hand painted red.

'Bet you'd like to vaporise him,' he says.

'Is that the ...?'

'Damn right it is.'

'So it's not on a timer.'

'Nope, it's on this.'

'Go on then,' I say. 'And take your pal with him while you're at it.'

'Yeah well, I was only saying wasn't I.' says Cousin Dan, huffily, and he takes the few steps over to me and snatches back the binoculars, and heading back to the far end of the hollow, says, 'I mean if I was you, I'd want to vapourise the guy who's boning my Mum.'

'... What?'

Cousin Dan stops short of putting the binoculars to his eyes and looks at me.

'The Egger guy and your mum.' he says, as if it were the most obvious thing in the world.

'... What about them?' I say, and Cousin Dan looks at my disbelieving face with a different kind of disbelief on his.

'What? Are they not doing it any more or something? Wait ...

No. No way. Fuck sake Cousin Findo, surely you know. The Egger guy's been humping your Mum for years.'

No. No way. No. But ... no ... years? ... no ... shit ... no ... Vincent Egger ... no ... and, Mum ... never ... not ... no ... surely not, no. No way no. I'm, no. But the look on Cousin Dan's face ... it's yes isn't it. It's all too much. Can't I talk to anyone any more without finding out something appalling? Mum and Vincent. It's just too horrible to ... oh shit, I imagined it. I need my brain to shut down right now. I need to drop into a coma for six months, no, a year, and then I need to wake up as someone else. Vincent and Mum ... at it ... oh for fuck's sake I imagined it again. Maybe I can ask Cousin Dan to bang me on the head only harder this time. Cousin Dan, who's looking at me with a mixture of incredulity and glee.

'Findo, you are such a dick,' he says.

I want it to be last week or a million years from now. Mum and Vincent. No, no, stop picturing it, stop picturing it. I shut my eyes to make it go. Not good. I open them. I look at what I see, maybe that'll help. The grass is rippling up the field in the wind. The Darwin-fish banner hanging from the steeple is flapping about. The church has a huge bomb and two small fighting people in front of it. Most of the town below is hidden beneath the hill but Chanonry point is sticking out into the firth and it'll have tourists at the end of it looking for dolphins. The sea's looking sparkly between the shadows from the sky, and on the other side, the fort and the towns and the all farmland and whatever the thing is that always pumps out steam, rise up to the hills and melt into the clouds.

'Shitwipes,' says Cousin Dan somewhere near me. He's back to looking through the binoculars. I return inside myself enough to focus on the figures kicking lumps out of each other in the churchyard. One of them is definitely getting the upper hand now, and there's not enough bulk about him for it to be Maxwell. Against the odds, it looks like Vincent's winning down there.

'Shitwipes,' says Cousin Dan again as he takes another magnified look at the situation, drops the binoculars, skids up over the edge of the hollow and races down the field, pausing only to grab the tripod of one of the cameras I passed on the way up. I assume he's going to hit Vincent with it. He reaches the fence, climbs over and as he disappears briefly behind the bank I move over to grab the binoculars. On picking them up, I see lying in a fluttering clump of grass in front of me, a big red hand-painted button. He's forgotten the remote control.

You always were a dick, Cousin Dan.

Chapter 49

Monday 15th April, 3.29pm

My thumb is lightly placed on the red button as I binocular the scene below me. Cousin Dan is circling Vincent, he's wielding the tripod like he's game for violence but he looks a bit unwilling to lunge straight in, in case he ends up like Maxwell, who bloody faced and woozy, is trying to regain his feet with the help of a gravestone. Vincent, less bloody than Maxwell and looking less likely to turn the other cheek than a rabid cage fighter, is stalking just out of Cousin Dan's reach, and is trying to assess whether he can finish Maxwell off before he regains his feet and his senses without exposing himself to Cousin Dan and his tripod, or whether he can somehow dispose of Cousin Dan before Maxwell's in a fit state to rejoin battle.

But their concerns aren't my concerns. I watch their silent dance impassively. I'm not Jason Bourne any more and I'm not James Bond. I'm God. I hold the life and death of those creatures inside a tiny movement of my thumb. And what kind of God am I? That's the question. Am I the fluffy and kind benevolent sort, or am I a proper Old Testament bastard? Well let's see.

Vincent Egger, that was a very nifty kick to the head you just re-floored Maxwell with, while avoiding a couple of mad swings from Cousin Dan's camera equipment: so while you're better at fighting than I could've ever imagined, you're still the worst kind of sanctimonious hypocrite mother-fucker. And I mean that literally. You've been fucking my mother. I find you guilty, no question. Starting to look like I'm an Old Testament bastard isn't it?

Maxwell, you may be half unconscious but you remain a shitty back-stabbing seller-outer. You nicked my idea, held me hostage and got my cousin to nearly kill me with a plank of wood. You're a fine and shining example of a cunt. Guilty.

Cousin Dan. Cousin Dan, Cousin Dan, Cousin Dan. You're a stupid dick and you've gone nuts. You're useless as a tripod warrior but you were good fun once: so I really don't mind about any of the

254

stuff you used to do to me with the nettles and the nail guns and the cow shit; the electric fences, the tripwire or the shovels and the fire. But this afternoon you used my head as a golf ball while I was tied up and being sat on, and you're supposed to be my cousin, Cousin Dan. I'm pretty sure you're supposed to be looking out for me in some way, not playing hench-dick to a psycho-bag because you think you have a right to be in 'Hello' magazine and you want to get on telly more than you want to get a job. I'm not sure it's entirely your fault, but you're still a dick. You're guilty too.

So, guilty, guilty, guilty. Three guiltys. It's just a question of the sentence then. My thumb settles on the red button and I lower my head a bit nearer the ground. They're all within twenty feet of the bomb, it's not as if they'll feel it. Should I? Will I? Just the tiniest little press. What would Jesus do? Or what would Hitler do? Or what would Elvis or Jason Bourne, or great great granddad the seal fucker do? What would Pingu do? More to the point: what would I do?

Chapter 50

Monday 15th April, 3.33pm

'Oi, Wankers!'

My shout makes Cousin Dan turn, and when he sees me he freezes. Vincent instantly takes the opportunity to whack him across the legs with the tripod he'd wrenched from him when I was half way down the field. As Cousin Dan drops to the ground, Vincent notices me, and on recognition, pauses just a moment, the tripod balancing near the top of a swing designed to take a lump out of Cousin Dan's face. Maxwell stumbles into view from behind the trailer, still looking pretty dazed but carrying a sizeable rock for throwing or hitting. As he sees me, he stops too.

I'm standing just inside the churchyard wall, smiling benevolently and drawing their attention to the remote control with the big red button I'm gently waving above my head. Maxwell's jaw drops, Cousin Dan groans a tiny despair, and Vincent gives me a questioning look before deciding I'm obviously entirely responsible for the way his afternoon's going. I move my thumb theatrically to the button. Cousin Dan opens his mouth but no sound comes out. If I press it at this distance we're all atoms.

'You wouldn't.' Cousin Dan manages to croak.

I stare directly at him.

'Yes I would.'

I lower the remote control, point it at the bomb like it's a TV and press the button. Click.

We're still here, the bomb's still here, nothing's happened. Click,click,click,click,click,click,click.

My benevolent smile hasn't left my face and I click away a few more times to make sure of my point. Maxwell gasps out a formerly final held breath, Cousin Dan looks like his bollocks have taken refuge in his throat and Vincent's looking a little bewildered.

'Cousin Dan, Maxwell.' I look at each of them in turn. 'Your bomb doesn't work. I tried it from up the hill, I tried it half way down, and now look, I'm trying it here.' I point the remote at the trailer once more and click a few more times for good measure. 'You've built a dud, you pair of twats.'

Cousin Dan and Maxwell exchange a look in which Cousin Dan accepts no responsibility for the bomb not working and Maxwell wants to know how the hell I ended up with the remote control anyway. I sense their partnership is at an end.

'Bomb?' says Vincent Egger quietly, taking a couple of small steps back, still wielding the tripod on the off chance, but now looking nervously about him for a ticking briefcase or something with a hissing fuse. 'What do you mean, bomb?'

I haven't the heart to tell him what he's looking for is the enormous thing that he's backing up against for safety.

'Ask your friends there,' I say. 'I think they've got something against the baby Jesus Mr Egger. Not that it matters, it doesn't work anyway.'

Vincent lets the tripod drop. The fight's gone from all of them. There's nothing more I want to say, so I turn to go and walk a few steps before I change my mind, turn back, and walk over to Cousin Dan where he's on the ground nursing his wounds. I hand him his remote control back and say, 'Better luck next time.'

I turn away again and without looking back I leave the churchyard through the gap in the wall gouged out by the trailer and I walk up the road towards the scooter, trying not to pick up my pace too obviously but keen to be away nevertheless. I'm sure none of them heard me click the batteries back into the remote when I had my back to them, and despite myself I'm walking faster than normal and seriously hoping the scooter's going to start first time. I reach it, push it off its stand, jump on, shakingly put the key into the ignition and fire it into life. I don't look at the scene in the churchyard. I turn the handlebars and the throttle, put my back to the lot of them and head for the trees. If Cousin Dan's as stupid as I think he is, he'll be sitting on the grass right now, looking at the remote in his hand and wondering what went wrong. Was it the wiring? The software? The detonator? What was it? I'm nearly at the trees and still accelerating. Cousin Dan will be feeling deflated and puzzled. Why didn't it work? Why didn't it work? And in a moment he'll be feeling tempted. I'm banking on him feeling tempted. He's seen the remote doesn't work so he'll idly press it. I'm at the green tunnel of trees now and nearly at the brow of the hill. Any moment now, any moment now. I'm approaching the top of the really steep bit, I may have to slow down, am I far enough away? Maybe he won't press it, maybe Vincent took it or Maxwell said something, or maybe they're all fighting again or just walking away. The road's about to drop away so steeply I can't see it below me, as I touch the brake lever the world goes impossibly bright and I'm hit on the back by something like a concrete hurricane, the air in my lungs is instantly driven out of my body which accelerates past where the air was faster than the blood inside it thought possible.

The world flashes nearly black as my skull hits speeds my eyeballs can't keep up with and still stay round. I imagine there's noise but it's far too loud to hear. As my sight fades back in, what I see makes no sense, but my brain insists I have to make it make sense and I have to do it now. I see my feet, I see the scooter, I don't know if I'm attached to it and I don't see any ground. I look where I think up might be, I see a wave of trees shattering away from me. I look down, I see the scooter handlebars descending out of reach, I find I still have arms and they work and I grab the handlebars before they're gone. I see the road through my outstretched arms, I seem to be a long way above it rather than on it. I look at my hands and the handlebars I've grabbed and my brain suddenly orientates me in space. The scooter is the comet and I'm the tail, we're flying down the tunnel of trees almost at the height of the canopy. I pull myself into the scooter and plant myself on it, realising as I do that it's not going to help, as the front of the scooter's pointing at the sky. I look behind me which is really down, I'm travelling straight along the road at maybe twenty feet above it. I'm dead. I look up to avoid seeing me die and notice the scooter's rolling forward bringing the road ahead and below slowly back into view, it's like I'm half way through some horrible giant ski jump gone wrong, as I'm dropping while tracking the fall of the slope below me, and now I'm dropping much faster than the road is. I become aware of being inside a monstrously loud roar like an earthquake in a thunderstorm and the scooter keeps rolling forward and here comes the tarmac to kill me. The scooter lands wheels down with a ball-jarring crunch and as the suspension bounces back my arse is sent back into the air, somehow the bike's still upright but I'm only attached to it by my fear assisted grip on the handlebars. I land back on the bike, bollocks re-crushed, it's wobbling madly and I'm about to be pitched off, for all the difference it's going to make I snatch at the brakes, I sense the back wheel skidding beneath me, and if anything, the fishtailing gets more violent. The road's not as steep as it was but I'm hardly staying on, hardly slowing down and there's a right-angled bend coming at the bottom of the hill. I'm either going to crash before I run out of road or run out of road and crash. Tarmac or tree. Maybe I've slowed a bit and maybe the wobbling's nearly under control, still far too fast though but slowing, wobbling, straightening up, running out of road, running out of road, there's the tree that'll kill me, slowing, slowing, tree, tree, slowing, tree, slowing. Holy mother of Jesus Christing cock shits: I've stopped. The roar above dies away. I'm still on the bike and I'm alive. Might be deaf though, and as I force my fingers to ungrip the handlebars I find my hands are shaking like the leaves falling all around me. I look back up the hill. Branches and twigs and leaves are raining down through the canopy, up at the top of the hill the trees are stripped and decapitated, and on the road, the single longest, most impressive skid mark I've ever seen, winds down to end at my back tyre. Mind you, I can't help thinking there's an even more impressive one waiting for me to discover when I get home. I jump as if I'm not deaf as something lands blatantly by me like a bag of wet cement and I'm splattered with something wet. I look. I can't help it. I've never seen anything like it. It's a small dog-sized blackened red semi-solid with extruding bits. Is that? Can't be, can it? Bone? No. Is that? No, maybe, it's ... and as I recognise it I look away as fast as I can: though far, far too late for it not to be burnt permanently into every future bad dream I'm ever going to have. It's a pelvis, ripped from both spine and legs with the loosely attached scorched remains of someone's cock. That's really, really, not nice. A flattened bollock, burst on the tarmac, is running white back into the pile of red and charcoal mess. And why am I thinking it's Vincent's? Why am I thinking that? I need not to look at it again. I'm looking at it again anyway but I really need to not. I need to not be here.

I turn to drive back into town. There are already a couple of people down the street looking up to the pall of smoke at the top of the hill. More people appear as I try to think what to do. They haven't turned to come up the road yet so I quickly duck the scooter up the side of the first building I get to, an old wooden shed or garage or something, and I park in the undergrowth behind it and turn off the engine. If the police were ever on their way here after I called them, they'll be getting a few hurry-ups now from all the people with bits of church coming through their ceilings. I can hear a few people making stunned 'What's happened? I can't believe it. Look up there.' noises as they come up the road. Well you're no more stunned than me missus, I can assure you of that. I'll let them go first, then duck back out so they can witness me passing them up the road back up the hill. That way I'll be first to arrive on the scene, tragically just too late to stop my cousin doing the terrible thing that I'd tried to warn the police about earlier. I'll also need to contaminate the hell out of the forensics, and if it feels appropriate, I may even cry a little. Then again, maybe not. I don't feel like it and I don't want to push my luck. I'll stick to what I decided when it turned out I was too well brought up to push the red button and murder three people in cold blood myself: but perfectly capable of inducing my cousin towards a kind of accidental suicide which took a couple of arseholes with him. It may be a fine line but at least I've got some morals. My hands have almost stopped shaking now I can sense I'm not going to be greatly troubled by feelings of guilt. I could have killed them myself, but didn't. I let luck and stupidity and Charles Darwin decide; so whatever else I may be, I'm not some animal. Well, apart from what I've inherited from my great great grandmother, who was an animal; a great big marine one. No, fuck that. I am an animal, of course I am, but a human animal exactly like everyone else, one hundred percent human and not even one sixteenth part something else. Fuck what Gran thinks, she needs to calm down on the drugs, and those doctors clearly don't know a seal DNA sequence from their arse. I reckon all those villagers in Kilmuir all those years ago had it right all along. The truth is whatever gets you through the day, regardless of what the truth actually is. So yes, Cousin Dan blew himself and some other knob-heads up. That is, simply the truth. And as for the other thing; great great granny Gask, the alleged source of my beautiful big eyes … Well, my great great grandfather couldn't really have started a family with some sexy female grey seal he kept locked in a boat shed, could he? I mean despite what Gran thinks she knows and despite what all the mirrors have been screaming at me every day of my life, I can't admit it's anything other than a ridiculous and impossible piece of nonsense and still have the slightest hope of expecting to stay sane. I just can't. And so if I'm to continue believing it can't be true, then where the hell does that leave me and all the inconvenient evidence to the contrary? I suppose if I think about it, it's pretty bloody obvious. She must have been a mermaid after all.

5606582R00148

Printed in Great Britain
by Amazon.co.uk, Ltd.,
Marston Gate.